God's Healing Love Series
Book One

REBECCA BORCHARDT

In His Arms: *God's Healing Love Series - Book One*
Copyright © 2023 by Rebecca Borchardt

ISBN
978-1-961601-75-8 (Paperback)
978-1-961601-76-5 (eBook)

In His Arms

Table of Contents

Chapter 1

On a beautiful October day, Stacey was on her way to lunch at school. While she was walking outside, one of her friends approached her. "Stacey, I'm sorry but I have to do this," she said as she punched Stacey in the face and ribs. Everybody outside, and even some people from inside, ran to watch as Abbey beat up Stacey, who was too stunned to fight back. By the time she snapped out of shock, she was on the ground, looking up at her friend.

Stacey watched as Abbey punched her in the face one more time, then got up and ran. However, Stacey wasn't watching where she was going and ran right in front of a moving car in the street.

Everybody rushed to her; she was unconscious. Aaron was the first person to make it to her. He checked her pulse; it was beating, but she was still unconscious. He had one of his friends call 9-1-1. The principal saw the crowd of people by the road and ran up to hear what happened. After he heard what happened, he ran into the school to call Stacey's brother, Adam, down to the office. By the time Adam got out to the parking lot, the ambulance had arrived. Adam ran to the ambulance and went to Stacey's side, but the police pulled him away. Adam struggled against them.

"Let me go, she's my sister!" he yelled. They let him go, and he knelt down next to Stacey, talking to her as the paramedics checked her over.

"She's still breathing, just not conscious yet," they informed him as they continued to examine her. They put a C collar on her and noticed some swelling around her knee, so they braced it before moving her onto a gurney. Adam assisted the paramedics in placing Stacey into the ambulance, then he called his dad.

"Dad, Stacey has been in an accident. We are in the ambulance on the way to the hospital, please meet us there," then he hung up. Christian went down onto his knees and prayed for his daughter, then got up, picked up his wife from work, and drove to the hospital. On the way, they called the Rysners, their friends.

"Allison, this is Christian. Stacey has been in an accident, and she is on her way to the hospital. Can you tell Derek? I know Stacey would want him to know and be here when she wakes up." There was a long pause over the phone, then Allison came out of shock.

"I will tell Derek, and we will drive down together," she agreed as they hung up. Stacey's parents made it to the hospital and found Adam.

"She was still unconscious when we arrived, but we only got here a few minutes ago," he said. They gave Adam a hug and sat down, waiting to hear news. A doctor came out a little later, and they stood up to talk to him.

"Stacey has a few broken ribs; she fractured her wrist, and she also tore her ACL. We are bringing in a specialist who is implementing a new treatment program for ACL injuries. We believe your daughter will be a good candidate. The specialist will come to examine your daughter and discuss the options with you," said the doctor. Stacey's parents nodded in understanding.

"Stacey is still unconscious, but you can go in to see her before the doctor gets here. We are flying the doctor in from Madison," the doctor added. They followed the doctor to go see Stacey, and then the doctor left.

"Oh sweetie," Christian said as he squeezed her fingers.

"Dad, school is getting worse for Stacey," Adam whispered as he looked at his twin sister. "Some of the girls have been really mean to her and torturing her pretty badly." Christian looked at his son.

"Why didn't she tell us? I mean, I know she was having some troubles but not this bad," Adam shrugged his shoulders.

"She was trying to take care of it herself. Aaron was telling me everything this morning during homeroom, and I didn't get a chance to talk to Stacey about it," Christian looked down at his little girl.

"My independent, stubborn baby girl," they sat with her until the specialist showed up to examine Stacey.

"I am Doctor Jayne Dolan. I'm here to examine Stacey to see if she fits the bill for our ACL treatment study. If I could get a few minutes alone with her, I'll come find you when I'm done," said Dr. Dolan. Stacey's family left the room.

"Hi Stacey, I would really like you awake while I examine you, but I can still do it with you out," Jayne started feeling the knee and Stacey groaned. "I should have warned you that this might hurt," Jayne continued her examination. Stacey woke up.

"Where am I?" Jayne smiled as she moved closer to the head of the bed.

"You are at the hospital in La Crosse. I'm Doctor Jayne Dolan. Please call me Jayne. I'm looking at your knee as it got hurt in the accident. Do you remember what happened?" Stacey bit her lip as she tried to remember.

"Abbey beat me up, and I ran in front of a car trying to get away."

"You are correct." Stacey lifted her arm and saw the splint. "A few broken ribs, a fractured wrist, and a torn ACL. You also have quite a few bruises from the encounter. We haven't fixed your knee yet, but that's what I was checking when you woke up. I am a lead doctor on a study of ACL surgeries and treatments. I think you are the perfect candidate for the study. The only thing is, you would have to relocate to Madison." Stacey smiled.

"I'm all for moving; not sure what my parents would say though," Jayne chuckled.

"Well, we need their permission, so we'll have to convince them," Jayne whispered with confidence. Stacey laughed, then groaned as her ribs caused her pain. "I'll check on when you can have medication again and grab your parents to talk about the study." Stacey laid back as she thought about everything that was going on.

"Stacey," Adam said as they walked in. "It is good to see you awake." He walked up to her and gave her a gentle hug.

"Hey Adam, Mom, Dad," they each gave her a hug. Jayne joined them.

"So, Stacey seems to be a good candidate for this ACL study." Their faces lit up. "This study does require her to put the work into her recovery and devotion to it. This means no missing sessions or check-ups."

"I can do that," Stacey said. Jayne smiled at her as she got ready to say the part that people reject.

"Stacey would need to relocate to Madison."

"Absolutely not," Stacey's mom said. Everyone looked at Laura. "I can't move my practice. I am well established in the La Crosse area." Stacey looked at her mom shocked.

"Mom, she didn't say you needed to relocate. She said I needed to relocate." Laura glared at her daughter.

"You aren't even 18 yet. You can't live on your own." Stacey opened her mouth to say something, but her dad put his hand on her arm.

"Doctor Dolan, it seems that we are going to need to discuss this as a family more. If you have information on paper that will give us more details, that would be appreciated; otherwise, we are going to need a while to discuss," Jayne gave them the information.

"Either way, we would like to do some more tests today as there isn't much swelling and I'm here already," Jayne said as she walked to the door. They all nodded their heads.

"Stacey, you are not getting your own place and living in Madison alone. You will just do the normal treatment," Stacey looked at her dad, looking for some help, and trying to hold her temper.

"What if I live with the Rysner's?" She asked quietly. Laura looked at her while shaking her head. "Mom, you trust them, I would be getting the best treatment for my knee, and I would be away from the bullies at my school. This would be a good move for me." Laura looked at the men in the room and saw they were agreeing with Stacey.

"I don't want you to be away from us. We are here to protect you," Adam laughed.

"Mom, how can you say that when she got hurt while being where you want her to stay? I'll miss Stacey, but I agree this would be the best after what Aaron told me about what these girls have been doing to her," Stacey looked at Adam, shocked he knew about it. "I had heard rumors about things but thought you would have come to me if it was real," he sadly shrugged his shoulders. Stacey looked at her dad to hear his thoughts.

"We will talk to Chad and Allison to see if they would be willing to take you in before we discuss this any further." Christian said and the discussion ended. Some nurses came in and started prepping Stacey for some tests.

Allison was packing some bags when she heard Derek call out, "Mom, where are you?" She paused to compose herself before she called out to him.

"I'm in my room Derek," she replied with tears rolling down her cheeks, not being able to compose herself. Seconds later, he walked into the room and saw she was crying. He walked up to her, trying to think about what could make his mom cry.

"What's wrong?" he asked while giving her a hug.

"Derek, Stacey…." she took a deep breath and pushed him back while rubbing Derek's arms. Derek looked at her, "Stacey is in the hospital, she was in an accident." Derek backed up in disbelief with his arms up as if he was afraid to touch something.

"No… no, I just talked to her before lunch, she's fine," Derek protested.

"Derek, the accident happened during lunch," Allison explained, trying to comfort her son. He pushed her away.

"Derek," his father said while walking into the room, "your mother is telling the truth, Stacey is in the hospital right now." Derek ran out to his car and made it to the door before his dad put his arm between him and the doorway. "Derek, we are driving down together, go pack some essentials," he said while motioning back towards the house, only to see Allison walking out with a few suitcases. Derek helped her put the suitcases in the car and jumped in. Chad joined them and drove to La Crosse. They went directly to the hospital. When they arrived, Adam greeted them and showed them the way to the waiting room.

"Where is she?" Derek asked as he gave Christian and Laura hugs.

"They just took her back for some tests." Derek sighed as he sat down. "She was awake and okay before they took her back for some tests but she is hurt. She has broken ribs, a fractured arm, and a torn ACL. Her face is pretty beat up as well," Christian informed him as they all settled in. They sat quietly for a while then Adam spoke up.

"Dad, are you going to tell them about the study?" Laura stood up and stomped away. Christian watched her leave but told them about the possible treatment and move for Stacey.

"So, we were wondering if you would be willing to house Stacey if we agree to let her participate." Derek looked at his parents with a hopeful look on his face. Chad and Allison looked at each other and did some whispering.

"Of course," Chad announced. Derek jumped up cheering.

"We haven't fully decided yet, Derek," Christian said with laughter in his voice.

"But, a hopeful possibility of her living closer, much closer," Derek settled back into his chair and leaned over to Adam. "Why did your mom leave when you started talking about this?"

Adam looked solemn for a moment while looking at his fingers, playing with the nail beds before responding, "She doesn't want her to move away. I don't really want her to leave either, but it would be so much better for her."

"I think she's just overwhelmed and worried about Stacey. She'll come around, don't worry." Derek encouraged him.

"Has Stacey told you about the troubles she has been having at school?" He looked over at Derek.

"Yes, I have been trying to get her to tell your parents or at least an adult about it, but she wanted to take care of it herself, and she seemed to be in a good place emotionally to not be overly concerned about her mental state," Adam slouched down into his chair. "We have been praying for guidance, and maybe this move is God's answer." Derek looked over at his parents and gave them a small smile.

"Maybe we should pray for guidance and healing," Chad suggested. They all nodded and bowed their heads as Chad started. "God, we are here waiting for Stacey to get out of testing. We know that You are with Stacey and will help her family make the best decision for her." He paused for a moment to let someone else jump in.

"I pray for guidance on the decision we have to make regarding the treatment for Stacey's healing. We know that she would be in good hands with the Rysners, but we love her and want her to be close," Christian added.

"I pray that she will be where it would be best for her, not for everyone else. She needs to be taken care of, not ignored and hurt because of selfish desires," Adam added as he heard someone approaching.

"I pray that she can obey her parents and be happy about it, even if the decision is not what she wants," Laura added, and everyone looked up at her. Christian raised his eyebrow at his wife, not sure he was agreeing with her prayer.

"In Jesus' name, Amen," Chad closed.

"Boys, let's go for a walk," Allison motioned for them to leave and followed them out.

"Laura, Chad, I think you two need to figure this out, but also take Stacey's feelings and physical needs into account as well," Laura sat down with her arms crossed.

"Why am I the only one that thinks our daughter should stay in La Crosse?" Christian sat down next to her and set his hand on her knee.

"I would love for Stacey to stay with us, but after hearing about her school problems and how it has now affected her physically, I don't think we should only keep her here because we desire her to stay close," Laura turned to look out the window.

"Why didn't she tell us about her problems before?" She asked.

"Because we trained her up in the way she should go. We taught her how to take care of conflicts on her own, and she was trying," Christian shrugged his shoulders. Laura took a deep breath and slowly let it out.

"I need some time to be okay with this," she stood up and went for another walk.

"Is she still struggling with her past?" Christian nodded his head.

"You'd think she could figure it out being a psychologist, but she won't talk to me about it anymore," Chad clapped Christian on the shoulder. Derek and Adam came back.

"Derek, where did your mom go?" Chad asked.

"She saw Laura going into the Chapel and went to join her," Derek responded, then threw his dad a candy bar.

"Dad, did you make a decision?" Adam asked as he handed his dad a candy bar.

"No, Adam, we need to give your mom some time to think it over, and we will make a decision together as a family," Christian replied. They all sat down and got something to occupy the time while they waited and prayed for guidance.

A while later, Jayne came out to talk to them. "Her tests went well. She is a perfect candidate for this study." Laura and Allison joined them. "We did discover that she got a concussion as well, and they would like to keep her overnight to monitor. She is getting moved into a room and was wondering if Derek was here." Derek stood up and waved to let Jayne know he was Derek. "I'll take you back to see her." Derek followed the doctor. Jayne went in to make sure she was situated, then let Derek in.

"Hi Stac," he said as he sat on the edge of the bed, holding her good hand. She smiled.

"Just the man I wanted to see," he bent over and kissed her gently. "So… do I get to move in with your family?" Derek chuckled.

"Last I heard, it was undecided," Stacey frowned.

"Do you think we could talk our parents into letting you stay here with me overnight?" Derek shrugged his shoulders.

"It might take a bit of convincing. Which decision would you rather them take your side on—the study or me staying here overnight?"

"Good point, but it doesn't hurt to try," Derek chuckled as he gently rubbed his fingers over her hand. "I think I hear them coming." A few seconds later, her family walked in.

"Derek, you can stay here if you want. I'll be staying here as well," Christian said as he showed Derek that he had his bag. Laura sat down on the other side of Stacey.

"Has my fate been decided?" Stacey asked quietly, looking at her mom.

"It has," Christian and Adam tried to object, but Laura held up her hand. Stacey gripped Derek's hand, hoping for the answer she wanted. "You will be moving in with the Rysners once you get released from hospital care." Stacey's eyebrows shot up in surprise, and the men froze in surprise. "Allison convinced me to let you go," Derek smirked as he looked at Stacey.

"Thanks, Mom," Laura stood up and brushed her thumb over the side of Stacey's face gently.

"Adam, let's go." Adam gave Stacey a gentle hug then followed his mom out.

"Dad, what just happened?" He was still staring after his wife. He shook his head to get over the shock.

"I have no idea. She didn't talk to us about it, but maybe we should thank Allison." Christian stood up and went out the door.

"I guess we didn't need to convince as much as we thought." Derek chuckled, as did Stacey, but she stopped immediately as her ribs were hurting from it.

"You should probably rest, Stac," she nodded her head in agreement and relaxed back into the pillows. Christian walked back into the room.

"You might want to rest too. With her concussion, they are going to be coming in multiple times as well as helping her get up to go to the bathroom." Christian suggested as he rearranged the couch to become a bed.

"Where are you going to sleep?" Derek asked. Christian pointed to the chair. Derek looked conflicted about taking the pull-out bed.

"I'll be working. I also have too much on my mind to fall asleep right now." Derek nodded his head, grabbed his bag to change into more comfortable clothes, and laid down.

⁓⁓∽◦✺⟊◦✺⟊✺◦∽⁓⁓

"Abbey, why are you doing this to me?" Stacey yelled out. Derek woke up and went to Stacey's side. She was still sleeping.

"Stacey, sweetie, wake up," he kissed her forehead and set his cheek against her head. She slowly woke up.

"I guess that wasn't only a dream…" she said with a groan as she tried to adjust herself. Derek stepped back and shook his head, looking into her eyes while helping her adjust the pillows. Christian joined them at the bed.

"Dreaming about what happened or other things that happened?" He asked.

"A mixture of both, it was a good day yesterday. No one had picked on me or done anything to me, then she just came up and started throwing punches," Christian closed his eyes.

"I feel like we should have noticed some kind of change in you," Stacey looked at her dad.

"When, Dad? You work 60-70 hours a week and volunteer another 10-20 hours. Mom works 80+ hours a week. You are wonderful parents, but you are both workaholics," he sighed then dropped down in his chair.

"I'm sorry, baby," he sat quietly for a while then stood up. "I'm going to go out for a bit. Text me if you need me." The teenagers agreed.

"That's one way to tell him," Derek whispered. Stacey chuckled.

"I had an opening, but I guess I could have used a little more tact," Derek moved to the chair her dad had previously vacated. "So, what do you think about me moving in with your family?"

"I think it's about time," Derek almost shouted. They both chuckled. "But seriously, I'm sad it had to take this, but it will be nice to not have to drive two hours to see you."

"You won't have to drive anywhere," they heard someone knocking on the door, and a nurse came in.

"Oh good, you're awake," she approached the bed. "I just want to check your eyes and ask you a few questions, then help you go to the bathroom if you need to go." The nurse did her exam, and Stacey passed. "Do you need to go to the bathroom?" Stacey nodded her head. Derek helped her sit up, then he went for a walk. "He could have stayed," the nurse commented.

"He left for my privacy, these hospital gowns show a little too much," Stacey said, and the nurse looked at her.

"He's never seen you… never mind, it is none of my business. Sorry I asked." Stacey looked at the nurse and smiled.

"We believe in saving ourselves for marriage. God intended for sex to be within a marriage relationship between one man and one woman," Stacey explained as the nurse quietly helped her into the bathroom. After she had Stacey situated back into bed, the nurse asked a question.

"What if you have sex outside of marriage? Does God reject you then?"

"Not if you put your faith in God and change your ways. He is the God of Mercy and Grace, which means if you are truly sorry for what you have done and ask for forgiveness, He will give it to you and give you a clean slate. But you have to truly mean it and try not to do it again. One of my favorite forgiveness verses says you are to forgive those that sin or wrong you, 7 times 70 times. And if we are to do it that many times, I believe God will do that for me as well. But that doesn't mean we can do what we want and just rely on being forgiven. We have to truly change and try not to do wrong," Stacey replied, giving the nurse a small smile. "I'm not going to be in the area much longer, but I can give you the name of my church and my pastor and his wife if you have any more questions. Or, you can call or text me," Stacey offered as she found a piece of paper to write down all the information.

"I'll go get you some ice for your ice pack," the nurse said and disappeared before Stacey could give her the paper. Derek came back into the room with the full ice pack.

"What did you do to her?" Stacey frowned.

"I got preachy," Derek chuckled. "Was she crying?" Derek nodded his head.

"She saw me and handed the ice pack to me and said, 'God can't forgive a person like me.' Then walked away." Stacey covered her face with her hands with a groan.

"I always push too far." Derek gently pulled her hands off of her face.

"I'm sure you did fine, some people need to think about it before agreeing or disagreeing." He sat in the chair and moved it closer so he could lean forward on the bed. He held her hand gently as he set his chin on his arms.

"I'll leave this paper here, and maybe she will take it on her own." Derek nodded his head. "Do you know if my phone made it here?" Stacey asked. Derek shook his head as he looked through her things.

"We can talk to your parents about it," Derek moved to be close to her then sang Stacey back to sleep.

⸙

Early in the morning, Stacey woke up disoriented, then she saw Derek. The room was dark except for the light coming in through the doorway. She looked at Derek's dark wavy hair and watched him sleep for a few minutes before she squeezed his hand and woke him up.

"Hi, Derek," she whispered with a raspy voice. "Can I have some water?" Derek grabbed the glass of water and let her take a sip out of the straw.

"Hello, sweetheart, how are you feeling?" Derek asked while setting the water back on the table.

"Sore," she replied as the nurse came in and turned a small light on to have enough light to see Stacey.

"I heard you are sore," the nurse commented as she moved closer to Stacey, watching for any signs of major pain.

"Just a bit," Stacey replied, while grabbing Derek's hand to hold for comfort.

"Let me do the last neuro check then I'll go get you some pain meds and some more ice for your knee." The nurse checked Stacey's eyes for any signs of head trauma then checked her knee for swelling.

"Where is the other nurse that was in here earlier?" Stacey asked.

"She went home early," Stacey looked at Derek concerned. "There is some swelling in your knee, so I'll get that ice for you. Do you need anything else?"

"Some water? And could I get some ice for my ribs too?"

"Of course," the nurse left to get everything.

"Derek, what did I do?" He gave her a small smile.

"You made her think, and she took your paper," Derek said as he pointed to the place where she left the paper. Stacey's expression changed from overly concerned to hopeful. The nurse came back in with the water, meds, and ice packs.

"I think Doctor Dolan will be in around eight o'clock. You should look at the menu for food and get some ordered as you haven't eaten anything since you got here," she handed them the cafeteria food menu. "Your boyfriend can order as well or go down to the cafeteria, but he will have to pay." Derek took the menu and started looking at it as the nurse left.

"What time is it now?"

"A little too early to order food, but let me know what you want so if you are sleeping, I can still order for you." Stacey took the menu and wrote out what she wanted, then looked for a clock. It was three in the morning, Stacey scooted over in the bed slowly and patted the space next to her; Derek smiled as he gently cuddled up next to her. A few minutes later, she was asleep.

The light from the windows sprayed a ray of light across her face, highlighting her smooth skin and brown hair. Then, the bruises were seen through the beautiful skin. He watched her sleep for a while, hoping he could sleep, but he couldn't fall asleep again. As he waited for sleep to come, he prayed, "Thank You for saving my girl, I love her so much. Please keep her safe." He held her in his arms as he waited for her to wake up again. He slipped out of the bed when he saw it was time to order food and ordered for both of them. He sat down next to her and laid his head on the bed again, waiting for her to wake up.

A little while later, Stacey woke up, realizing what had all happened the day before, and saw Derek watching her. "Well, hello Derek," she greeted with a smile.

"I was just thinking about my life if you wouldn't have made it," he said, setting her right hand in-between his and rubbing her fingers.

"But I am alive," she declared as Derek stood up and gave Stacey a gentle hug and a kiss. Stacey saw Jayne walk in behind Derek. She looked hesitant as she saw their intimate moment.

"Stacey, may I check you?" Jayne asked.

"Yes, may Derek stay?" Stacey requested.

"Yes, he can stay." She smiled then examined Stacey's knee, ribs, and head. "Please don't put any pressure on your knee until we start therapy, here are a set of crutches and a wheelchair, you can pick and choose which one you want to use." Stacey's mind went to all the changes that are going to be happening in the next few days. "Your parents signed the papers to come to Madison. We are going to take you by helicopter for ease and comfort for you then we are going to keep you at the hospital for a few days to continue to monitor the concussion but also do the surgery after the swelling goes down, which means you really need to stay off your knee." Jayne started heading for the door.

"Hey, Jayne do I need to stay in the hospital gown?" Jayne paused in her step and turned around.

"No, and I brought clothes we give our participants that are easy to get on and off with the brace and such."

"Thanks Jayne," Jayne left and came back a few minutes later with rip away pants. "I think my parents brought over some clothes?" Derek handed the bag to Stacey. Jayne shooed Derek away, disconnected the IV from the IV port in Stacey's arm then helped her get dressed. Jayne let Derek back into the room when they were done and left the room. He walked over to Stacey and gave her a kiss. She let the kiss linger then she pushed him a few inches away.

"Derek, did you order something to eat?" she asked with his face inches away.

"Yes, it should be here any minute." He moved to brush her cheek but paused. "Your face is so bruised. I'm scared to touch it." Stacey put her hand up to stop him and brought his hand down and held it.

"Just wait a few days then it won't hurt as much." She played with his hand, massaging his fingers. She watched her fingers move along his.

"I know I'm just scared that every time I touch you, I'm hitting a bruise or your ribs or your knee and I know it probably hurts." The tenderness in his voice made Stacey look into his eyes. She placed her hand on his face, and brushed her thumb along his cheekbone.

"Yeah, it might, but I still want to cuddle with you and receive hugs and kisses, just be gentle." She looked into his eyes to make sure he had listened to her, and he did. Someone knocked on the door.

"Come in," Stacey said and the food service worker walked in with her tray. They asked for her name and birthday then set it on the table. Derek paid for his food and set his tray on the table with hers as he helped her get situated to eat then sat across from her.

Jayne walked into the room with Stacey's parents. "The helicopter is on its way to bring us up to Madison. You have about an hour to say good-bye to your parents. We got permission to bring one extra passenger." Derek's hand shot up.

"Me, me, pick me," he said like an overly excited child and the adults were laughing at his antics.

"We assumed you would want to go. Your parents signed off on it and are already on their way back to Madison." Christian announced. Jayne left them.

Thanks Mom and Dad for letting me do this, I know this wasn't an easy decision but I appreciate you giving me this opportunity." Stacey saw her mom still wasn't very comfortable with the idea. "I love you guys." Christian gave her a hug.

"We love you too. We expect updates on how everything is going and we would like you to come home for holidays." He held up a phone. "You can use this phone until we either find your phone or get time to replace it." Stacey agreed as he set it in her hand. "Adam and I will be coming up with some more of your stuff soon." He stepped back and Laura stepped in.

"I will miss you, Mom," Laura gave her a hug.

"Stay in touch," she whispered then stepped back and left.

"As distant as ever," Stacey said under her breath and she saw that her dad heard her. "I…"Christian raised his hand to stop her.

"She's going through some things," Stacey rolled her eyes.

"She's always going through something," Christian patted her shoulder then gave her another hug and followed his wife out the door. Derek stepped up to the bed. "I'm surprised I didn't get a lecture for that." Derek chuckled.

"There's a lot going on and they are forgiving." Derek looked at Stacey. "This accident has seemed to take away your filter." Stacey chuckled carefully.

"Is that a good thing or a bad thing?" Derek shrugged his shoulders.

"Let's pray before we eat and travel back to Madison in a helicopter." They bowed their heads. "Dear God, thank You for some healing and peace You have given us during this situation. We know You have a bigger plan in our pain and You have given us wonderful parents to help us through all of this. Please keep us safe as we take a helicopter back to Madison. I pray for this food to nourish our bodies and please bless the hands that prepared the food."

"God, please help the nurse that was in here earlier. I pray that You can help her heart and be there for her. In Jesus' name, Amen." They both started digging into the food. They ate their food quickly then Derek packed up their things to be ready for the Helicopter ride. Jayne came a few minutes later.

"Let's get you onto a gurney and to the helicopter pad." Jayne and a nurse helped Stacey move onto a gurney then they pushed her out to the helicopter. Jayne and the nurse moved her gurney into the helicopter. They clicked the bed into the helicopter then sat the bed up so Stacey could look out the windows. Derek hopped into the helicopter and buckled himself in. They both received headsets and held hands as they waited for the helicopter to go up.

"You two ready for this ride?" the pilot asked through the headset.

"Yes," they both replied. Jayne smiled at their excitement. The helicopter started up and off to Madison.

"My friends will be so jealous to hear that I was able to get a ride on a helicopter." Derek said as he looked out the window.

"Too bad the Grand Canyon is too far away." Stacey commented. The pilot chuckled. "The fall colors are beautiful though." They watched the scenery go by as they continued on their way to Madison.

"Stacey, how are you feeling?" Jayne asked.

"This is all exciting, but I'm starting to feel a headache coming on." Jayne checked her pulse and oxygen levels.

"I'm guessing it's kind of like car sickness, especially with the concussion." Stacey nodded her head.

"We don't have too much longer to go before we are there," the pilot commented. Stacey leaned against Derek and closed her eyes. Derek rubbed his thumb over the back of her hand and started softly singing to her. The helicopter landed a little while later, and Stacey was moved into her new room. Derek went to make a few phone calls.

"Can I get some pain medication, please?" Stacey asked as they settled her into her new bed.

"Of course," Jayne said as she transferred all the information from Stacey's treatment from the La Crosse hospital to the Madison hospital. Derek came in a few minutes later and sat down next to Stacey.

"Mom and Dad just arrived. I'm going to go home and take a shower, then I'll come back with my vehicle, if you are okay with me leaving." Stacey gave him a small smile and a nod.

"I'm super tired right now, so don't rush. I'm going to try to get a nap after Jayne gives me my next dose of pain meds. I'll text you when I wake up; try to get some rest too." Derek kissed her cheek then left the room. Jayne left and came back with Stacey's pain meds and some water.

"Do you want ice packs right now too?" Stacey nodded her head. Jayne helped Stacey get situated then left her to sleep.

"God, I know this is what You want for me but it is scary. Please give me some peace about this whole situation." Stacey prayed then put her headphones in to listen to Christian music as she fell asleep.

—∿∙◦⌇◦⊙⌇◦∿—

Derek jumped into his parents' car. "How is she doing?" Chad asked as he pulled into traffic.

"I think she is doing well, but I think during the helicopter ride she started feeling overwhelmed and tired."

"Understandable," Allison commented. Derek stared out his window. "What are you thinking about?"

"I'm really excited she will be here, but I don't like what brought her here, and I know it will be a lot of changes for her and a long recovery." Allison turned to look at him.

"It is good you understand that; it will help you help her." She reached back and squeezed his knee. Derek gave his mom a big smile. "We will get the spare room set up for her since it is on the main floor, so she doesn't have to do stairs."

"Have you told Joanna and Ariel?" Chad chuckled.

"Yes, they are super excited to have her come live with us. Joanna said, 'Now he can't complain about not being able to see her all the time.'" Derek laughed hard.

"Do I really complain that much?" He asked as he caught his breath.

"I think she was just teasing you." They arrived at their house. Derek jogged into the house and found his sisters waiting for him.

"How was the helicopter ride?" Joanna asked.

"It was really cool." He sat down between them and wrapped his arms around their shoulders. "I hear you are excited for Stacey to come because I have been complaining all the time about not being able to see her." The girls' eyes grew to the size of golf balls.

"You weren't supposed to hear that!" Joanna said as she tried to get up. Derek trapped both of them and started tickling them. "You win!" Joanna yelled. Derek relaxed his tickling fun and sat back with his sisters.

"Are you really excited she's coming besides the decrease in my complaining?"

"Yes," Ariel said. "You really don't complain that much, but you are on the phone with her all the time. But, seriously, we love Stacey." Derek gave his sisters hugs.

"Thanks," He stood up. "I'm going to go take a shower."

"I was going to say something about the smell, but…" Derek threw a pillow at Joanna's face. "Hey!" Derek walked away and got into the shower.

Stacey woke up around three in the afternoon and looked around the room. She found her phone and texted Derek, "I just woke up. You don't need to rush over, just wanted to let you know I was awake." Stacey was looking at her phone when Derek walked into the room. "I said you didn't need to rush over," Derek smiled.

"I woke up a little bit ago and just decided to come over instead of waiting for your text." He approached the bed and gave her a kiss on her forehead. "If you are up for the company, Joanna and Ariel want to come for a visit. They said they would bring food."

"I'm up for some company and food, I skipped lunch. But, I do want to see if I can get cleaned up a bit before they come." Derek texted his sisters to come in an hour as Stacey got the nurses to help her get cleaned up. Derek went into the waiting room as the nurses started helping Stacey. Jayne saw Derek in the waiting room.

"Is she still sleeping?" He smiled as he shook his head.

"No, she's getting a shower, and you don't need to tell her how long I was sitting here waiting for her to wake up," she chuckled.

"You aren't going to be able to relax until she's at your parents' house, are you?" Derek shook his head.

"She doesn't like hospitals, and it is all strange. I'm surprised she didn't ask for my mom or dad to stay with her while I went to take a shower." Jayne sat down next to him.

"She did sleep. The nurses went to check on her a few times. I heard her praying for peace after you left, and I believe God gave her some." Derek took a deep breath.

"I guess I should be laying down my anxiety at His feet as well." Jayne squeezed his knee. Derek saw his sisters coming with some food. "Jayne, these are my sisters, Joanna and Ariel, and sisters, this is Stacey's doctor, Dr. Jayne Dolan." They all shook hands.

"I'll go see how the shower is going." Jayne left to check on Stacey.

"Does Stacey know how long you have been here?" Derek shook his head.

"And you don't need to tell her." Ariel lifted her eyebrow with a mischievous grin. "Ariel…"

"I won't, but you should have rested longer at home." Derek saw Jayne motion them over. They went over to the room and walked in.

"So, what food did you bring me?" Stacey asked as they walked in. Joanna chuckled as she set the bag of food on the tray and moved it over to the bed. Stacey opened the bag and smiled. "Chinese, either Derek told you or you remembered from other times I have been up here."

"We remembered; Chinese is your favorite take-out." They all started digging into the bag and separated the food.

"Dear God, thank You for this food that is about to nourish our bodies and for the safe trip to Madison," Derek said as Stacey had a pile of food heading to her mouth.

"Sorry," she said after she ate the bite. "I missed lunch." They all chuckled and started filling their own mouths with food. "Your parents didn't want to come?" Joanna smiled.

"They did, but they had an event at the church they needed to go to." Stacey nodded her head in understanding. The girls stayed for a few hours then headed out. Derek saw the sunset through the blinds and opened them so they could watch the sunset together. The sunset skittered across the spans of the Earth in their beautiful mixture. The colors reflected onto Stacey's face, and Derek watched her. "Did you know that God made you and the sunset very beautiful?" Stacey turned her head away.

"What about all the bruises on my face?"

"I see through them," Derek said as he turned her face back towards him. "I know you are hurt, but you are still as beautiful as the day I realized I loved you." Stacey looked at Derek in the eyes and kissed him.

"What day was that?" Derek laughed because she knew the answer.

"The day you came to camp for the first time." Stacey laughed.

"We were like five, how did you know you were in love with me?" Derek shrugged his shoulders.

"I just knew." They cuddled together, continuing to watch the sunset. Jayne came in a little while later to check on her knee.

"If the swelling remains down, we can do the surgery in the morning," she announced. Stacey took a deep breath. "A little bit of nervousness in that deep breath?" Jayne asked.

"Yes," Stacey said.

"Well, I'll be with you the whole time, and I'm guessing this guy will be here for the before and after part as well. If it goes well, you will be able to leave the next morning, which would be Saturday."

"Did you tell my parents?" Jayne nodded her head.

"They said they would be coming after work and school," Jayne said quietly. Stacey sighed as her phone went off.

"Oh, sweetheart, I wish I could be there for you." Stacey was annoyed as her mother ranted and raved about not being able to be at Stacey's side even though she could be there if she took time off.

"Mom, it's fine, I'm fine, but thanks for calling." Stacey rolled her neck to relieve some tension. They hung up after a few more words. "I'm going to go to sleep. Derek, are you going to school in the morning?" He shook his head.

"I'm going to be right here with you. I talked to Mom and Dad about it, and Joanna already grabbed my homework." He lifted a backpack. "I didn't know you were going into surgery, but I didn't want you to be in the hospital alone." Stacey gave him a huge smile with a relieved sigh. "Mom and Dad will be here praying while you are in surgery." Stacey sat back and relaxed into the bed.

Chapter 2

The next morning, Stacey woke up to someone knocking on the door. She slowly sat up as Jayne walked in. "Good morning, sleepy head. I heard you slept through all the nurse checks last night." Stacey smiled while slowly stretching.

"I guess I was tired." Derek sat up from where he was sleeping.

"I randomly checked to make sure you were breathing a few times because you didn't move with them coming in," Derek said as he rubbed his eyes. Stacey gave him a small smile. Jayne moved the blankets off Stacey's legs and looked at her knee.

"Looks good," she covered Stacey's knee. "No breakfast, we will do the surgery as soon as they get you prepped." Stacey took deep breaths to calm her nerves. Jayne squeezed her hand. "You are doing great, and God will be with you." Jayne slipped out as Derek moved to be closer to Stacey.

"Should we pray?" Stacey nodded her head. "Dear God, thank You for giving us another day together. Please ease our anxiety as Stacey goes into surgery this morning. We know Your healing hands are guiding the doctor's hands. In Jesus' name, Amen." Derek leaned forward and kissed Stacey's forehead. Stacey's phone started ringing. It was her dad's mom, Grandma Rosemen.

"Hi, Grandma, how are you?" Stacey asked, not sure if she wanted to know why her grandmother called--their past was not the best.

"I'm fine and here in Madison. Come help me bring my stuff in." Stacey's eyes grew in horror as she looked at Derek, praying for help.

"What stuff, Grandma?"

"I'm coming to help take care of you." Stacey bit her lip, holding back all of her comments. She wanted to forgive her grandmother, but the past event that happened was still fresh in her mind.

"Grandma, I'm fine. I have my friends helping me, and Adam and Dad are coming later anyways." The fear of what happened in the past made Stacey feel like hitting a punching bag. She didn't want to be sick like she was when her grandmother took care of her.

"Well, they need to work, so I am here to take care of you."

"Grandma, I am old enough to take care of myself, and I am in a hospital anyways. They can take care of me if I need help."

"Come help me," she said as Chad and Allison walked in.

"Grandma, they are starting to prep me for surgery, I can't help you bring stuff in. Come with just what you need and go wait in the waiting room." Stacey heard her grandma huff in anger as she hung up. Stacey slumped in her bed, feeling defeated and tired of her grandma's games. Stacey called her dad.

"Dad, I might need you to come earlier. Grandma Rosemen is here and trying to take over my life again."

"Oh boy, this is going to be fun," Christian said sarcastically. "I'll grab Adam out of school and run some interference. Could Chad and Allison help out?" Stacey looked at them.

"I'll ask them too." She said good-bye to her dad. "So, my Grandma Rosemen is here at the hospital. I don't really want to see her before the surgery, or even really after but I will see her after. My dad is coming earlier than originally expected but if you could help keep her out of trouble while I'm in surgery, I'd appreciate it." Chad chuckled.

"I remember your dad's stories about some of her extremeness, or intensity may be a better word. We will help as much as we can. We just wanted to come in to say hi before you go in." They gave her hugs and prayed for her then left as the nurses came in to prep her. Derek stayed in the room with her until they took her back to the operating room then he joined his parents in the waiting room.

"Hi Mrs. Rosemen," Derek said as he saw Stacey's grandma in the waiting room. She didn't say anything to him. Derek skirted over to his parents and raised his eyebrow at them.

"She doesn't want to acknowledge that other people are here for Stacey," Chad whispered. "Did you get any sleep last night?" Derek shook his head. "Do you think you could get some sleep now, in Stacey's room, since no one will be going in and out until her surgery is done?"

"No, I'm struggling to relax but was praying for her all night last night." Derek glanced over at Stacey's grandma.

"Do you know the story between Stacey and her grandma?" Chad asked.

"She was helping take care of Stacey when she got pneumonia really bad one year after falling through the ice. I think she was 12 or 13. Instead of really helping her get better, she did things to keep her sick so the family would need her to stay. It took months for Laura and Christian to figure out it wasn't just pneumonia anymore, and Stacey was the one that convinced Adam to get a video of grandma prepping her food and discovered she was putting something in her food. I think that was the only year Stacey missed camp because she was recovering from the pneumonia and other stuff her grandma gave her. She had lost a lot of weight and was not healthy." Derek said quietly. Chad's eyes were the size of saucers.

"Wow, now I understand why Stacey doesn't really want to see her." They talked a bit more then relaxed as they waited for Stacey's surgery to be done.

Christian and Adam walked into the hospital. "Dad, why weren't we here earlier before Stacey went into surgery? I feel like we aren't supporting Stacey in all of this." Christian looked at his son.

"You're right, we should have been here before she went into surgery. I think your mom and I need to start getting out of our workaholic mindset that work can't survive without us." Christian wrapped his arm around Adam's shoulders and squeezed him in a quick hug as they entered the elevator.

"Are you ready to see your mom?" Adam asked his dad as he watched the floor numbers go up.

"Not really, I'm kind of surprised she is here. We haven't really seen her since the whole thing with Stacey." They both took deep breaths as the elevator doors opened. They walked out and found the waiting room. Adam sat down next to Derek as Christian headed to his mom.

"Mom, it has been a while," he said as he looked her over as she was knitting.

"About six years, not sure why I haven't heard from you." Christian's jaw dropped.

"Mom, you know exactly why we haven't talked to you. You kept Stacey sick for months to feel needed." She ignored his comment and continued knitting. "Mom, I need you to look at me and listen to what I am saying." She huffed and put her knitting stuff down in anger.

"I'm here to see my granddaughter. I don't need to listen to you."

"You do need to listen if you want to see her." She looked up at him with sharp eyes.

"You would continue to keep my grandchildren away from me?" Christian sighed as he collected his thoughts.

"I will. You hurt my daughter, and I'm not going to let you do that again. If you don't follow the boundaries I set, you will not be seeing them again." She sighed.

"What are these boundaries?"

"You will not be staying here. You will not be in the room alone with her. And you will only stay for an hour a day. We are not expecting her to stay in the hospital for long." She started packing up her knitting stuff.

"You are cruel, but I guess I can do this to see her." She looked over at Adam, and he looked over at Christian who nodded his head. Adam walked over.

"Hi Grandma," he said quietly as he gave her an awkward hug.

"Hi Adam," he sat down across from her. "How have you been?"

"I've been good, Grandma." She was going to ask another question when Christian saw Doctor Jayne walk into the room. He stood up and went to her.

"I wasn't expecting to see you here, Mr. Rosemen." Christian smiled sheepishly.

"Unexpected visitor who isn't allowed to see Stacey without me here, and we realized she shouldn't have been doing the surgery without us here." Jayne looked behind him and saw Adam coming up too. "How's Stacey?"

"Surgery went well. Everything got repaired the way we wanted it, and she is in her room now," Adam started heading that way. "She was still out of it when I left her." She warned him. Adam and Derek went to her room together. "Will I need to get security to help with your unwanted visitor?" Jayne asked. Christian looked back at his mom.

"Hopefully not, I set boundaries, and she momentarily agreed to them." She nodded her head then went back to work. Christian went back to his mom. "Stacey is out of surgery. I'm going to see if she is up for company. I'll let you know." She pulled her knitting stuff back out of her bag as Christian walked to his daughter's room.

"Derek, was Stacey upset that we weren't here this morning?" Christian overheard his son asking when he got to the door.

"Honestly, yes. Your mom called shortly after Jayne told us they would be doing the surgery in the morning and Stacey was annoyed with your mom because she was saying she wished she could be here when she really could have been here if she wanted. I think Stacey understands there are other obligations, but your parents put their work ahead of you guys a lot," Christian started heading into the room.

"I tried to get them to come earlier, but they pulled rank on me. I couldn't concentrate at school. I almost drove here myself." Christian paused. "You know, sometimes I wish I wasn't a good person but a troublemaker." Derek chuckled.

"Why?"

"Because the only real attention I get from my parents is when I get in trouble, which isn't often." Christian cleared his throat as he finished walking into the room. Adam looked up at his dad. "She hasn't woken up yet." Christian looked at his daughter then back at his son.

"Derek, I know you won't mind, but could you stay with her? I need to talk to Adam." Derek agreed and watched them leave. Derek moved closer to Stacey and held her hand.

"God is answering your prayers," he whispered as he gently moved his thumb across the back of her hand.

"And what prayers would that be?" He looked up shocked that she heard him.

"I think your dad is starting to understand that family should be before work. I believe he overheard Adam and I talking about it, and they just went off to talk. It might be a while… or not, depending on if they find something to talk about." Stacey smiled. "How do you feel?"

"I think I'm okay for now, but a little fuzzy still. Was it a dream, or is Grandma Rosemen here?"

"She's here, knitting the blazes out of whatever she is making. She's hardly moved except when your dad confronted her." Stacey sighed.

"I love you, Derek… going back to sleep." She whispered as she drifted back to sleep. Derek chuckled at how fast she fell asleep. Jayne popped in.

"Did she just wake up?" Derek laughed.

"For like a minute," she went to the side of Stacey's bed and looked everything over.

"Let me know when she wakes up again. We need to get the knee mobilizer going, but we don't like doing that until after she is fully awake." Derek nodded his head.

***

A few hours later, Stacey slowly woke up and found Derek sleeping with his head on her hand. She smiled as she slowly moved her hand and ran her fingers through his hair. He slowly lifted his head then smiled as he set his chin on his hand.

"Hey you," he said. Stacey smiled.

"I'm glad you finally got some sleep." He chuckled as he sat up and ran his hand through his hair. "Is my dad here?"

"Yes, I'm not sure where though. I'm not sure if they have been back since they went off to talk as I've been sleeping." Stacey tried to adjust herself but stopped when pain radiated up her wrist. She winced. "You okay?"

"Yeah, just forgot about my wrist being hurt."

"You should hit your nurse call button. Jayne wanted to know when you were awake." Stacey hit the button then looked at Derek.

"I'm so glad you are here, and that your parents let you stay out of school to come." He leaned forward and grabbed her hand, kissing her knuckles.

"I think I would have risked getting in trouble to be here." Stacey giggled, trying to imagine him disobeying his parents. Jayne walked into the room and smiled when she saw Stacey awake.

"Surgery went well. I'm going to look at your knee, and if everything still looks good, then we will put your leg in a mobilizer machine. It will slowly move your leg to keep your knee moving." Jayne focused on what she was doing, and a nurse came in with the machine. They set it up and started it.

"That's an interesting feeling, my leg moving without me having to do it." Derek laughed.

"You still have a catheter in, but we will take it out later tonight, and then you will start trying to move around after that. I know it will be a little more difficult with your injured ribs and wrist, but we need to get you up and about now that the surgery is done." Stacey nodded her head, then heard a knock on the door. Jayne headed out the door and let the people in.

"Hi Grandma," Stacey said when she saw her. She sat down next to Stacey and grabbed her hand.

"Hi Stacey, how are you feeling?"

"I'm fine, Grandma. They said the surgery went well, but there will be a long recovery before I'm back to normal." Stacey tried to get her hand out of her grandma's grip, but the IV port was making it difficult. "Grandma, can you let go? It kind of hurts with the IV port." Her grandma looked down at their hands and slowly let go.

"I guess you still don't want me around…" Stacey looked at her dad with some fear in her eyes.

"Grandma, if you were truly taking care of me without hurting me, there would be nothing to forgive, but you kept me sick for months. I have forgiven you for that, but it doesn't mean I can't have boundaries to protect myself from getting hurt again." She abruptly stood up and grabbed her bag.

"I guess I'm not welcome here." She huffed and stomped out of the room. Stacey took a deep breath.

"I didn't…" Christian stopped her.

"It isn't you, honey, she still doesn't believe she did anything wrong, and I set up boundaries out in the lobby. I'm actually surprised she stayed and came in." Stacey sighed and closed her eyes to think, then opened her eyes with a smile.

"Just needed to collect your thoughts?" Adam asked.

"Yup, I'm really glad you came." Adam and her dad came and gave her hugs. "Did Mom come?" They shook their heads.

"She's coming after work tonight, and we should all be here for the weekend." Christian said as he noticed the sadness on her face. "Derek, Adam, can you give us a few minutes?" They nodded their heads then gave Stacey kisses on her forehead as they left.

"Dad, I'm not sure I have the energy to have the talk you want to have at the moment." He sat down where Derek had been sitting.

"We can wait for the big talk, but I do need you to listen." Christian picked up her hand and stared at it. "I have realized in the last few days that there has been a lot of emotional neglect on our part, and I am truly sorry. We have missed a lot of opportunities to be together as a family and to truly be there for you. I don't want to make excuses for your mom, but she does have some stuff from her past that she is still trying to work through, and sometimes she hides in her work helping other people."

"Dad, she's had this stuff from her past for a while. I feel like it should be worked out by now." He sighed.

"That may be true, young lady, but she hasn't given it all up to Christ." Stacey's eyebrows rose in surprise.

"Mom isn't a believer?" Christian sighed.

"She knows about God and what Christ has done for us, but she hasn't done the believing part. She has been just going through the motions. I thought she had, but realized it a while back that there wasn't true faith there and confronted her. If she knew I was telling you, she would not be happy." Stacey looked down where her dad was holding her hand.

"It changes things, but kind of explains a lot..." she looked up at the ceiling to think. "Except it doesn't explain why you work so much." Christian sighed.

"The more we were together, the more we fought. So, to avoid the fighting, I just stayed away and you two were so self-sufficient. This is also the reason why most decisions are made by me. She decided she wanted her kids to have what I have and gave me the decision-making rights, although I do still look for her input." Stacey was shocked.

"I feel like… actually I'm not sure what I feel at the moment." Christian nodded his head in understanding. "Does Adam know?"

"Yes, we talked about it while we were waiting for you to wake up." Stacey wished she could just get up and walk away. "I think I'm going to give you some time to yourself. I can see you want to think alone." Stacey nodded her head. Christian stood up and kissed her forehead, then headed for the door.

"Can you tell Derek he can come back in?" Christian nodded his head then left. Stacey laid her head back and stared up at the ceiling.

"God, that was so much information, but as I'm processing it, it kind of all makes sense." She continued to think about past situations with her mom. Tears started running down her face. Derek walked in, and she looked up at him with tears. He joined her on the bed and quoted her favorite verse from the Bible.

> *"The Lord is my shepherd; I shall not be in want.*
> *He makes me lie down in green pastures, He leads*
> *me beside quiet water, He restores my soul.*
> *He guides me in paths of righteousness for His name's sake.*
> *Even though I walk through the valley of the shadow of the death,*
> *I will fear no evil, for You are with me; Your*
> *rod and Your staff, they comfort me.*
> *He prepares a table for me in the presence of my enemies.*
> *He anoints my head with oil, my cup overflows.*
> *Surely goodness and love follow me all the days of my life*
> *and I will dwell in the house of the Lord forever."*
>
> *Psalm 23*

Stacey started reciting it with him towards the end then turned into his chest and cried.

"Hey you," he whispered. "Can you tell me what's going on in that beautiful head of yours?" She took some slow deep breaths.

"So much information, emotions, pain both physically and mentally…" Derek brushed his hand through her hair and kissed her forehead.

"It has been a few exhausting days." Stacey looked up at him.

"Did Adam tell you about what he talked to my dad about?"

"Some,"

"I feel like I've been lied to most of my life but at the same time Mom's reaction to things and some of the fights we have had make so much more sense. I don't know but this is a lot." Derek continued holding her best he could with the knee mobilizer and small bed.

⸻ ⁓⌇⌇⌇⁓ ⸻

A few minutes later, Derek's family walked into the room and noticed the two of them on the bed. Stacey turned to them with tears in her eyes. "Are you okay Stacey?" Joanna asked while she went up to her and brushed her hair out of her face. They stood around as Derek explained.

"She just hasn't had time to realize her situation enough to be able to process it and she's learned a lot that has kind of shocked her." They nodded in understanding. Then Stacey started sniffing the air.

"Did you bring food?" They laughed as Ariel moved forward with the bags of food.

"We did, and we cleared it with Jayne before bringing it in here." They ate some food and enjoyed the afternoon together. The nurses came in to check on her a few times. Then, Jayne came in.

"You have a few visitors, but I thought it would be a good idea for you to try walking down to them." Stacey hesitantly nodded her head. "I'll be with you the whole time while you are walking." Derek's family said goodbye, then Jayne helped Stacey get disconnected from her IV, put her knee brace on, and some clothes. "Are you ready to go?"

"As ready as I'll ever be." Stacey stood up with Jayne next to her and slowly put pressure on her knee.

"So, you will be walking with crutches, but this might be difficult with your rib breaks and sprained wrist. We can try a few things." Stacey set her foot down on the ground and used the crutches to help her stand up on her good leg. "Good, now gently set your foot down on your bad leg and just stand for a little bit." Stacey winced a little bit but then relaxed into standing.

"This is going to be a slow walk," Stacey said.

"Good, and we don't really have far to go. The cafeteria is directly below us, and we just have to make it to the elevator." Stacey slowly started walking with her crutches while listening to the instructions Jayne was giving her, while Derek followed. They made it to the elevator, and Stacey leaned back into the wall to relax. "How are you feeling?"

"It feels okay but hurts slightly. It is just taking a lot of energy, and my ribs and wrist are hurting a little bit."

"I can get you some pain medication now that your IV meds are no longer going. I'll grab them while you are talking to your visitors in the cafeteria." Stacey nodded her head, then pushed off the wall as the elevator doors opened. She made her way to the cafeteria and saw her visitors immediately.

"Hey, Aaron, Mrs. Williamson, how have you been?" She sat down with her crutches and set them up against the wall behind her.

"Better than you, I suppose," Aaron commented while staring at Stacey.

"Well, thanks for coming to visit me." Stacey introduced them to Derek. "I'd like you to meet my boyfriend, Derek. Derek, this is Aaron and Mrs. Williamson." They shook hands as they sat down. Derek held Stacey's hand as they started talking, and Aaron stared at their hands. Derek looked over at Stacey then wrapped his arm around her shoulders. He distracted everyone by getting them to tell him stories about Stacey, and they were laughing and having fun telling stories. Jayne came with her meds and told Stacey to page her when she was ready to go back to her room. They talked for hours, then Jayne came to get her.

"We should get you back to your room," she said as she grabbed her crutches for her. Stacey stood up.

"It was nice seeing the two of you. I'm not sure if you heard, but I'm moving to Madison for my knee treatment, so I won't be coming back to school." Aaron looked like he was about to object, but Mrs. Williamson interrupted.

"Well, you will be missed by many," Aaron stared at Stacey, a little shocked. She gave him a little smile.

"There will be some people I miss but I think this will be a good move for me." Mrs. Williamson looked at her confused. "I was a target of some major bullying, which is what caused the accident."

"Oh, I didn't know that," Mrs. Williamson said quietly.

"Aaron can fill you in if you want." Stacey saw Jayne and Derek getting antsy to go back up. "I should go, bye." Stacey went back up to her room, and Jayne got her settled back into her bed then left.

"I didn't realize you were so close to Aaron," Derek said softly.

"He is about the only one who didn't abandon me while I was getting bullied." Derek looked out the window past her.

"Am I reading something, or does he have a crush on you?" he asked as he continued looking out the window.

"I believe you are right, but he has never said anything to me or done anything. He has never really believed you have existed." Derek looked at Stacey.

"Well, I'm glad you will be closer to me." He leaned forward in his chair and grabbed her hand.

"Me too." She raised their hands to her face and set his hand on her cheek. "I don't think of him like that. You are the only one I love." He smiled then leaned forward to kiss her, but they were interrupted by a knock on the door. A man entered the room.

"Hello, Stacey, looks like you're doing better."

"Hi, Mr. Thompson. Derek, this is my gym teacher, Mr. Thompson. Mr. Thompson, this is my boyfriend, Derek."

"Well, it's nice to meet the boy Stacey always talks about." Derek blushed as he went to sit on the bed while Mr. Thompson took the extra chair.

"So, what are you really doing here?"

"I came to check on you, but I also had another reason to be in town. My wife just got a new job here in Madison, so we are moving here, and I am going to be the new gym teacher at the High School, just down the road."

"Really, that's cool, then you just met one of your students." Mr. Thompson nodded his head in acknowledgement towards Derek. They continued talking for a while longer, then he had to leave to go home with his wife and relieve the babysitter of his kids.

"I think you need to go to bed early," Derek whispered as she started drifting off to sleep. She nodded her head and curled up with her pillow.

Stacey woke up and looked over at the pull-out Derek was sleeping on. She smiled as she thought about all he has done for her while she has been in the hospital and even before all of that. "God, thank You for the wonderful man You made in Derek. He will do great things for You. Please help us with the new journey we are about to begin. It will be different living away from my family but nice to be closer to my second family. Please give my mom some peace about the things she is struggling with so she can join Your family. Thank You for everything. In Jesus' name, Amen." She tried to adjust herself and saw Derek's head pop up. "Sorry," Stacey whispered as he sat up and moved to help her.

"Don't be sorry, I'm here to help you." He helped her adjust into the incline position and put an extra pillow behind her.

"Are you ready to be going home today?" Stacey asked.

"Yes, hospitals are not fun to sleep in. So many interruptions." Stacey chuckled.

"Are you ready to be moving into my parents' house?" Stacey nodded her head. "I think they are giving you the room they added onto the house as it is on the main floor with a bathroom in it, and you won't need to do stairs all the time."

"Isn't that the new four seasons room they built for having company over?"

"It is a multipurpose room, but it would be used as a guest room." Stacey looked down at her hands as she fidgeted with the fringes on the pillow her dad brought her from home. "Stac, it isn't a big deal for them to give up that room for you. They felt the need to build it, and apparently, it was well-timed because now it is needed for you." She looked up at him.

"Okay, but after my leg starts getting better, if they need the room, I can bunk somewhere else in the house." Derek smiled as he gave her forehead a kiss.

"You are not an inconvenience; you are an addition to the family," Stacey looked up at him and gave him a big smile. There was a knock on the door, and Jayne walked in.

"Derek," she said, "why don't you go home and get cleaned up? I'm going to be helping Stacey with her shower and other stuff." Derek kissed Stacey, then grabbed his bags.

"About an hour?" he asked. Jayne nodded her head.

"Why don't you order your breakfast? Then, it should be here by the time we are done getting you a shower." Stacey grabbed the menu and ordered her food.

⸻ ∽∾⌇⊙⌇∾∽ ⸻

An hour later, Stacey was clean and eating when Derek came back in.

"You look refreshed," Derek said as he sat down on the chair next to her.

"So do you, and you are no longer sporting the five o'clock shadow." Stacey reached out and touched his smooth face. He smiled.

"That is the longest it has been in a while." Derek stole some of her food. "Did Jayne say when you were being discharged?"

"In a few hours, she wants to do a test before I go, and she wants me to meet my physical therapist." Stacey took a few more bites. "Was my mom at your house?" Derek nodded his head while finishing the bite he just took.

"Yes, she had just arrived when I got there. I think they were talking about coming here, but they were also thinking of just seeing you when you got to the house because you were being discharged." Stacey nodded her head in understanding.

"It would be a lot of waiting around with me not being here." Derek kept eating her food. "Didn't you eat before you left the house?"

"Stac, I can always eat, but I can stop if you want it all to yourself."

"You are fine, I ordered in case you wanted some as I didn't know if you would take the time to eat at the house." He chuckled as he stole another bite. Jayne came back into the room shortly after they finished breakfast.

"I got the testing room ready, and the physical therapist is there. Are you ready?" Stacey nodded her head. "We will take a wheelchair this time as we don't want you tired before the testing." Derek helped her into the wheelchair, then sat on her bed with the TV remote as Jayne pushed Stacey out.

"You look like you have a secret," Stacey said as they waited in the elevator.

"I kind of do…" Stacey looked up at her. "Your physical therapist is my husband. I still get excited to see him." Stacey chuckled.

"Does he have more patients than just your case study?"

"Yes, but he does mostly lower extremity injuries." They made it to the room, and Stacey looked around at all the exercise equipment.

"Stacey, I'm Dallas," they shook hands. "The tests we will be doing today are the same strength tests you had done before you came here for the surgery, but then the rest of our times together, we will be doing full-body strengthening. We will also be in a different room." Stacey nodded her head in acknowledgment, then started doing the tests with Jayne and Dallas helping her around the room.

"Why are we doing full-body strengthening when it is my knee that needs the work?"

"It is part of our study; part of the difference is the surgery, and part of it is the physical therapy. So, for the physical therapy part, we have seen a difference in our patients who do full-body workouts with us compared to the ones that just work on the specific area of pain. So you will have physical therapy five days a week, a combination of arms and core, legs and core, then after the incision heals, we will do some swimming too."

"So, because I injured my leg, I'm going to be in the best shape of my life?" Dallas chuckled.

"Something like that. We have some workout clothes for you to wear that will make it easier for you to get them on and off with the knee brace. And over the weekend, you will have some exercises you will need to do at home. We will give you the equipment for that as well." They helped Stacey back into the wheelchair.

"Am I allowed to drive?" She asked both of them.

"After about a week, you were on some narcotics through your IV, so you have to be completely off those to be able to drive. Now, you will need to ice your knee and take Tylenol and ibuprofen alternatively as needed," Jayne said as they got ready to leave. Stacey said goodbye to Dallas, then they went back up to the room. The nurses came to do a final vitals check, then gave them the rundown of the information with her injury and her discharge information. Stacey's dad came to sign her out.

"Hi Dad," she gave him a hug. He signed the discharge papers, and Derek pushed her in a wheelchair as Christian carried their bags out.

"How are you feeling?" Christian asked as they started going to the Rhysner house.

"A little sore, but I was moving a lot this morning. I should ice my knee when I get to the house." They arrived at the house, and Stacey crutched her way into the house.

"Look who is up and about!" Allison exclaimed as she gave her a hug.

"Hi Allison," Stacey squeezed her then saw her mom behind Allison.

"Hi Mom," Allison moved out of the way, and Stacey gave her a hug.

"How are you?" Laura asked.

"A little sore but doing pretty good." Her mom moved out of the way, and Stacey crutched into the living room and dropped onto the couch, putting her leg up. Derek went into the kitchen and got her some ice. They wrapped the ice pack around her knee, then Derek relaxed on the couch next to her with his arm around her shoulders.

"So much more comfortable than any of the hospital furniture." Derek exclaimed. Stacey chuckled. The families sat in the room with them, and they watched a movie. Both Stacey and Derek fell asleep shortly after it started.

"They've been through so much together already at such a young age," Allison said to her husband as they watched them sleep.

"They will probably have more to go through, but seeing how they handled this gives me high hopes for their future together."

⁓⁓

Stacey and Derek woke up a few hours later and found the living room deserted. "I guess I was tired," Stacey whispered.

"Me too," Derek said as he kissed her forehead. They saw Adam's face pop into the room.

"They are awake," he announced as he came in and plopped down on the ottoman in front of them.

"What do you want?" Stacey asked. He just sat there with a huge smile on his face. "Adam…" she said as she saw his mischievous smile.

"They want you to come see your new room. They have been working on putting it together to have a homey touch." Stacey smiled, then set her legs down and reached out to Adam to take her hand. He pulled her up, and Derek handed her the crutches. Adam led the way. They made it to the four seasons room that had just been added onto the house, and Stacey stared in awe. She looked around and saw a bed with a nightstand on each side. Then, she noticed there was a door to something and she went to it. When she opened the door, she discovered a closet; it was like another room—a mini-mall. All of her clothes were in there and they didn't even fill a fourth of the closet.

"I guess you will be working on filling up the rest of the closet," Derek said when he found her in the closet.

"Yeah, that will be my goal for the rest of the year," Stacey replied sarcastically. He walked up to her and wrapped his arms around her waist.

"It is nice to see you standing up again, even though you are using crutches."

"It's nice to finally not be so short, even though I am short anyways." Stacey walked out of the closet, then saw the huge painting of the two of them.

"Who painted this picture of us?" She asked as stared at the picture.

"Joanna painted it from memory of all the times we go out and watch the sunset."

"That is an amazing replica of us." She moved closer to look at it in more depth.

"Yeah… she caught your beauty,"

"And your good-looks," Stacey said as she smiled at Derek, then she finished looking around her room, which was when she noticed the little reading area with a skylight. "This is beautiful," she said as she sat down on the big chair and looked up into the sky. She noticed all of her personal belongings were put away in their respective places.

"Did my mom put all of this away?"

"I believe she did,"

"She knows my routines well, which is more than I can say about my personality." Allison popped into the room.

"Derek, your dad needs your help for a little bit, then lupper should be ready." Derek kissed Stacey on the forehead, then followed his mom, as Stacey chuckled at the word lupper and the first time she heard about the word from Derek's family. "It is lunch and supper put together." Derek had told her the first time she heard it.

A little while later, Joanna joined Stacey in her room. Joanna started the conversation.

"Please don't break his heart," she pleaded.

"I'll try not to," Stacey replied, seeing the concern in Joanna's face and wanting the concern on her face to disappear.

"Derek has loved you for a long time, and I think you are the only person for him; the two of you are perfect for each other." The comment was received with a sigh of relief.

"Joanna, I have loved him for a long time as well. I don't know what I would do if I lost him. My friends don't believe him to be real because he seems too good to be true, but he is so real to me." Joanna gave Stacey a hug as Laura walked into the room.

"Joanna, can I have a moment with my daughter?"

"Yes," Joanna stood up and left the room.

"Thanks for setting up my room, Mom," Laura looked around the room and sunk into a chair close to Stacey.

"You're welcome." She remained quiet for a little while longer.

"Mom, you said you wanted to talk." Laura looked down at her hands.

"I heard that your dad let out my little secret." She looked up at Stacey to see a reaction.

"Yeah, and it is kind of a big secret, Mom," Laura looked back down at her hands.

"Sorry," Stacey wanted to get up to get closer to her mom but was too tired to move.

"Mom, can you come closer?" Laura got up and moved her chair closer. Stacey leaned forward and held her mom's hands. "Mom, I understand that something may have happened in your life that is keeping you from accepting Jesus' sacrifice and love, but it doesn't mean you need to hide that from us. I wish you wouldn't have hidden this from us because it makes me feel betrayed. I thought I was following in both my parents' footsteps when I became a believer, and I looked up to your belief. To find out that it was fake makes me rethink things, but my faith in Jesus is not something I am rethinking. I love you, Mom, but I've lost a little bit of respect for you." Laura nodded her head.

"Thanks for letting me know how you feel. I really want to believe, but I can't get over what happened in the past." Laura dropped Stacey's hands and stood up.

"You know, He could help you if you let Him." Laura shook her head as she walked out. Stacey joined the two families in the dining and living room for the evening.

⸻⸻

Stacey woke up the next morning in her new room and smiled as she looked around again. She slowly moved about to get ready for church, then sat in the reading chair with her Bible to do her quiet time. A little while later, Stacey heard a knock on her door and saw Derek pop his head in. He saw her on the chair in the reading area and walked into the room.

"Happy Birthday," Stacey whispered as he bent down for a kiss.

"I thought you forgot about my birthday."

"I wouldn't forget my boyfriend's birthday," Stacey said as she tipped her head up to see him better, and he continued to bend down to meet his lips with hers. They had just separated when Joanna walked in.

"Happy Birthday, Joanna," they said as she joined them.

"Thanks, Mom sent me in here to get you for breakfast." Everyone ate breakfast, and then they all went to church. Stacey rode with Derek in his car, and their families went in separate cars. When they got to the church, Derek carried Stacey inside the beautiful sanctuary with stained glass windows and the wooden cross in front of the many pews. They sat in the front row so Stacey wouldn't have to worry about anyone bumping her knee. Derek's father, Chad, stood up front as one of the pastors in the church to start the morning with announcements.

After the announcements, the worship leader started the morning with a few worship songs. Chad delivered a wonderful sermon about God's miracles, and then they sang a few more songs. When the service was over, Stacey met some people and saw old friends from camp. As Derek picked Stacey up and they headed toward the car, they were stopped many times to talk and greet Stacey. In the parking lot, they realized Derek's car was gone, but Christian's car was there with Adam and Joanna in the front seats. Derek helped Stacey into the car, and then he got in on the other side. Adam took a scenic route back to the Rysners' house. Eventually, Adam received a call, and they headed straight to their house.

"I will get Stacey out of the car; you guys go ahead," Adam suggested as he parked. Joanna and Derek went inside, and when they opened the door, they were met with a big SURPRISE! Adam and Stacey were right behind them. Derek turned around and grabbed Stacey; he kissed her because he knew she was in on the surprise. They went inside, and Derek carried Stacey around while giving hugs. He almost set Stacey down on the ground, but she placed her good leg down before she could get hurt.

"Derek, why don't you put me down in a chair before you hurt me?" Stacey suggested.

"But then I couldn't be holding you all the time," Derek replied.

"Derek, just put me down in a chair and go visit people or sit down by me." He gently set Stacey down on a couch, and he went off to get some food for himself. Then he sat down next to Stacey. When Derek wasn't looking, Stacey playfully stole some of his food... he caught her once.

"You're stealing all of my food, Miss Rosemen."

"Oh, I thought you brought the food for me," Stacey replied innocently as her family started laughing. Adam brought her chocolate-covered strawberries, some other fruit, and a cup of punch.

"Thank you, Adam," Stacey said as she took the plate and cup from him. Joanna sat next to Stacey, and they talked for a while until she spotted her boyfriend. Then Stacey engaged in a conversation with one of her friends from camp, when suddenly, Derek gently turned her head with two of his fingers and kissed her for a while. When they stopped kissing, Stacey looked around and noticed that the room had cleared. She realized why they had cleared out. He kissed her again and pulled her closer to him. Then Christian entered.

"There are other people who came here to see you, Derek." Derek started to pick Stacey up, but Christian stopped him. Derek gave Stacey a peck on the lips before he left. Stacey's father sat down next to her with an ice pack. He wrapped the ice pack around her knee and then held her. "You know, I haven't been able to hold my baby since she got hurt." Stacey laid her head on his shoulder, cherishing the peaceful time with her father.

"Dad, you know I will always be your baby, and I love you very much," she reassured him.

"I feel like I am losing you, honey."

"You will never lose me, Dad, my love is always right here," Stacey said as she pointed to his heart. They sat there in silence for a while, and then Adam joined them on the couch for a cuddling session. The couch was crowded. After some time, Adam gently picked up Stacey and headed outside to where the party was. He grabbed her crutches so she could move on her own. Derek introduced her to some of his friends.

"Stacey, there are a few friends who couldn't come today, but they would like to meet you soon. Would you like to come to school with me early tomorrow to meet them?" Derek asked, with some of his friends close by.

"Sure, I'm not sure how I'll get back, but I'm guessing you have that figured out." He nodded his head, and they spent a good part of the evening hanging out with friends and family.

⁓⁓∽•ᴐᴇᴛᴑᴄᴛᴇᴑᴑᴠᴠ⁓

The next day, Stacey got ready to go early and was relaxing when Derek came to check on her. "You look beautiful," he whispered, pulling her up onto her feet and handing her the crutches. They went out to Derek's car and drove to his school. Stacey was wearing a skirt and a nice shirt, with her knee wrapped up and her new knee brace on. Three guys were waiting for them when they arrived. Derek carried Stacey out of the car to meet them. "Dennis, Chase, and AJ, this is Stacey," Derek announced as he walked towards a picnic bench. The three guys followed Derek to the picnic table and sat across from Stacey and Derek.

"The way Derek always talked about you made us think he was lying because it was all too good to be true, but you are here now," Dennis said, looking at Stacey. She glanced from the guys to Derek as her face turned red.

"How are your knee and ribs doing?" Chase asked, having talked to Derek every day, hearing updates, and praying for her.

"They are doing fine, thanks for asking." They continued chatting until school started. Then Derek saw his mom pull up, and he helped Stacey into the van and gave her a kiss. He stood next to the van with his head inside the door.

"I don't want to leave you," Derek whispered.

"Well, you have to go to school, and I need to get back for a little bit of physical therapy," Stacey declared. Derek gave her another kiss. "Derek, leave. You need to get your diploma." Finally, Derek left, and Stacey headed for her meeting with Jayne before her physical therapy. When she arrived, Stacey used her crutches to get out of the van. "Thanks for the ride, Allison," she waved as Jayne appeared next to Stacey, and they went inside.

"Why are you giving me all of this attention?" Stacey asked as they headed to the cafeteria.

"Stacey, with this study, I only have a few patients. Right now, you are my only patient for this study. I just finished the intense rehab with my last patient, and he graduated from his therapy. He still has to come in for check-ups every so often, but he is doing much better." Jayne helped Stacey get some food and got some for herself, then they headed to her office.

"So, I am your only patient right now?"

"In a way, yes. I still have patients from the past years of this study, and I have patients who come in for their check-ups. But otherwise, you are my only patient. I do help with shortages of staff and such, but my study is my priority. While I was waiting for a new patient for the study, I picked up a few patients for regular exams and procedures. The only time I will be called away is for an emergency or if I have a scheduled appointment. You will have daily physical therapy with my husband, which I might help with, otherwise, I will come in and check on you often, because you are my first priority." She took a few sips of her drink and observed Stacey, watching for signs of fatigue.

"That sounds like fun," there were no signs of fatigue that Jayne could see.

"Yes, especially when you start school again." They finished eating and talked a little more about the schedule before heading to her physical therapy session. Dallas greeted them at the door, and they had fun working on getting Stacey's arms and core stronger. As Stacey neared the end of the session, she texted Allison to let her know she was ready to be picked up. When she reached the front door, she saw her dad with a bouquet of red and white roses, a pile of mail, and a few other boxes on the counter for her.

"Dad, what are you doing here? I thought you left earlier."

"I'm having a hard time leaving, and the hospital called to tell me about all this stuff that just showed up. So, I told Allison I would pick you up." Her father explained as he gave her a hug, then grabbed the pile of items as they headed back to the Rysners' house. She went to her room to read all the mail and opened the packages. One of the packages contained her cell phone—the school had found it and sent it to her. There were many messages on her phone as well. The roses were from Aaron, and the letters were from her friends from school. Adam entered and plopped down next to her on the bed.

"Lots of well wishes?"

"Yeah, from people I barely even know. I guess a lot of people knew about what I was going through and liked how I was handling it until it escalated. I also have some apologies in these letters and a few confessions." Stacey handed him a few of the apology letters and confessions. Adam read them.

"Wow, I guess God had some good coming out of all your pain." Stacey gave him a small smile. "These roses kind of worry me." Adam said as he finished reading the card that came with it.

"I agree. I'm not sure how else to tell him I'm not interested." Adam laid back on the bed and looked up at the ceiling.

"I'm not sure either."

"I thought you needed to go to school." Adam rolled over with a huge grin on his face.

"I guilt-tripped Dad into staying a little longer." Stacey chuckled then looked at her twin brother.

"Are you really okay with me moving here?"

"Yes and no, I'll miss you, but I know Derek will take good care of you." He got off the bed. "Let's go watch a movie before we have to leave." He pulled Stacey off her bed and helped her to the living room. Christian joined them, and they watched a comedy together.

Two hours later, she woke up to see Adam smiling in her face, "Adam, what are you so happy for?"

"It's nice seeing you awake and happy. You seem happier than you have been in the last few months, even though you're in pain."

"Adam, you always seem to find good in all the pain in the world."

"Is the pain tolerable?"

"Most of the time. It wouldn't be so bad if I could get around a lot easier, but that will come."

"But Derek loves carrying you around." She giggled as she thought about how safe she felt when Derek picked her up. She changed the subject to Adam's girlfriend and how school was going. Then Adam saw the clock.

"Dad and I do need to get going though. I have a test and a speech I need to give." Stacey stood up on her good leg and gave her brother a tight squeeze.

"Call or text me whenever you want," she whispered to her brother, then she gave her dad a hug.

"Don't be a stranger," her dad whispered.

"Same goes for you," he kissed her cheek and then she handed him the phone she had borrowed. "I got my phone back; you can have this one back."

"Thanks, I love you, Stacey."

"I love you too." Christian and Adam left, and Stacey followed them out and stood by a porch post, which is where Allison found her.

"Are you doing okay?" Stacey looked at Allison with a tear going down her face.

"Yeah, I'll just miss them." Stacey went inside and grabbed an ice pack on the way to her room. She worked on answering the letters and messages she received from her friends and family while waiting for Derek to come home.

Chapter 3

Stacey headed to the hospital for her physical therapy. "Hey Dallas, are you ready to torture me?" Stacey asked him as she crutched into the room.

"I don't torture you; I just make you work on building muscles." She shook her head as she moved onto a block.

"That's the same thing to me. So, what are we doing today?"

"We are doing leg and core strengthening." Stacey groaned as she started working out. Half an hour later, Stacey was all sweaty and smelly but feeling great about what she accomplished. She was heading out the door when she saw Aaron in the lobby. She also saw Chad waiting for her. Both of them approached her as she continued moving towards them.

"Hi Aaron, how are you?" She asked as he stood in front of her.

"I'm fine... can we talk alone, please?" Stacey looked at Chad, and he nodded his head as he went back to the chair he had vacated and sat down again. They went outside, and Aaron sat on a bench with Stacey next to him.

"What did you want to talk to me about?" Stacey asked, even though she knew the answer to her own question.

"Stacey, will you go out with me?" Aaron asked as he showed Stacey a diamond necklace. Stacey studied the necklace as she tried to think of what she could say to him.

"Aaron, I can't. I have a boyfriend. I have told you many times that I have a boyfriend already." Stacey watched as Aaron's jaw clenched from trying not to cry. "Aaron, there is a girl out there for you, but that girl is not me."

"I think the only time my mouth has or ever will touch yours was when we were in that play together. Keep the necklace; it is your birthday present." Aaron said as he ran away. Stacey sat on the bench thinking. Her thoughts were interrupted when she felt someone sit down next to her.

"I'm guessing he didn't get what he wanted," Chad whispered as he looked at the necklace. Stacey continued staring at the necklace and shook her head. "You care about him but not in the same way he does?" Stacey nodded her head again.

"I think of him like a brother. He has been great while I've been dealing with my bullies, and I kind of feel like I used him to have an ally in school." Chad placed his hand over the necklace to get her to look at him.

"From what I can tell, you told him many times you were dating someone, and he stayed with you. You did not use him." Stacey gave him a small smile.

"It still hurts to hurt him, even if I didn't want to hurt him."

"That just means you have a great heart." Chad placed his arm around her shoulders and remained quiet.

"Can we go home now?" Stacey asked half an hour later.

"Yes." Chad helped her to his vehicle, and they went home. Chad stopped Stacey from getting out of the vehicle. "Do you want to talk about it more?" Stacey sighed.

"I don't think it will make me feel any better." She handed the necklace to Chad. "I don't want this, though." Stacey went inside and retreated to her room.

⁓⁓◦ᕬⱺᕬ◦ᕬⱺᕬ◦⁓⁓

Derek came home from school and looked around for Stacey. Chad saw him and motioned for Derek to join him in the office.

"Where's Stac?" Chad motioned for him to sit down.

"She's been a little down today. Aaron came to visit, and she had to turn him down." Derek smiled. "I wouldn't have that attitude when you go in to see her. It really bothered her to have to hurt him. They were really good friends." Derek frowned as he thought about it.

"I guess I understand, but their relationship has always kind of bothered me." Chad looked at his son.

"Maybe you need to pray and confess your selfish thoughts before going in to see her. She has been in her room since she left her physical therapy session this morning." Derek looked concerned.

"Has she eaten?" Chad shook his head. Derek stood up and went to the kitchen.

"Dear God," he started praying as he made a charcuterie board for Stacey. "I know I have been jealous of Stacey's relationship with Aaron, but I need help putting that aside to help her through her current pain. Please help me not say something that will stress Stacey or make her even more upset. She has been through enough this last week, and she may be losing another friend who has been there for her." Derek continued cutting up some cheeses and meats, grabbing some crackers, nuts, and dips to add to the tray. His sisters started stealing some of the food as he began carrying it to Stacey's room.

"Where are you taking all of that?" Ariel asked.

"To Stacey. She hasn't eaten all day. I guess she has had a rough day. I'll text you ladies when or if it is okay for you to join us." They agreed. Derek moved to Stacey's door with the tray and knocked before slowly entering the room. He saw her curled up with her pillow on her bed. He left the door open as he walked towards the bed. "Can I join you?" Stacey lifted her head and saw the tray, then gave a small nod. Derek set the tray on the bed and sat across from her.

"I didn't hear you come in." Stacey whispered as Derek looked at her and noticed tear tracks going down her face.

"It looks like you've been crying." He reached across the bed and brushed the tears off her face.

"Yeah, Aaron came to the hospital to ask me out. I turned him down, of course, but it was hard to watch his reaction. He's been a good friend, and I just hate that I had to hurt him." She took a few bites of the food Derek brought.

"Is that all you've been thinking about?" Stacey shook her head as new tears appeared in her eyes.

"I know Adam was just here a few days ago, but I do miss him, even with his constant array of messages. I'll get used to it, but I guess I needed a crying and thinking day." Derek took a few bites of the food while he looked over at her. "Did your dad warn you about Aaron?" Stacey asked quietly.

"Yeah, why?"

"I was kind of expecting a different reaction when I said he was here and I rejected him." Derek frowned.

"I'm sorry, and you are right. If I had come in here before talking to Dad, you would have received a different reaction. But my dad is right, I needed to get over my jealousy of your relationship to really hear what you are saying. I confessed everything to God as I prepared this tray of food." Derek noticed his sisters poking their heads in to see them. "Are you okay with my sisters joining us, or do you want some time alone?" Stacey saw their heads pop in and out.

"You can come in now," Stacey announced. They ran into the room and hopped onto the bed. "How was school?" She asked them.

"It will be better when you start coming," Joanna said as she shoved some food into her mouth. Stacey smiled as she ate some food.

"Do you know when you are going to school?" Ariel asked.

"Hopefully soon. I won't technically be behind because of changing schools, but I will have to catch up on the curriculum of your school." They all nodded their heads in understanding. After they finished the tray, they moved into the living room and watched a movie.

⎯⎯∿∘◦⊙◦⊙⊙⊙◦⊙◦∘∿⎯⎯

Stacey awoke feeling rested and relaxed. It didn't take long for her to realize the significance of the day. "It's my birthday and Adam's as well. We're now 18 years old."

Shortly after, Stacey noticed a large box in her room. Curiosity piqued, she reached for the box, eagerly tearing it open. Inside, she found a massive teddy bear. "Wow, this thing is huge! What's that on its arm? Oh, it's a bracelet. This is stunning." Stacey thought to herself, removing the bracelet from the bear's arm and slipping it onto her own wrist. As she admired the gift, she sensed she was being watched.

"Adam, I love you. Come in, I won't bite." She reassured him. Adam cautiously entered the room and sat down on the bed beside her.

"Happy Birthday, Stacey," he said, embracing her warmly.

"Happy Birthday, Adam." Adam got up to give Stacey some privacy, grabbing her clothes before leaving. Stacey changed into a navy-blue short-sleeved dress and flat shoes. When she was ready, she headed to the kitchen, where Derek greeted her with a kiss and a tight embrace.

"Happy Birthday, Stac," Derek said, his arms encircling her waist. Stacey leaned her crutches against the wall and returned his embrace.

"Thanks, Derek. So, what's the plan for today?" Derek scooped her up gently and carried her into the living room. As they entered, Stacey was met with a chorus of voices exclaiming, "SURPRISE!"

"I told you I'd get you back," Derek whispered mischievously in Stacey's ear, her family forming a circle around her. Stacey's Aunt Addison whistled to get everyone's attention.

"Let's head out for breakfast." The whole group piled into their cars and drove to a breakfast buffet. After everyone had settled into their seats, Derek stood up to make an announcement, capturing the attention of everyone in the room. He tapped his glass with a knife to signify an announcement.

"I'm happy we are all here to celebrate Stacey and Adam's birthday. Just enjoy the time together." They all ate and talked for a while, then Laura asked Adam and Stacey if they wanted to open their presents, and they both enthusiastically nodded their heads.

"This is from all of us," Laura said as they handed each of them a huge box. They opened the boxes, and there was a laptop, laptop case, games, digital cameras, cases, and money for each of them. They both said thank you to everyone, gave them hugs, and continued talking until noon.

Later, they went to the park to walk around. The park was beautiful. Chad had brought a wheelchair for Stacey, so she wouldn't be worn out. Derek picked Stacey up and sat down in the chair. Derek started wheeling Stacey away, but Aunt Addison caught them and she asked to talk to Stacey. Derek stood up and put Stacey back in the wheelchair. He gave her a kiss and left. Addison wheeled Stacey to a bench, and she sat down.

"Stacey, you really do like Derek, don't you?"

"Yes, I do," they continued talking for about half an hour. After a while, Stacey saw Derek approaching hesitantly, afraid of interrupting their conversation.

"Sorry to interrupt, but I would like to steal her away." Addison gave Stacey a hug and whispered to Derek to come back and talk to her. As he was pushing Stacey's wheelchair, he bent down and whispered into her ear.

"Aaron wants to talk to you." She agreed to talk to him as they headed towards Aaron's location. Derek stopped pushing the wheelchair, came in front of Stacey, and gave her a loving, longing kiss to show Aaron that Stacey was his. Derek waved at Aaron as he left to go talk to Aunt Addison. Aaron walked up closer.

"Happy Birthday, Stacey," he whispered as he slowly inched closer. Stacey became uneasy as his face became unemotional and fearless.

"Thanks, Aaron. How have you been?"

"Horrible. How have you been?"

"Aaron, I have been great," Stacey said as Aaron walked closer and closer, and Stacey got more and more uncomfortable. Aaron came so close that their noses were two inches apart. Stacey tried to back up, but he grabbed the wheelchair. She was about to scream when he kissed her. Stacey pushed him away, but he wouldn't let her leave as he gripped harder onto the wheelchair. She let out a scream.

⸻⁕⸻

Derek was talking to Aunt Addison about Stacey when they heard a scream, and they both looked at each other.

"Derek, did I just hear a scream?"

"Oh no," Derek said as he ran towards Stacey.

Aaron panicked when Stacey screamed. He picked her up and tried to run, but Stacey's family caught him. Everybody tried to get Stacey, but Aaron wouldn't let her go. Stacey screamed from the pain in her knee. A few minutes later, the police arrived and told everybody to back away. Everybody took a step back, cautiously hoping Aaron wouldn't do anything to her.

"Put the girl down," the police ordered him. Derek walked up to Aaron to get Stacey from Aaron, but the police yelled for him to stay back.

"Sir, I can't walk without some help," Stacey explained to the police as Aaron's grip became tighter and more painful.

"Okay, sorry… go get her then." Derek walked up slowly, but Aaron dropped her before Derek got to them. When he dropped Stacey, her bad knee hit the ground first, then Derek caught her. Christian ran up to her, hoping nothing else got hurt or re-hurt.

"Are you okay?" Christian asked her while she looked up at him.

"No," she whispered as she fainted. When she woke up, she was in her parents' car lying on Derek's lap. When she saw Derek, she grabbed his neck, pulled his head down to hers, and kissed him, then she fell back to sleep. When they arrived at the hospital, Jayne had Derek put Stacey on her bed, and she checked Stacey's knee. Jayne put Stacey on some morphine, and Derek went in to sit with her. Jayne walked out to Stacey's family to inform them of the effects of the day's adventures.

"Nothing got torn, but the hit stretched the stitches, so she is going to have to take it easy like she has been the last few days." The family sat down and talked with Jayne. "I think we will keep her overnight. I don't think she will wake up until tomorrow anyways, and we should take it slowly." Everyone agreed.

"I think we should all go home and get some rest. Laura, Christian, and Adam, you can use Stacey's room as she will be here tonight," Allison said. They all agreed to go get some rest.

⸻ ♦ ⸻

The next morning, Stacey woke up drowsy and in acute pain. Derek walked over and laid next to her as she scooted over for him. She laid her head on his shoulder, feeling warm and safe. She listened to his heartbeat as she fell asleep again. About two hours later, Jayne came in to talk to them. She woke Derek up and told him the plan. A few minutes later, Stacey woke up, and Derek went to her and sat on the edge of the bed.

"Hey darling, how are you feeling?" She looked at him and observed the concern on his face, unsure of how to alleviate his worry.

"I'm feeling better, but my knee is still in pain," she answered. Derek moved off the bed, moved closer to her, and sat down again.

"I think it will be in pain for a while longer."

"Don't you think I know that?" Stacey asked, irritated with her situation.

"Yeah, I know that you know that, but I'm trying to make myself feel better about you being in pain. I don't like seeing you in pain." She felt bad about her reaction when all he wanted was to take care of her.

"Oh, Derek, I'll live," Stacey said as she leaned against his shoulder.

"Kiss me, please," Derek whispered in her ear. Stacey complied, turning her head to kiss him. She pulled away when she felt a shot of pain going up her leg.

"Stacey, are you alright?" He jumped off the bed and backed away, afraid he had caused the pain.

"Derek, can you go get Jayne, please? I need my pain meds." He nodded his head and bolted out of the room to find Jayne. A few minutes later, Jayne ran in with with a numbing shot and a pill. After Stacey took the pill, Jayne checked her stitches and found that a few of them had opened up.

"Stacey, I am going to have to re-stitch your knee; a few of them have ripped. I can do it now because your whole leg is numb from the shot I just gave you. Derek, can you distract her again, like you did the other day?" Derek nodded his head as Jayne prepared herself to sew up Stacey's knee. Ten minutes later, Jayne finished up by cleaning Stacey's knee and wrapping it up. Jayne left the room after she cleaned everything up, and Derek carefully laid himself down next to Stacey as she fell asleep.

At noon, Christian went to check in on Stacey. When he entered the room, he saw Derek holding her, and he slowly walked in to see that she was sleeping.

"Derek, is everything okay?" Christian asked in a whisper, wondering why she was sleeping and hoping not to wake her up.

"I'm not sure. We were just cuddling, and she turned her head to give me a kiss, but she pulled away in pain." Christian relaxed as he sat down on the empty chair in front of Stacey.

"Hi, Daddy," Stacey whispered as she slowly woke up, feeling less pain.

"Hi, sweetheart. How are you feeling?"

"I'm fine for now. The pain meds are still working, so I can't feel anything in my left knee." Christian watched her face for any sign of pain, but there wasn't any there.

"Well, do you feel like going out to eat with everybody?"

"Do I need to get discharged?" Jayne joined them with the discharge papers. "I think I'm up for it, but I would like to get cleaned up and change." Christian handed her the bag of clothes he brought, and Jayne went to grab some things as Derek slipped out of the bed and gave her a kiss before Jayne came back. Jayne helped Stacey get cleaned up, then dressed her in some clean clothes. When they were done, Derek came in with the wheelchair, and he helped her get into the chair. He pushed the chair to the front entrance as Christian pulled up with the car. Derek gently picked her up and set her in the car. He left the wheelchair at the hospital and brought the crutches with them. He jumped into the car as they went to a nice sit-down restaurant.

The rest of the family joined them at the restaurant, and they ordered their food. Then they made plans for when Stacey's family would visit her and when she would go visit them in La Crosse. After they received their food, Stacey just sat back and watched the antics of her family and Derek's family.

"My darling, you're being quiet," Derek whispered into Stacey's ear, noticing she hadn't talked in a while.

"I'm just trying to relax, and it's fun watching you guys tell stories." The family in front of them didn't seem to notice their private conversation as their stories continued.

"Okay, as long as you're okay. You're just being really quiet," Derek kissed her cheek.

"I'm fine, Derek, but thanks for asking." They finally left the restaurant at two o'clock in the afternoon. The Rosemen's, with the exception of Stacey, went back home to La Crosse, and the rest of them went to the Rysner's house. When they arrived at the house, Stacey used her crutches to limp to her room.

Around five o'clock, Jayne came by to check on Stacey's knee and inspect her room. She stayed for supper, then left when they finished. However, she left some prescription pain meds for Stacey to take before bed. After dinner, Stacey helped clean the dishes, then she went to lay down in the living room to watch a movie with Joanna, Ariel, and Derek. Finally, when the movie was over, Stacey went into her personal bathroom and took a Jacuzzi bath, but she had to keep her left leg out of the water. She relaxed into the water and almost fell asleep as the jets were going. About half an hour later, she heard a knock on the door.

"Stacey, are you okay?" Joanna asked, having been sent in by Derek to check on her.

"I'm fine, just relaxing in the Jacuzzi," she replied as she heard Joanna laughing on the other side of the door.

"I'll check on you in half an hour."

"Okay, thank you, Joanna." Stacey continued relaxing for 10 more minutes, then she got out of the Jacuzzi and put on a dark-green top and a pair of black shorts. Joanna kept her promise and checked on her within 20 minutes after Stacey got out of the tub.

"Hey, you're not incapable of doing everything yourself."

"Yeah, Jayne has taught me how to get dressed without hurting myself." Stacey moved to Joanna with her brush in her hand. "Joanna, would you like to play with my hair? My wrist is sore."

"I would love to. Let's go out to the living room," Joanna suggested as Derek walked in. Joanna, Stacey, and Derek went into the living room. Stacey sat on the floor with ice for her knee next to Derek, while Joanna sat behind them and played with Stacey's hair.

A while later, Stacey noticed that Derek was sleeping. "Derek, go to bed."

"Do you want help going to bed?"

"No, Derek. I'm fine, but you need to go to bed." He gave her a kiss as he got up to go to bed. A short while later, Stacey went to bed as well and fell asleep shortly after she laid herself in the bed.

In the middle of the night, she woke up in a hot sweat from a nightmare. She slid from her bed and used her crutches to go into the bathroom for a drink of water. Then she went to the reading area and sat down on the lounge couch, watching the stars in the sky. She retrieved a blanket and fell asleep on the chair, praying for a peaceful sleep from God.

⸎

In the morning, Derek came in to check on Stacey, and he panicked when he didn't see her on the bed. "Dad, where is Stacey?" Chad looked up to see panic on Derek's face.

"I don't know. I saw her go into her room last night. What is her favorite thing to do?"

"She loves reading." His face lit up as if he had the best idea in the world. He ran back to her room and checked the reading area to find her sleeping on the lounge chair. Chad slowly followed.

"Dad, I think this is her favorite spot in the house."

"Derek, let her sleep. She needs it to heal." Derek left the room, and Stacey continued sleeping. At nine o'clock, she woke up to the smell of bacon. She got her crutches and went into the kitchen. Everybody was in the kitchen, making breakfast. She watched them work together until Derek saw her. He walked up to her, gave her a kiss, and led her to a chair to sit down.

After breakfast, Derek took Stacey to the hospital for her physical therapy session. When she arrived, Dallas greeted her with a big smile.

"Good morning, Stacey. This must be the boyfriend," Dallas walked up to Derek and shook hands with him as Stacey sat down on the bench to get ready.

"Yes, this is Derek," Stacey said as she put on her weight lifting gloves. Then Jayne slowly took the brace off her knee to examine the wound.

"It is looking better, but it is still swollen. So when you get home, you should elevate your knee and put some ice on it." Jayne wrapped it back up in gauze with her brace, then she patted her shoulder as she left the room.

"Dallas, are you ready to torture me yet?" Stacey asked when she was ready to go.

"I'm always ready to torture you," Dallas said with a huge smile on his face. "Today, we are going to do little leg workouts with your left leg, but we cannot bend it too much to break the stitches again. Have you taken the pain meds today?" Stacey shook her head. "Take them now, then you won't be as sore or in as much pain later." Stacey took the pills, then started her physical therapy; Derek didn't like seeing her in pain. The first part of the workout was the leg work, then strengthening the core was next. An hour later, Stacey was exhausted, and Derek carried her to the car and into the house when they arrived home.

"I never imagined physical therapy to be so painful or hard," Derek said to his mother after he put Stacey into bed.

"Derek, hard work is the whole point of physical therapy," Allison replied as she cleaned up the kitchen, preparing it for lunch preparations.

"I know, but watching someone you love go through physical therapy is heartbreaking to watch." He picked up an orange and started peeling it.

"Yeah, but that is the best thing for her knee to get full functionality." The two of them looked at each other. Derek finished peeling his orange, then headed to the living room to watch TV.

An hour later, in Stacey's bedroom, she woke up and checked her emails. One of them was from Abbey.

> *Dear Stacey,*
>
> *I am so sorry I did that, my heart told me not to do it but my mind told me to do it. My mind won, you know I have always wanted to be popular and now I am sorry for ever wanting to be popular. I am now only popular for the wrong reasons; the people who put me up to this don't even want to be my friends. Apparently they didn't think I would actually do it because you were my best friend, they didn't know how desperate I was to be popular. I am so sorry for hurting you. Please forgive me."*
>
> *Abbey Knowmen*

After Stacey read the e-mail, she continued reading the rest of her e-mails and replied to all of them but Abbey's. "God I don't know what to say to her. She hurt me but I am still alive. Please give me the words to forgive her." She fell asleep reading a book.

───∽∾∾⁛∾∽───

Outside Stacey's room, Derek was talking to his dad. "Dad, why is it so hard to leave the person you love when that person looks sad or in pain?" Derek picked up a book in his dad's office and paged through it.

"Derek, that feeling is called love," Chad put his pencil down and set his hands on his desk while watching his son. "When you love someone, you always want to be there for them and comfort them." Derek looked up from the book to see his dad watching him.

"So, the feeling is normal for a person in love?"

"Yes, by the way, Mom wants to go out tonight, dressed up."

"Did the girls get the dress?" Allison answered his question by carrying the dress in for him to see.

An hour later, Derek walked into Stacey's room and woke her up. "Stacey, get up, we are going out to eat." She turned around and noticed he was wearing a suit.

"Wow, you look nice."

"Yeah, I do clean up well," Derek said sarcastically while adjusting his jacket, "Just wait until the girls get you in your dress." He winked at her and left the room.

"What dress?" She asked as the girls then came in with a beautiful red lace and satin dress with flare at the bottom. They did her makeup and hair. When they were done, Stacey put on a pair of flats, and they slowly walked into the living room to show everybody the dress. Derek walked up to Stacey.

"You look beautiful," he said as he swung her into his arms.

"Your arms are going to be strong and tired if you carry me like this all night."

"I don't care," he said as they left the wheelchair and crutches at home. They went out to eat; Stacey ate a tenderloin steak with French fries and sparkling red grape juice to drink. They were all having fun, laughing. Under the table, Derek and Stacey were holding hands; Derek placed something on Stacey's left index finger. She pulled her hand out, and she saw a beautiful ring. He pulled the ring off and put it on her right hand on the ring finger, then he whispered.

"This is a ring of our commitment to each other." Stacey smiled, but it was covered with a long, passionate kiss. At eight o'clock, they left the restaurant, and they went to an aquarium. They watched the sea creatures, then they went home. When they arrived home, Stacey went into her room, changed into a pair of shorts and a sweatshirt, then she grabbed her laptop and turned it on as she sat on her bed. A few minutes later, Derek walked in and jumped onto the foot of the bed.

"I had fun tonight, how about you?" Derek asked as he adjusted her pillows for her to be more comfortable up against the headboard. Then he sat back at the foot of the bed.

"It was amazing; thank you for bringing me," Stacey said as Derek climbed up from the foot of the bed to get closer to her.

"Stacey Marie Rosemen, you are so easy to please," Derek said as he leaned into her and gave her a kiss. While they were still kissing, Stacey put her hands on his stomach and tickled him. "Stacey, you're asking for trouble," Derek whispered as he grabbed her hands to stop her from tickling him.

"Ouch, Derek, you can't hold onto that wrist," Stacey said as Derek released her wrist. Then she tickled him again.

"Stacey, I don't want to hurt you."

"Then don't," she replied as he attempted to tickle her. She held in her laughter as he continued to try to tickle her. He stopped and looked her in the eyes.

"You know there is one thing I hate," she tilted her head as she put her hands on his chest.

"What is that?"

"I hate that I can't tickle you." Stacey laughed as she pushed Derek off of her. Derek looked at Stacey's right hand, smiled, then he explained,

"My mom received this ring from my father when they were dating; she gave it to me today to give to you." Stacey smiled as she pulled Derek's head towards her and gave him a kiss. He said good-night and left the room. Stacey checked her email and played a few games on her computer before she went to bed.

⎯⎯∿⦿⟲⟳⦿⟲∿⎯⎯

The next day she woke up to her alarm and took a quick shower before she put on some nice clothes. Derek came in 10 minutes later to wake her up, but he was surprised to see her up and ready to go, sitting on her bed.

"Hey, I was going to wake you up, but you are already awake," Derek said as he approached her. He cupped her head in his hands as he bent down to her eye level.

"Derek," Stacey said sweetly, "Can you give me a kiss?"

"That is easy enough to comply with," he said as he leaned down to kiss her. Stacey stood up on her right leg as they were still kissing, and she wrapped her arms around his neck. Derek then picked her up and spun her around as Stacey kept her left leg straight.

"Stacey, I love you."

"I love you too," they whispered as Derek stopped spinning. Then Stacey went into the kitchen to eat, and Derek finished getting ready for church. When Stacey was done eating, she sat down in the living room with her Bible and read until everybody else was ready to leave. They left for church a little early; when they arrived, Chad introduced Stacey to Pastor Jeff.

"Would you be willing to tell everybody your story and sing a song? Derek told me you have a beautiful voice," Stacey looked at Derek then answered Pastor Jeff.

"Yes, I would love to sing a song and tell my story." Stacey went up to the front of the sanctuary and told her story after they sang a few songs. She shared her story while standing up with her crutches and explained everything through her own life and the last two weeks, as well as how God had helped her through her troubling times. After she was done talking, she sang a song for them while playing the piano, then she went to go sit down next to Derek. A few more songs were sung before the service was over, and many people came up to her with praises.

"God has blessed you." Eventually, Derek and Stacey made it out of the church, and then they went home to relax. Stacey went into her room and changed into some comfortable clothing and grabbed an ice pack for her knee. Once everybody was in the living room, they picked out a movie together and watched it. Because everyone was comfortable, they decided to order pizza; nobody wanted to make supper. While they were waiting, Stacey built a fire in the fireplace, and Derek brought drinks into the living room. About 20 minutes later, the pizza arrived delivered by a delivery boy, and they all ate the pizza while watching another movie. After the movie was over, Stacey and Derek went outside to the backyard and watched the sunset. What they didn't know was that Chad was watching them watch the sunset.

"Chad, why are you watching them?" Allison asked in a whisper when she found him watching the young couple.

"They remind me of when we were first in love," he whispered with his arm around Allison's shoulders.

"Well, when we were first in love, we wouldn't have wanted anyone watching us in our private moment. Let's leave them alone." Allison suggested as she pulled him back away from the window.

"You know, ever since we met the Rosemen family, I have wanted Derek and Stacey to fall in love, and they have." Allison looked at Chad, and their eyes locked.

"Have I told you lately that I love you, Chad Rysner?" Allison wrapped her arms around his neck as he backed her into their room. She kissed him before he could reply.

"Yes, but I don't mind hearing it all the time." Finally, they went to bed, and they fell asleep in each other's arms.

Chapter 4

The next morning Stacey woke up, opened her Bible, and read Psalm 23; that is when she found the note from Derek.

Dear Stacey,

I had to go to school, but I didn't want to. Have fun at Physical Therapy and think of me. I love you!

Derek Rysner

Stacey went out to the living room to find Allison. "Can you give me a ride to the hospital for my physical therapy session?" Allison agreed, and a few minutes later, Allison dropped Stacey off at the hospital. Dallas was in the entrance waiting for her, as she used crutches to walk.

"Are you ready to be tortured?" He asked as he offered a wheelchair.

"As ready as I will ever be," Stacey replied as she sat down in the wheelchair he had for her. Before the session started, Jayne came into the room and checked Stacey's knee to make sure the stitches were still intact.

"Stacey, everything looks fine. The swelling is down, and everything is intact," Jayne announced, then stood up to leave.

"Jayne, do you think she can start walking if she doesn't overdo it?" Dallas asked his wife. She turned around and looked at him.

"Yes, she can walk, but if it hurts too much, she should stop." Stacey looked at both of them, wondering why they were talking to each other and not to her.

"The both of you do know that I am right here, and you can talk to me." Jayne and Dallas laughed as they got the room set up for her workout. Stacey went between the parallel bars and walked with both legs. She used the bars to hold her body up as she set her left foot down. "It feels good to use my left leg."

"Stacey, slowly bring your foot up and bend your knee," Dallas said. She did just that and felt a little pull on the stitches, but other than that, it felt great. "Now, take a few more steps slowly." Stacey walked a little longer before she did her core and arm workout. When she was done, Dallas gave her a list of things to work on daily to improve her mobility in her knee. "Stacey, just do these things to help you."

"I will, thanks for helping me, Dallas."

"You're welcome, Stacey. You are so easy to push; you work so hard." Stacey used the wheelchair to get to the entrance, and then she used her crutches to get to the car.

"Hey Stacey, how was physical therapy?"

"Tiring. I just want to go home and sleep."

"Okay, we'll be there in a jiffy," Allison said as she drove home. A few minutes later, they were home, and Stacey went directly to her room to sleep. Before she fell asleep, she called her father and talked to him until he got a business call. Then she fell asleep. She woke up at noon and moved to the reading area to watch the clouds and birds overhead.

A little later, she heard a commotion out in the front area of the house. She went out to see what was happening. When she arrived in the front area, she saw the last person she wanted to see: Aaron. Stacey tried to run to her room, but she collapsed. Aaron saw her run and fall, then he tried to get in, but Chad kicked him out. Allison helped Stacey into her room, but she couldn't calm Stacey down; she was trembling and shaking.

"Stacey, you need food," she didn't answer, just sat there staring out at nothing. Chad then came in with Detective Kent and his partner.

"Are you okay, ma'am?" He asked, breaking her trance.

"As fine as can be expected, but my knee is bothering me again." The detective's partner went out to grab Stacey an ice pack, then came back with an ice pack, a glass of water, and a few ibuprofen. Stacey thanked the officer as she took the items.

Around three o'clock, Derek came home. When he saw the police cars, he ran inside. "Stacey," he yelled out.

"Derek, I'm in my room," she yelled back. Then Derek ran into her room. He froze when he saw Stacey. She sat on the bed and waited for him to come to her. He stood there frozen. She slowly walked up to him and wrapped her arms around his neck.

"Hold me, Derek," she said, as her legs were giving out on her. Derek caught her and carried her to the red chair; he laid her down and then laid himself down next to her.

"Honey, you're trembling,"

Outside the house, Aaron was planning his next escapade. "I want her with all my heart. I want her, and I'll do anything to get her," he thought. He sat outside Stacey's room, getting angrier as he watched her cuddling with Derek the whole time. She wasn't alone until 6:30, and Aaron started moving in to get her, but she received a phone call. She went into her closet and changed while talking on the phone. Once she was done, she walked back into her room, and at that moment, Aaron grabbed her. A little squeak came out of her mouth before he covered it. Then, he carried her out to the car and threw her into the trunk. She started screaming, and Aaron knocked her out to silence her.

After about 20 minutes, Aaron stopped the car and took Stacey out of the trunk. He tied her up in the front seat next to him. "Aaron, why are you doing this?" Stacey asked, trying to stay calm in the situation.

"Stacey, I am doing this because I want you," he replied. She remained silent for a few minutes. "We're almost there." Stacey became more uncomfortable as she saw where they were going. However, before they stopped, she prayed to God for help. A few minutes later, he parked the car and went to Stacey's side of the car.

"I am untying you, and I am going to trust that you are going to cooperate," he said as he untied Stacey and carried her into the hotel. Once they got inside the door, she started yelling and struggling against him.

"Let me go! I don't want to be here with you!" She hit him in an attempt to break free, but he held on tight.

"Settle down sweetheart," Aaron responded, barely keeping a hold of her.

"I am not your sweetheart," she said as she slapped him but barely hit him because of the way he was holding her. The receptionists saw her struggling with Aaron and Stacey mouthed "Help" to them as Aaron set her down on a chair. One of the receptionist's went into the back as the other receptionist was figuring out the room arrangement. While Aaron was at the desk with the receptionist, Stacey got her cell phone out and turned the sound off then she text Derek and told him where she was and to not text back. Stacey then put it away right before Aaron turned around. He was walking towards her and attempted to kiss her but she slapped him and attempted to kick him but he caught her foot. The receptionist tried to stall him but he pushed passed them. He threw Stacey over his shoulder and carried her to the room. Stacey was so scared, she prayed for help. "God please help me through this and help Derek find me." They arrived at the room and Aaron slammed the door shut and threw her onto the bed.

"Stacey, how could you do that to me," Aaron yelled,

"Because I don't want this, how could you do this to me?" Aaron charged at Stacey and she backed away as much as she could but she was cornered and her knee was in pain. He tore her clothes off and tied her hands to the headboard and raped her. She struggled as much as she could but she couldn't get away, Aaron was much stronger than she was. A few minutes later—which to Stacey it felt like forever—the police came in. They pulled Aaron off of her. Jayne came in with a blanket and covered Stacey then she moved her to a different room. She checked her knee and the stitches were stretched again. Jayne gave her some pain medication and did a rape kit assessment if Stacey wanted to press charges. When the physical pain subsided in her knee, Jayne ordered her to the shower. Stacey just stared out the window.

"Stacey, take a shower," Jayne said with a stern voice but Stacey didn't move or react to anything. Jayne left the room for a second.

"Jayne, I need to see her," Derek said when he saw her coming out of the room.

"Derek, she needs to clean up." Jayne whispered as memories went through her mind.

"Jayne, I have some clothes for her and I need to see that she is okay."

"Just hold on a second Derek." Jayne went back into the room and Stacey was still in the same place and position. "Stacey, let's get you cleaned up, so you can see Derek." Stacey looked at Jayne, surprised,

"He is here now?" Jayne looked at her surprised that she responded.

"Yes, but you need to clean up and put some clothes on." Stacey agreed as she headed into the bathroom, took a shower and put a long sleeved shirt, sweatshirt and sweatpants on, while Jayne got her a new blanket. When she was all cleaned up, Jayne let Derek come in; he slowly walked in.

"Stacey, I am here," he said. Then she hopped into his arms; he picked her up and held her as he sat down on a chair. A few minutes later, Jayne came in and saw him alone. Derek saw her face and pointed towards the balcony. "She said she wanted some time alone, outside."

Outside on the balcony, Stacey was crying out to God. "God, I love You, but this hurts. He took my virginity. My body hurts. I don't feel comfortable around Derek. It was hard to take his comfort, even though I know he won't hurt me. Please help me to be able to take comfort from the people I love." After she prayed, she went inside. Then Derek put his arm around her waist. "Let's go home." They headed down the stairs. Stacey collapsed on the way down, and Derek caught her and carried her to the ambulance that was waiting for her. Jayne came out and took care of Stacey as they went to the hospital.

While they were in the hospital, Jayne put an IV into Stacey's arm to give her some meds. Then they let her sleep. While she was sleeping, she saw the whole thing over again. She saw Aaron kidnapping her, tearing her clothes off, and raping her. She woke up in a cold sweat, screaming. Jayne came running into the room and held her—Stacey wouldn't let Derek hold her. When Stacey settled down, Jayne got up and brought Derek into the hall with her.

"Derek, it is going to be hard for her to get over this. She might not be comfortable around you or any other guy. You are going to have to go slow unless she says that she is okay with it."

"Okay, Jayne, can we bring her home tonight?"

"Yes, I was just waiting for her to wake up. Be slow and gentle, Derek. This was hard for her; soon you will have your Stacey back." They went back into the room and got Stacey ready to leave. Derek carried Stacey to Jayne's car and put her in it, then Jayne drove them home. When they got to the Rysner's house, Allison, Chad, Joanna, and Ariel were waiting for them. When she got out of the car, Allison ran up to her and gave her a hug, but Stacey was still feeling weak, so Derek picked her up and carried her into the house. He set her down on the couch, everyone else joined them, and they played cards. When Joanna was getting ready for bed, she asked Stacey if she wanted her to sleep in the room with her.

"Yeah, I think that would make Derek feel better," Stacey replied. Joanna went into Stacey's room and fell asleep, then everybody else went to bed as well. Stacey stayed up and made herself a cup of hot cocoa. Then she went into her room and sat down on her reading chair. She read the Bible until she fell asleep. At midnight, she woke up cold. Joanna came over with her comforter.

"You were screaming and talking in your sleep. You retold what happened to you tonight in the hotel. Do you want to see Derek?" Joanna asked as she watched Stacey calm down from the nightmare.

"Yes, but…"

"But you don't want the intimacy," Joanna finished for her. She went out the door, and Derek was there. "Derek, she wants to see you, but that is just it." Derek understood. While Joanna was talking to Derek, Stacey prayed.

<hr>

"God, please make this go away. Every time I go to sleep, it comes back. Just make it go away." A few minutes later, Derek walked in and kissed Stacey on her forehead. He held her hand and sat on the floor.

"Stacey, I know this is hard for you, but it is killing me because I can't help you. When I heard you screaming, I wanted to run in here and hold you, but my dad stopped me. We listened to you and heard everything. It hurts me to see you hurt." Stacey scooted over, lifted the blanket, and patted the spot next to her for Derek to lay himself down next to her. "Are you sure?" Derek asked, surprised she was letting him hold her.

"I'm sure," Stacey replied as Derek stood up and laid himself down next to her. Stacey lay on her right side facing Derek, and he held her. Tears started rolling down her face, but no sound was made. She fell asleep thinking about Derek holding her.

"Derek, you have to leave," Joanna said after he had held Stacey for an hour. He scooted out of the chair and kissed Stacey on her forehead. He watched her sleep for a few minutes until Joanna pushed him out of the room. When he was outside the room, he leaned against the wall, slid down to the floor, and he prayed.

"Dear God, please give me the old Stacey back, she is scared of me, she cried in my arms. She wouldn't even hug me back. Please help us in this time of emotional turmoil."

The next morning, Stacey woke up exhausted and sore. "Dear God, I think I hurt Derek last night because I cried in his arms. Thank You for not replaying what happened again. Please help me be more relaxed around the guys that I love. I want to be held, but it brings back the memory. Please help me forgive Abbey and Aaron. In Jesus' name, Amen."

In the middle of the prayer, Stacey heard knocking, but she ignored it as she was praying. However, Joanna opened the door and let Derek in. "Hi Derek."

"Hi, sweetheart," he replied as he slowly walked up to her. Stacey got up and met him in the middle of the room. When they were close, Stacey put her arms around his neck and kissed him. He was surprised, but he responded quite nicely. When they stopped kissing, Derek held her and kissed her forehead. Stacey opened her eyes and saw that Derek's eyes were moist.

"Oh Derek, you are going to make me cry." She held his face with both of her hands, and she went on her tiptoes and kissed him. She was about to stop when he pulled her closer. She finally got a breath as she glanced at the clock. "Derek, you have to go to school."

"Can you call me every hour?"

"Maybe," she answered, knowing that she was going to forget at some point in the day.

"I don't like that answer, Stacey," she brushed his hair out of his face.

"Well, I won't promise you anything." He gave her a sour look. "Derek, if you don't leave now, I won't call you at all." He ran out of the room instantly as Stacey followed him. She paused at the door and was grabbed by Derek, she squealed.

"Stacey, I'm sorry for scaring you."

"It's okay, just…" Derek covered her mouth with an affectionate kiss, then he let her go and went to school. Stacey went to physical therapy and was working really hard, so hard she forgot to call Derek. He called her, but she didn't get to the phone in time. She waited for him to call again. A few seconds later, he called, and this time she picked up.

"Hi Derek."

"Are you okay, Stacey?"

"Yes, Derek, I am fine, tired but fine." He asked for an explanation of why she didn't pick up right away, and she answered his questions, then they hung up.

"Stacey, was that Derek?" Dallas asked as she came back from the phone call. She nodded her head, exhausted. "You do know he is just trying to protect you."

"Dallas, if this happened to Jayne, would you be acting the same way Derek is?"

"It did happen to Jayne, and yes, I did check in on her, and I was worried about her emotional state, as Derek is with you." She stared at him but didn't ask for an explanation.

"I just don't know how to stop the way I am feeling." She sat down on the ground and pulled her good leg up to her chest and hugged it.

"Well, it is kind of hard stopping the way you are feeling when you were hurt in that kind of way," Dallas said as he helped Stacey stand up and walk.

"Thank you for listening to me, Dallas." She sat down to take a break.

"You're welcome, Stacey. You didn't deserve to be hurt, but you will live." Jayne gave Stacey a ride home when her physical therapy session was over. Stacey limped into the house, and she volunteered to make supper for the family. She pulled some steaks out of the freezer and defrosted them. When Derek came home, he helped Stacey peel the potatoes and cook the steaks over the grill. Stacey finished the steaks on the grill; they were perfect. At the same time, her mashed potatoes and vegetables with melted cheese over them were done. Joanna put the food on the table as Stacey grabbed the drinks. They were all seated around the table when Chad said a prayer.

"Dear God, thank You for this wonderful meal, as well as the person who prepared it. Please help everyone know how to help her and to get the pictures out of her mind. Thanks, in Jesus' name, Amen."

All the food was passed around and eaten. "Stacey, how did you learn how to cook like this?" Ariel asked as she took another bite.

"Mom taught me, and Grandma Rosemen as well, but she only taught me to control me."

"I don't quite remember everything that happened with that. Can you tell me?" Allison asked as she watched Stacey take another bite of food then started explaining the situation.

"Well, she lived with us for a while, and when someone would come over, she would be rude to them."

"Why did she live with you?" Joanna asked while cutting into her steak.

"The year that I got really sick from falling through the ice at my other grandparents' house, and my parents couldn't afford to take any more days off of work. She came to take care of me, but she basically put me on house arrest. When my parents came home from work, she would tell them I was getting fresh air and getting out, when I was really stuck in the house all day."

"Why would she lie?"

"She wanted to have control over something, and I was weak, so she had control."

"When did your parents find out she was controlling you?"

"About four months later, when I was still sick. Grandma had been giving me placebos, so I was getting sicker, not better."

"I think I remember you being really sick. That was the only summer you guys missed camp."

"Yeah, I missed camp because I was in the hospital trying to recover."

"Did your Grandma get in trouble?"

"Kind of. My parents sued her for the amount of the hospital bills, but they are slowly letting her back into our life again." They all remembered the fight Christian had with his mother at the hospital during Stacey's knee surgery. They were all amazed they were letting her grandmother back into their lives. "Yeah, it is hard to let her in, but we are trying."

"That would be hard, but you guys are trying. That is all God can ask," Chad commented as he thought about everything she had been through.

"Well, I'm going to clean up," Stacey said as she stood up.

"No," the Rysner family said in unison, "Joanna and Ariel can clean up; you need to rest your knee," Allison said. Stacey agreed while laughing as Derek whisked her off to the living room. They were sitting on the couch holding hands when everyone else joined them.

"What movie do you want to watch?" Joanna asked as she handed Stacey an ice pack for her knee.

"It's your pick today, Joanna," Derek replied. Joanna picked a movie, and they watched it, but Stacey fell asleep halfway through. Derek carried her into her room and laid her under the covers, kissed her on the forehead, and left the room with a prayer of sweet dreams and safety for his girl.

The next morning, Stacey woke up with the feeling of someone in her room. She slowly turned around to find Derek staring at her. "Derek, what are you doing in here?" Stacey asked in a whispered voice. She was surprised to see him in her room. She looked at the clock to see it was super early in the morning and sighed as she looked at him.

"I wanted to see you to make sure you were okay." Stacey saw his face and knew there was something else bothering him. Then he continued to explain. "I couldn't sleep because I was worried about you."

"Let's go into the living room so you can sleep," Stacey suggested. Derek picked her up and carried her to a couch in the living room. They laid themselves down, and ten minutes later, Derek was fast asleep. Stacey just enjoyed lying in his arms for a while before she slid out of his embrace and cleaned the whole kitchen top to bottom. At six o'clock, Stacey started cooking breakfast when she heard Derek yell her name. She went to the doorway between the kitchen and the living room. "Derek, be quiet, you don't need to wake the whole house." Derek took a deep breath as he walked up to Stacey.

"Stac, I'm scared I'm going to lose you."

"Not if I can help it," Stacey said with a smile on her face; Derek covered her smile with a kiss. She grabbed his hand and pulled him into the kitchen and made him sit down as she made him breakfast. They were enjoying their breakfast when they heard a gasp behind them. Stacey turned around to find Allison staring at the kitchen.

"My dear, do you know how my kitchen got so clean?"

"Yes, the cleaning fairy came in and cleaned it all up," Stacey said with a smirk on her face.

"Well, the next time you see this cleaning fairy, tell her thank you for me." Stacey agreed as she started preparing some more breakfast food as the rest of the family walked in. Stacey watched her boyfriend's family eat as she cleaned up. She went to her room to relax. She was on her laptop when she heard a knock at her door.

"Come in," she yelled; Derek walked in and laid himself down on the bed next to her.

"Derek, why aren't you going to school?" He told her about the professional work days for the teachers, which means the students have no school. "Oh, I wanted another day alone," Stacey said softly, acting disappointed.

"Why? What's wrong?" Derek asked urgently as he backed away, scared he pushed her space bubble.

"It's nothing, it's just…" that is when Derek looked into Stacey's eyes, they were sparkling.

"Stacey, you're good, but not that good. You can never lie, and your eyes give you away."

"But I had you going for a while."

"True, but I figured it out. So, what do you want to do today?" They talked about a few options then decided they wanted to go on a picnic before it got too cold outside. "Well, my dad is at work, so it will be four ladies with me. We should ask them if they want to come." Derek carried Stacey into the living room. "Mom, can we have a picnic today?"

"Yeah, your dad is off for the rest of the week, so he can hang with us. Go ask your sisters if they want to bring their boyfriends." Derek turned around and walked into the kitchen.

"Ariel, Joanna, where are you?" He said in a sing-song voice. They were hiding from him, then he informed them that they were going on a picnic, and they came out of their hiding spots. The girls loved picnics, then Derek continued explaining the plans for the day and that they could bring their boyfriends.

"Jeremiah will drive Kenny, Ariel, and me to the park," Joanna announced as Allison finished packing up the basket. Joanna smiled at Derek.

"We'll meet you there, then," Derek said as he smiled back at Joanna. Stacey watched the two of them and knew something was up.

"What's up with you two? You keep on smiling at each other."

"Nothing," Derek said. "Can't we just smile at each other?"

"No, it's not natural," Stacey said with a straight face. "You're up to something, and I'm going to find out what it is." She waited for him to give away his secret, but he kept his mouth shut. "Tell me, please," she pleaded, with a pout on her face.

"No, I will wait. By the way, you are a really cute pouter, but I won't tell because I like seeing it." He tapped his finger on her rounded nose as he picked up the basket.

"Well, then I will stop pouting," Stacey said with an angry face and crossed her arms in front of her chest.

"I don't know how I am going to deal with you; you are cute no matter what face you make." She turned her face away from him so he couldn't see her cute faces. "Don't hide your face from me, Miss Rosemen," Derek said as he turned her face toward him. "I love you, and I want to see your face."

"Well, I don't like you very much because you're not telling me what's going on," Stacey said with a serious face. Derek kept his mouth shut and smirked at her. They slowly walked towards the door.

"You will find out when we get to the park," he whispered. As soon as she heard him, she tried to pull him to the car while using the crutches. "Stacey, we don't have the drinks," he said with laughter in his voice.

"Fine, let's go get the drinks," Stacey said in an exasperated voice. Derek laughed at her antics as he ran into the house to grab the drinks and a few other things they had left behind. They got in the car with Allison and Chad and drove to the park. Stacey looked out at the park, searching for her surprise, but she didn't see anything out of the ordinary.

"Where is my surprise?"

"Just wait, it will be coming soon," Derek, Stacey, Chad, and Allison got out of the car and were unpacking the basket onto a blanket when Stacey saw Ariel walking up with a puppy in her arms.

"Derek, whose puppy is that?" Stacey asked as she looked at it. Derek looked at her with a huge smile on his face. "Really! That's my puppy!" He nodded his head as Stacey jumped into Derek's arms and gave him a huge hug and kiss before Ariel came over to hand the puppy to Stacey.

"Hey puppy, how are you?" Stacey asked as Ariel handed her the puppy. "What kind of puppy is this?" Derek told her the dog was a male Finnish Spitz. "Does he have a name yet?"

"No, he doesn't, but I have been looking at names for him, and I like Wylie and Rory." Stacey looked at the little guy and picked a name.

"I like Wylie," Stacey said as she continued holding her puppy and petting him.

"Well, you can still hold him while you eat," Allison said as she laid out the food. Stacey sat down and put Wylie down in her lap with the leash on. Stacey thanked Derek for the puppy and continued to eat.

"Were you surprised?" he asked as he pet Wylie on the head.

"Yeah, I wasn't expecting a dog; we never talked about it, but you know I love dogs."

"So, Stacey, how much do you love my son?" Chad asked as he took a bite into his sandwich.

"I think he is right at the top of guys that I love," Stacey said while she looked at Derek. "Well, you are my number one outside of my family." Stacey said as Derek leaned over to kiss her.

"You're my number one outside of my family too. Stacey, I love you."

"Hey, guys, quit the mushy stuff. I'm trying to eat," Joanna said as she made a disgusted face. Derek looked at Jeremiah and Joanna and raised his eyebrows.

"It's not more than you do," Derek answered back.

"Okay, I think I'll eat quietly now," Stacey said as she watched Joanna and Derek bicker for a while. They finished their picnic, then Derek and

Stacey went for a slow walk with Wylie; Derek carried Wylie as Stacey used her crutches. Stacey paused at the swings and sat down on one of the swings; Derek stood in front of her and kissed her.

"Stacey Marie, I love you so much. I can't wait to marry you." Stacey looked at her hands and fiddled with her ring.

"Well, you have to ask me first," she whispered before she looked at him.

"True, but I will when I feel the time is right." He answered while brushing her hair out of her face and behind her ear. She looked at his face then looked back down at her hands.

"So, you think we are ready?" She bent down when she saw Wylie looking up at her.

"Yeah, we have known each other our whole lives, and we have been dating for three years." Stacey told him about other people who had been dating longer but they weren't ready to get married. "Stacey, I love you. I have wanted you my whole life, first as friends, then I wanted to date you, and now I want you to be my wife." She commented about their age. "I think we can get through everything together no matter what happens. I want you in my life."

"I love you, Derek. I just wish Aaron didn't hurt me and I felt better about everything now. Something doesn't feel right, and it is scaring me. I want you in my life, but I am just hurting now."

"I know you are hurting. I know he hurt you, and I know it will take a while for my old Stacey to come back. I also know we might not ever get the old Stacey back because of what has happened to you, but I will love you no matter what happens. You are a big part of my life." Stacey hid her face in Wylie's fur to hide her tears; Derek put his finger underneath her chin and lifted her head so he could see her eyes. "Sweetheart, what's wrong?" Derek asked as he wiped the tears from her face as he knelt down in front of her.

"Derek, I don't deserve you; you're so nice to me. You give me gifts I don't deserve. You commit your life to me even though I am now damaged goods." Tears started falling more quickly down her soft cheeks. Derek kissed her cheeks, kissing the tears away.

"Stacey Marie Rosemen, you are not damaged goods. It's not your fault. I love you. Yes, I wish this didn't happen to you, but you are still my girl. The girl I will love for the rest of my life." Stacey stood up and set Wylie down on the ground while she pulled Derek up.

"Derek, I love you, and I want to be back to my normal self, but it's too fast to be back to normal," Stacey said as she gave him a hug. He held onto her as he whispered into her ear.

"I know that sweetheart. I was planning on giving you the puppy for our anniversary, but I thought you would want him now." She pushed against him and looked him in the eyes. Derek gave her a kiss then she sat down on the swing again and she picked up Wylie as Derek pushed them on the swing. Ariel and Kenny walked over to Stacey and Derek and joined them on the swings.

"Stacey, how did you like the surprise?" Ariel asked as Kenny pushed her swing.

"I loved it. How did you guys pull this off?"

"We have been planning this for a long time," Ariel replied. "As soon as Derek found out that Kenny's dog was having puppies, he has been planning this. Wylie is just old enough to be away from his mother.

"Thanks, Kenny, and everyone else for this wonderful surprise." She set Wylie down on the ground and grabbed her crutches. "I think I am going to go for a walk." They all watched as she slowly made her way to the shore of the lake and sat down on the grass.

"Derek, why aren't you going after her?" Kenny asked.

"I will in a little bit, but she needs some time alone," Derek said with a huge sigh as he dropped onto one of the swings and started pumping his legs to get the swing going high.

"What were you talking about?" Ariel asked.

"She thinks of herself as damaged goods and thinks she doesn't deserve all of this."

"She deserves more than this," Kenny said as he got his swing as high as the bars.

"I know that, but I have to convince her." Derek was even with Kenny and stopped pumping his legs. They stayed quiet for a while longer.

"Now it is time for you to go after your girl." Kenny announced. Derek jumped off the swing and started after Stacey slowly. When Derek caught up to Stacey, she didn't hear him and he heard her talking; he didn't interrupt but he listened.

"God, I know I can be strong and get through this, but it hurts me and everyone around me. Can't You just take this pain away; take the memory away at least? Every time Derek holds me, I think of what Aaron did to me, and I want to run. Please, God, help me be strong to get through this without hurting anyone in the process. Please give me peace," Stacey prayed softly as tears ran down her cheeks, and she held Wylie. When she became silent, she heard leaves rustling behind her and turned around to find Derek walking up to her. Derek sat down next to her and held her hand; they just sat there quietly until Joanna and Jeremiah walked up to them.

"Hey guys, we were wondering if you guys wanted to play a game." Derek looked at her for the answer and she nodded her head. Derek picked Stacey up with Wylie in her arms, and Jeremiah grabbed her crutches. They went back to the blanket and played a few games before packing up and heading back to the Rysner's house. When Stacey arrived back, she went directly to the hospital for her Physical Therapy. She greeted Jayne as she entered the hospital and explained the whole day, how Derek surprised her with a puppy.

"Derek got him for me to help me recover from Aaron. He was going to wait until our anniversary, but he thought I would want to cuddle with the puppy and play with him."

"Well, that was nice of him. Pets like to cuddle." Dallas walked in, "Are you ready to be tortured?" She looked behind her to see Dallas in the doorway.

"Yes, I am ready if you're ready to torture me." Dallas smiled as he set up the room for her Physical Therapy session. She used her crutches to slowly walk with minimized weight on her left leg to the area Dallas set up for her.

"How's the knee feeling?" Jayne asked as she observed Stacey's body language and saw some pain and more limping than normal.

"It's feeling sore," Jayne inspected it.

"No more walking on your left leg. It is swollen. You need to rest it." Jayne declared. They did an arm workout including the bench press, triceps extension, bicep curls, dips, and pull-ups. Then, they did an abdominal workout. At the end of the session, Stacey dropped to the floor in exhaustion. Jayne and Dallas sat down next to her, laughing.

"I love that you're laughing at my pain," she said with a smile as she tried to get up. She got halfway up then fell back down laughing.

"Dallas, can you help me up, please?" Dallas laughed as he stood up, he wrapped one arm around her waist as she put her arm around his neck. He helped her stand up and sit on a chair. Derek walked in,

"It looks like someone is worn out." He commented as he leaned against the doorway.

"Yeah, my bed is calling my name."

"Wow, you can hear your bed speak to you?" Dallas asked.

"Oh yeah, can't you hear your bed speak to you?" Dallas laughed.

"No, but I'll listen for it to talk to me from now on." They were all laughing. Stacey stood up with her crutches and hobbled over to Derek. She stumbled a little then recovered before someone could help her. Derek followed her out the door while waving goodbye to Dallas and Jayne.

"They are such a cute couple." Jayne declared.

"I hope Stacey recovers from the attack quickly so they can get back to normal."

"You noticed that too?"

"She was uncomfortable with me helping her until she was too exhausted to do it herself, then when Derek showed up, she didn't give him a hug, kiss or anything." He remembered the time when he wasn't able to hold his wife because she was afraid of him.

"She'll get better as time goes by." Jayne confirmed as she too remembered the past.

"Yeah, but for the both of them, I hope it will be sooner than later." Dallas said as he gave Jayne a kiss.

⸺⁓⁓⁓⁓⁓⁓⸺

Out in the parking lot, "You're family is here." Derek announced as he set her crutches behind them in the car. Stacey rolled her eyes as she set her head against the head piece on the passenger seat. She stayed silent as he started driving the car to the house. Derek stopped the car in front of the house and as Stacey started getting out of the car Derek grabbed her arm.

"Stacey, are you alright?" She looked into his eyes.

"I'm fine but I am not looking forward to my nagging, psychoanalyzing mother." Derek searched her eyes to make sure she was telling the truth.

"If you want a break from your family, we can go for a car ride or something." She nodded her head in agreement as Adam showed up by her door. She opened the door and gave Adam a hug then he carried her into the house. Derek slowly followed with her crutches as he watched Stacey being surrounded by her family. Adam set her on a couch as they started talking.

"What's going on in La Crosse?" She asked them as she pulled a blanket over her legs.

"Abbey went to trial and was just charged with a fine." Stacey took a deep breath and shrugged her shoulders.

"That's fine. She didn't push me in front of the moving car. I ran in front of it." Stacey looked at her mother and saw that she was irritated.

"How can you say that? She beat you up." She stood up and started pacing.

"Mom, I'm turning the other cheek. She only gave me a few bruises. A fine is all she needs besides my forgiveness." Everyone but her mother agreed as she stomped out to the porch. They were all silent then Allison looked at Stacey.

"When are you starting school?" Allison asked to change the subject.

"Well, school is out the rest of this week. So, I think everything is ready for me to start on Monday."

"What are your plans for tomorrow?" Chad asked as Laura came back into the room and curled up on a chair with a blanket.

"Well, they still have school in La Crosse so I was planning on going to La Crosse to see my friends and hand in my books." Stacey looked at Derek for approval of the plans. He nodded his head in agreement as Wylie jumped into Stacey's lap. Everyone laughed as they watched him play with Stacey. After a while she excused herself from the room and went outside for fresh air. Derek started to follow her but Laura stopped him so she could go out to talk to her.

"Stacey, why won't you talk about what happened between you and Aaron?" Stacey looked out at the street, ignoring her mother. Laura turned Stacey toward her, "Tell me what happened. Aaron was a good friend, he wouldn't rape you." Laura declared. Stacey raised her eyebrows,

"Mom, no matter what you think Aaron would or wouldn't do doesn't matter because he raped me. He did what you didn't think he would, so that's my fault?" Stacey paused. "Yes Mom, I seduced Aaron and called it rape. Is that what you want to hear? Well that's not true." She turned away from her mother.

"Stacey Marie Rosemen, don't turn away from me when I'm talking to you," Laura yelled as Stacey walked away from her.

"Mom, I'm done talking and listening," Stacey proclaimed calmly. Laura became angry as she turned Stacey around.

"Don't talk to me like that; I'm your mother." Stacey ignored her, then she saw a hand coming towards her face and felt a slap. Her head moved with the slap, and then she looked at her mother as she touched the left side of her face. She watched as her mother's face turned from anger to horror. Derek ran out to Stacey as Laura ran to Stacey's vehicle and drove off. Derek tried to hold Stacey, but she pushed him away and hobbled with her crutches to her room. About ten minutes later, she heard a knock on her door.

"Come in," she yelled. Adam walked in with a bag of frozen peas.

"Here, this is for the new red mark on your face," he commented while handing her the bag. She thanked him as she put the bag of peas on her face. Adam sat on the edge of the bed. "How are you holding up?"

"Alright, I guess. I want to be held, but it brings back the memories, so I have pushed Derek away. I'm trying to let him hold me, but the last time I did, I cried in his arms until I fell asleep. I don't want to hurt him like that, but I guess I'm hurting him either way." Adam rested his hand on her leg.

"Just do what you are comfortable with," he declared. Stacey smiled as Adam sat next to her on the bed.

"Adam, why did this happen to me?"

"Stacey, I don't know, but everything will be fine." She leaned into his shoulder as tears rolled down her face. He pushed her hair out of her face and brushed the tears away.

"Why is Mom denying that this happened?" Adam thought for a while.

"I think she wants to believe that nothing happened to you." Stacey sat up when she heard a knock on the door. She yelled for them to come in, and Derek and Christian walked in. Derek walked up to the bed and sat at the foot of the bed as Christian stood next to the bed facing Stacey.

"So, we will drive up to La Crosse early tomorrow morning so Adam can go to school, and I can get to work on time. Then, the two of you can pick up Stacey's car and visit the school or whatever your plans were to do tomorrow." Derek and Stacey agreed.

"What time are we leaving?" Stacey asked.

"We should leave at five in the morning so we can pick up our belongings from home." Stacey's eyes grew knowing she wasn't going to sleep well during the night.

"Just wake me up and carry me to the car before we leave."

"Won't you want a change of clothes?" Adam asked. She thought for a moment, then she ordered him to pick out some clothes for her to wear the next day and pack it up. Adam looked at Stacey with one eyebrow cocked up. "What did you just say?" He asked, amazed that she was ordering him around.

"Did I mumble or something?" Christian laughed at the twins.

"Adam, go pack a change of clothes for your injured sister." Adam complied as he jumped off the bed, found a small duffel bag, and packed a small amount of clothes along with a few things to do in the car. He set the bag on the bed; Stacey inspected it.

"Those are some nice clothes, thanks Adam." Adam smiled as Christian kissed her cheek and led him out of the room. Stacey watched them leave as Derek sat at the foot of her bed. She looked at him and smirked. He moved up closer to the head of the bed.

"How's my girl feeling?"

"I'm feeling alright. My face aches, and so does my knee, but other than that I'm good." Derek set his right arm on the left side of Stacey, so their faces were at the same level.

"Derek?" He looked into her eyes, "I love you."

"I love you too, Stacey dear," he inched his face closer to hers, watching for any anxiety. Then he felt her hand on the back of his neck, pulling his face towards hers. They closed the distance between them as Stacey relaxed into his arms and closed her eyes. Derek gently kissed her on her beautiful lips, and Stacey kissed him back. Derek pulled away to catch his breath.

"Derek, come hold me," Stacey asked as she moved over in the bed, and Derek lay next to her. He put his arm under her neck as she laid her head on his shoulder. They laid in each other's arms in silence for a few minutes. "Derek, what are you thinking about?"

"Umm… I'm thinking about you, the events of the last few weeks, and our future." The door opened a few inches as Wylie ran into the room and jumped onto the bed.

"Wylie," Stacey yelled as she sat up to hold him. Derek sat up next to her to pet the dog. Then he held Wylie's head.

"You have the worst timing, little guy. I just got to cuddle with her, and now she wants to cuddle with you," Derek whined as Stacey held Wylie. Stacey moved back against the headboard, and Derek moved up to be by Stacey while wrapping his arm around the back of her waist. Wylie moved to Derek's lap and played with him for a while, then he got bored and laid himself down on Stacey's lap.

"Thank you for giving me Wylie, he's so cute."

"What about me?" Derek whined with a pouty face.

"You're cute as well," she said as he gave her a cheesy smile. He held her for another hour, then he gave her another kiss as he left her for the night.

"God, please give her a nice dream so she may sleep well and be rested. Thank You for putting her into my life; she is the love of my earthly life. I love You for everything You have given me. Love, Your devoted son, Derek." Derek went to his room to sleep.

Chapter 5

The next morning, Derek woke up to his alarm clock at 4:30 in the morning. "I don't want to get up," he thought to himself as he rolled out of bed and jumped into the shower. Christian woke up when he heard the shower and hopped into one of the other showers. After their showers, Christian woke Adam up for him to take a shower.

At 4:55 in the morning, Derek woke Stacey up just enough for her to hold onto his neck as he carried her to the car. Christian and Adam followed with her crutches, her bag, and their bags. Derek set her into the seat and buckled her in as the other guys packed the vehicle. Then, they were off. Stacey slept the whole way to La Crosse, while the guys talked.

"Adam, how's Nicole?" Derek asked, knowing Adam was close to asking her to marry him.

"Oh, she is wonderful. She has been so helpful the past few weeks while Stacey has been in Madison. She is my beautiful girl."

"Like the girl in my arms," Derek said as he looked down at Stacey lying on his lap.

"Speaking of Stacey, when are you going to ask the girl to marry you?" Christian asked. Derek's eyebrows lifted, surprised by the question.

"That is weird coming from her father. The question a father usually asks is 'when are you going to leave my daughter alone?'" Christian laughed then explained that he liked him.

"So, when are you going to ask her?" Christian asked again.

"Soon, very soon," Derek replied while brushing her hair out of her face. They arrived at the house; Christian and Adam unpacked the vehicle while Derek carried Stacey into the family room. Adam and Christian rushed around the house to get ready for work and school then rushed off. Derek set Stacey on the couch and sat by her feet on the couch as he watched TV. About ten minutes later, Stacey woke up slowly.

"Good morning, Stacey dear," he whispered, not to startle her.

"Hey Derek," she slowly sat up and leaned against Derek.

"What are our plans for today?" Stacey thought for a while,

"Well, a shower for me then school to drop off my books and talk to my friends then I don't know." Derek rubbed her arm.

"Okay, how about I make you some breakfast while you take a shower?"

"That sounds good, but breakfast and a shower can wait a few more minutes." Stacey announced as she snuggled into Derek's arms.

"I think they can wait since I finally get to hold you without any fear in your mind." Stacey smiled slightly as she turned her face towards his.

"Derek, I know you won't hurt me like Aaron did." She stated as she sat up and turned toward him, sitting across his lap.

"I don't know why God allowed me to get hurt, but I will let Him use my injury in any way He wants. I'm in His arms. Those first few days, I had tried to push Him away. I still talked to Him, but I was accusing Him in anger. But I gave up because I was hurting too much. I let Him back into my heart, and He gave me peace. I am still hurting a little, but I am doing better. I have people who love me and need me more than my anger towards Aaron and God, so I let it go." Stacey shrugged as Derek gently kissed the tears off of her cheeks.

"You are my wonderful woman. You have gone through so much in the last few weeks, and you are calm with Jesus' strength, God's strength. You inspire me to be better than I am. I love you, Stacey." She hid her face in his neck and held him. Derek kissed her forehead, then Stacey lifted her head and kissed him.

"I should go take a shower," Stacey whispered as she slowly stood up, then she noticed her crutches were across the room. She looked at Derek, then at the crutches. He laughed as he stood up to get the crutches. Stacey hobbled to the bathroom as Derek went into the kitchen. Stacey took her knee brace off, then she took the gauze off. She put a low amount of water in the tub, cleaned up, and put her skirt and ¾ sleeve shirt on. She sat down with clean gauze, hydrogen peroxide, and some lotion. She poured the peroxide onto a piece of cloth and set it on the inflamed cuts on her knee from falling a few days ago. She clenched her teeth, and a little squeal came out. She heard a knock on the door. "Derek, you can come in," he walked in.

"Are you all right?"

"Yeah, I was just cleaning my knee." Derek stood there looking helpless. "Don't burn my food," she said to give him something to do. Derek ran back to the kitchen as Stacey laughed. She gently rubbed the lotion around her stitches, then rewrapped her knee, put her brace back on, and hobbled to the kitchen. Derek set the plates on the table as she arrived in the room. He gave her a quick peck on the cheek, then helped her sit down.

"God, please continue to give us the strength to make it through our next few weeks and months. We want to grow in Your Love. We are in Your arms. Love Your kids."

"Amen," Stacey whispered. They dug into the fried eggs with sausage and orange juice. When they were done, Stacey packed her school books into a backpack then made a picnic for lunch. Derek helped her pack her car, then he drove her to the school. When they arrived at the school, Derek dropped Stacey off at the door, then parked the car. Stacey waited for him as he carried her backpack up to her. She gave him a quick kiss before they walked into the school. Derek opened the office door for Stacey.

"Hi Joanie," she announced her presence.

"Stacey, it's so good to see you." Stacey smiled.

"I need my transcripts, please." Joanie looked at her with an eyebrow raised. "I'm moving to Madison for a new study on knee injuries, but they need me in Madison." She nodded her head as she started typing into the computer.

"Okay, I'll get that for you, and Principal Hane wants to see you. I'll see if he can talk to you. By the way, do you know where Aaron has been? He's missed a lot of school." Stacey contemplated telling her the truth.

"Joanie, he's in jail." Joanie gasped, then Stacey explained why. "He raped me. He kidnapped me from my room and took me to a hotel and raped me. He should be in jail for a while." Joanie was surprised as she tried to understand it. "Joanie, you know he's been obsessed with me for the last few years. He was my shadow; everywhere I went, he was there." Joanie agreed,

"So, who's this handsome fellow?" She asked, as she eyed him up and down.

"This is Derek Rysner, my boyfriend of 3 years, friend of 12 years." Again, she was surprised. "Joanie, I don't flaunt my life, and no one believed me because when we saw each other, I wanted to see only him, not my friends."

"Well, it is nice to meet you, Derek." She stood up and shook hands with him.

"It's nice to meet you as well, ma'am." Joanie smiled at his manners. Then, Principal Hane walked in.

"Stacey Rosemen, it is nice to see you."

"Hello, Principal Hane. I'd like you to meet my boyfriend, Derek. Derek, this is Principal Hane."

"It's nice to meet you, sir," Derek said as he shook hands with the principal.

"So, this is Derek Rysner, the once invisible boyfriend, not so invisible anymore." Derek laughed. Principal Hane commented on her leaving them and how lucky the school was to have her. Stacey smiled, then the bell rang.

"What period is it?" She asked, wanting to go to Choir to say goodbye.

"It's your Choir period," Joanie answered, then sat down to answer the phone.

"Okay, I'm going to go hand my books back, go to Choir, then I'll come back to pick up my transcripts." They acknowledged her statement and watched her hobble out the door with Derek as her shadow.

"How does Principal Hane know you so well?" Derek asked as she led him to her classes.

"I worked in the office as an assistant, so we became pals." Stacey stopped at her math teacher's class.

"Stacey, come in," she crutched into the empty classroom.

"When are you coming back full-time?"

"I'm not. I'm moving to Madison. I'm just here to drop my books off and say goodbye."

The teacher congratulated her and sent her off with good tidings. Derek handed the math teacher the book, then they went to the next room. They returned all of the books and then went to the Choir room. Stacey hobbled in while joining them in the song they were practicing.

Mrs. Williamson continued playing until the song was over, then she told everyone to turn around. The girls screamed as they rushed over to Stacey. The guys came more slowly, including Adam. She gave each of them a hug, then they all sat on the risers as Derek, Stacey, and Mrs. Williamson sat in front of them.

"So, what was the prognosis?" One of the boys asked.

"I tore my ACL, broke a few ribs, sprained my wrist, and acquired a few bruises on my face."

"Adam told me you're not coming back," Nicole stated.

"That is true. The Madison hospital has an ACL study. They are trying a new method, and I am one of the patients, so I am moving to Madison." All of their faces looked saddened by her statement.

"Oh, have you heard from Aaron? I'm getting worried about him," Mrs. Williamson said.

"I have heard from him and last I knew he was in jail." The girls gasped. Then Stacey opened her mouth to explain but Adam interrupted her.

"He raped her," Adam answered for her in anger. The whole class gasped. Mrs. Williamson knelt in front of her.

"When did this happen?" She asked in concern.

"It happened Tuesday." All of her friends were speechless; she waited for someone else to speak.

"So, who is this handsome guy?" Another girl asked. Stacey turned to look at Derek,

"Oh, he's just my boyfriend," she said sarcastically with a huge grin on her face.

"Just your boyfriend?" one of the girls asked.

"Well, he is the guy you never acknowledged as my boyfriend but we've been dating for 3 years and my best friend for 12 years. His name is Derek Rysner." Stacey announced as the door opened and Abbey slipped in. When she turned around, she froze. Everyone was silent as they waited.

"Hi Abbey," Stacey said into the silence,

"Hi Stacey," she slowly walked up to Stacey. She knelt in front of her and laid her head in Stacey's lap. Tears ran down her cheeks, "I'm so sorry," everyone but Derek, Adam, and Mrs. Williamson cleared out of the room.

"Abbey, everything is alright." Abbey looked up at Stacey with an eyebrow raised. "I forgive you." Stacey raised her hand to wipe Abbey's tears away. Abbey backed away,

"How can you say that?"

"Abbey, you just gave me a few bruises. My knee injury was my own fault. Anyways, you didn't hurt me as much as Aaron did." She scrunched up her face in confusion then Stacey explained what had happened. Abbey's jaw dropped then she slowly re-approached Stacey to give her a hug. Abbey released Stacey out of the hug and Stacey wiped the tears off of her own face.

"I know this may be asking too much but can we still be friends?" Stacey thought for a few seconds and smiled

"As long as there are no more punches or hitting involved." Abbey looked at her and was flabbergasted. "Everyone should get a second chance." The bell rang dismissing the class. Stacey gave everyone a hug as they left.

"That was an amazing thing you just did there." Mrs. Williamson declared.

"I don't want to hold a grudge against her and she was sincere in her apology." Stacey explained, and stood up with her crutches. She headed towards the piano and sat down to play. She was playing one of their songs then Mrs. Williamson asked her a question.

"Do you think you will be able to forgive Aaron?" Stacey pondered the question for a moment while playing her song then paused in her playing and looked up at her teacher.

"I think yes, after the freshness of this pain goes away, but I couldn't let him into my life again." She began playing the piano again, and Derek placed his hands on her shoulders.

"You're an amazing girl," Mrs. Williamson said, then looked directly at Derek. "Derek, make sure you take care of this loving woman."

"I will, ma'am. I love her so much. I don't want to see her hurt again," Derek replied, earning an approving look from Mrs. Williamson.

"Well, we should get going," Stacey announced, finishing her song and standing up. Mrs. Williamson gave her a hug and then turned to Derek.

"It was nice meeting you, Derek," she said, offering her hand for a handshake.

"It was nice meeting you as well, ma'am," Derek replied, shaking her hand. He opened the door for Stacey, and they headed towards the office once more. In the office, Stacey was greeted by balloons, streamers, cake, and a banner. Her friends and teachers had gathered to surprise her.

"What's going on?" Stacey asked.

"Adam warned us you were coming today, so we're giving you a send-off party," Principal Hane explained. Stacey looked at Adam and motioned for him to come closer. Adam walked over, and she gave him a warm hug.

"Adam, you're the best."

"I know," he replied with a smug grin. Stacey took a seat on the couch while people talked to her and mingled around. Derek draped his arm around her shoulders. Joanie approached with a large bag and placed it in front of Stacey. When she looked inside, she found a bag of Hershey Kisses, pens, two small notebooks, and a La Crosse Schools sweatshirt.

"Now, don't forget us," Principal Hane said, pointing his finger playfully.

"I won't forget you. Adam's still here to keep you on your toes," Stacey responded, playful in tone. Joanie handed her a piece of cake, and Stacey continued to chat with everyone until the next bell rang. They all gave her another round of hugs as they headed to class. Principal Hane and Derek worked together to carry her presents, cake, and school supplies out to her car.

"So, are you going to take care of our Stacey?"

"Yes, she's the love of my life, she is my life."

"You really do love her." Derek nodded his head, and then shared his plan for the evening as a surprise for Stacey. Principal Hane gave his approval and congratulated him.

"Well, good luck," he said, patting Derek on the shoulder. They walked back into the school, and Stacey and Derek left for a picnic by the river. Derek spread out a blanket on the ground and set the picnic basket down. Stacey used her crutches to hobble over to the blanket, and Derek helped her sit down. Then he took a seat across from her and began unpacking the basket. He brought out two sandwiches, crackers, cheese, grapes, and apple juice. Stacey helped organize the food and drinks, and then Derek held Stacey's hand as they both bowed their heads.

"Dear God, thank You for this wonderful day and Stacey's wonderful friends who love her. Please continue to help her heal and help us grow together in Your arms…"

"Please help my transition from school to school be smooth and bless the Rysners for their hospitality and Jayne and Dallas for their healing, helping hands. We are in Your arms. Amen." They released hands as they grabbed their sandwiches. "What are our plans for the rest of the day?" Stacey asked him.

"Well, we will relax here for a while, then we can go to your parent's house and hang out with them. Then, around seven o'clock tonight, we should head back to Madison."

"Could we stop up at Granddad's Bluff?" Derek tried to act normal, hoping she didn't find out about his plan. He agreed, and they finished their sandwiches. Then Derek sat behind Stacey as she leaned back into his chest. "Derek, what are our plans for the future?" Derek composed himself while trying to figure out what to say without giving away his plans.

"I think our plans include getting you healed and both of us graduating."

"Yeah, I guess." Derek kissed her cheek. She put a piece of cheese on a cracker and fed it to him. Derek laid his hand on her abdomen. Stacey turned slightly so she could see his face. "You're being quiet today, why?"

"I'm enjoying you in your element and when you forgave Abbey; that amazed me. You amaze me." Derek took a drink of his apple juice as Stacey retrieved the grapes. She sat across from him and threw a grape up, and he caught it in his mouth. Stacey laughed as Derek took a few grapes from her and she attempted to catch the grape in her mouth, but it bounced off the corner of her mouth. They laughed, then they tried again, this time she caught it.

"Yay!" Derek laughed at her excitement. She moved back to sit in front of him.

"How are you feeling today?" Derek asked.

"I'm having a wonderful day with my boyfriend." Derek picked Stacey up slightly and had her sit across his lap.

"How are you, Derek?"

"I'm great." Stacey wrapped her left arm around his neck and laid her head on his shoulder.

"We should have brought Wylie with us," she realized.

"But then I wouldn't have you to myself." Stacey lifted her head and looked at Derek. He turned his face towards her, and he closed the space between their lips. They were in their own little world until they heard people approaching. Stacey looked behind Derek to see Adam and Nicole walking up to them with the Rosemen's Golden Retriever, Rusty.

"Rusty!" Stacey yelled. When the big pup heard Stacey, he ran towards her. "Hey bud," Stacey whispered as she pet him on the head.

"Sit, Rusty," Adam yelled as Rusty tried climbing on top of Stacey. Rusty sat down immediately, then Adam and Nicole sat down with them.

"How was school?"

"It was a normal day except for you coming to visit and that party," Nicole answered.

"Derek, do you want to play Frisbee?" Adam asked. He agreed and set Stacey back onto the blanket. Stacey and Nicole watched them throw the Frisbee as Rusty tried catching it.

"Nicole, how long have the two of you been dating?"

"Um…we have been dating each other about as long as the two of you have been dating." Nicole said then continued to reminisce. "We have known each other since kindergarten. I think we met each other the same year you and Derek met."

"That's weird. We met and started dating around the same time as each other. Do you think we'll get engaged, married, and have kids around the same time?"

"That's possible." Nicole watched the boys for a while. "If Derek asked you to marry him today, what would you say?"

"Yes, definitely yes. If Adam asked you today, what would you say?"

"I would say yes. I love him so much." Stacey smiled, "Well, we are both happy. How do you feel around Derek since Aaron hurt you?" Stacey took a deep breath while fidgeting with the food on the blanket.

"At first, it just brought back the images, but then I would remember whose arms I was in, and I would feel safe. He doesn't know this, but I still dream about that night and it scares me. But I just wake up and read God's Word. He comforts me; I lay in His arms." Nicole thought for a while, then she grabbed a few crackers with cheese. A few minutes later, Adam, Derek, and Rusty ran back and dropped to the ground on the blanket. Stacey's phone rang, and she answered it.

"Where are you guys?" Christian asked.

"We are by the river. You and Mom can join us if you want." Stacey suggested.

"Okay, we are on our way." Stacey laid down on the blanket, then Rusty started licking her face.

"Rusty, sit," Stacey ordered as she continued lying on the ground. He sat up and looked down at her with his tongue sticking out. "Mom and Dad are coming to join us."

"That means I have to behave," Adam complained. They all laughed at him, then Stacey threw grapes at him, and he caught them. Nicole tried catching them, but it took her a while to finally catch one. Adam looked behind Stacey,

"Here they come," Adam warned the group. Stacey turned her body to wave at her parents. Christian whistled, and Rusty ran towards him. He ruffled his fur as they continued walking towards the blanket. Laura sat down next to Stacey,

"Hey guys, could I talk to her alone, please?" They grabbed the Frisbee and walked away. The four of them plus the dog went out onto the field to play Frisbee.

"Stacey, I'm so sorry for slapping you. I was angry at Aaron, and I took it out on you."

"Mom, it is fine," Stacey avoided eye contact, knowing the next question.

"Could you tell me what happened?"

"I'd rather not. I want it to be the past and not hold me back in the future." Laura stared out at the water.

"I feel helpless. I wasn't there to comfort you, and you won't let me help you now." Stacey took a deep breath as she looked into her lap.

"Mom, you know me. I like being alone and facing my troubles on my own. I didn't let anyone comfort me that first night. I tried to let Derek hold me for his sake, but I couldn't. I like my space when I am angry or sad. I don't want to talk about it because it makes the memories fresh, and I don't want to deal with that." Stacey watched her mother's facial expression and body language change.

"Oh, Mom, don't even start with me," Stacey exclaimed as she tried to get up.

"What do you mean? I'm not starting anything," Laura asked.

"Don't start psychoanalyzing me. I'm not a patient or client. I am your daughter, and you're not really listening to me," Stacey retorted. Laura's mouth gaped open.

"I just want to understand, Stacey."

"You know, for a psychologist, you don't listen very well. I've told you I don't want to talk about it. That's me talking to you." Stacey gave up trying to get up and whistled for Rusty, who ran towards her. Adam and Derek followed seconds later. Stacey buried her face into Rusty's soft, fluffy fur. Derek knelt next to her and held her, but she pushed him away, mistaking him for her mother.

"Stacey, it's me," Derek whispered as he wrapped his arms around her again. Christian walked up to the scene and gave Laura a knowing look. Laura stood up and walked away; Christian followed.

"You tried being the psychologist again, didn't you?" Laura nodded her head in regret. "Laura, you know Stacey hates it when you become the psychologist to her. If she wants to talk, she will talk."

"I just hate not knowing what happened to my own daughter. I've helped many women get over their attacks, but she won't let me help." Christian turned Laura to look at him.

"She seems to be coping better than the rest of us. We need to let her be and not force her to dwell in the past." Laura took a deep breath and let it out.

"Fine, I'll leave her alone." They walked back to their kids.

"Hey, before the two of you leave, we want to take you out to dinner at your favorite Italian restaurant." Derek looked at Stacey; she nodded her head while petting Rusty. They packed up the picnic basket and blanket in Christian's vehicle, then drove to the restaurant in separate vehicles as Christian dropped Rusty off at home. Stacey held Derek's hand as he followed Adam to the restaurant.

"Stacey, what did your mom say to upset you?"

"She wanted me to retell what happened and she wanted to psychoanalyze me. I really dislike it when my mom turns into a psychologist. Psychologists shouldn't try to fix their own children's problems." Derek smirked.

"I think you're great," he said, suppressing his laughter. Stacey smiled as they parked the car. Derek turned the vehicle off, then turned towards Stacey. He placed his hand underneath her chin and gently turned her head towards him. "We'll have fun," Derek declared as he moved closer to her. She smiled as he kissed her, then she pulled back.

"I love you, Derek. You keep me sane." Derek laughed as he opened his door and moved to Stacey's side to help her out of the car. Adam and Nicole waited for them at the entrance.

"You guys took long enough," Adam joked.

"Yeah, we were talking... Could you help me keep the subject off of me tonight?"

"Yeah, I will. I don't like it when Mom does her job on us." Derek laughed.

"Is she a good psychologist?"

"Oh, she is an excellent psychologist, but we hate it when she does it to us. We just want a mom who doesn't overthink or analyze everything." They walked into the restaurant and requested a table. Stacey sat down on the bench while waiting for their table. Derek looked at her and smiled, brushing the hair out of her face. Christian and Laura walked in as their table was ready. Stacey chose a corner seat to avoid getting hit, with Derek beside her and Adam on the other side. They ordered their food and shared funny stories from the past. Stacey shared her Chicken Alfredo with Derek as he shared his Spaghetti. They enjoyed their dinner, talking and joking. Around 6:30, Stacey got up to go to the bathroom. After she left, Nicole asked Derek.

"Are you asking her tonight?" He smiled and nodded his head. He took the ring out of his pocket and showed it to his future family.

"She will love it," Adam said. Laura was the only one out of the loop.

"What's going on?"

"I'm asking your daughter to marry me on our way back to Madison at Granddad's Bluff." Laura stayed quiet as Stacey returned to the table.

"Hey babe, are you ready to go?" Stacey asked Derek. He nodded then gave everyone a hug, and they went to her car.

"We are going up to Granddad's, right?"

"Yep, I want to watch the sunset with you." Derek drove up the Bluff, parked her car, and carried her to a bench. Their arrival time was perfect; the sun was just ten minutes away from setting. They watched the sunset, and right before it fully set, Derek knelt in front of her.

"You are the love of my life. You give meaning to my life, and I want to grow old with you and have kids with you." He pulled the box out of his pocket, and Stacey gasped as he opened it to reveal a diamond ring. "Will you do me the honor of becoming my wife and marrying me?"

"Yes, I will marry you, Derek Rysner." Derek took the ring out of the box and placed it on her left ring finger. Then, Stacey wrapped her arms around his neck as he stood up and spun her around. He gently set her back down on the bench. They finished watching the sunset, and Derek carried her to the car. He set her on the seat and gave her another kiss. He closed her door and walked to the driver's side, then jumped in. Stacey called her parents, "Hey Dad, I'm engaged!"

"That's great, baby. I knew he was asking tonight." Stacey smiled, "Well, I guess I'll see you at Thanksgiving." Stacey hung up the phone.

"Does everyone know?" Stacey asked Derek.

"No, only your family knows. I wanted to surprise my family." He replied as he started the vehicle and maneuvered down the Bluff.

"How do you want to surprise them?" They came up with a plan to keep it quiet until they saw the ring on her finger.

"So, do you want a spring, summer, or fall wedding?" Stacey thought for a while, trying to catch a glimpse of her ring, but it was too dark to see the details.

"An early-midsummer wedding would be nice." Stacey watched Derek drive, then a thought crossed her mind, "Eloping would be much faster and a lot easier." He glanced over at her and shook his head. "Yeah, I know, our parents would kill us." They both stayed quiet, taking in the moment.

"Did Adam talk to you about asking Nicole?" Derek asked Stacey.

"Yeah, he's proposing on their three-year anniversary of dating, which is just a few days away." Derek nodded, and they sang and talked all the way back to Madison. Upon arriving at the house, Derek parked the car. Stacey got out of the car, and Derek grabbed her bag. They walked up to the door together and opened it. Derek placed her bag in her room as Wylie ran up to Stacey. She picked him up.

"Hey, Wylie. Where is everyone?" She asked the dog before setting him down. He scampered off towards the family room. Derek joined Stacey as they entered the family room, where the entire family along with the girls' boyfriends were watching a movie. Stacey and Derek quietly found a couch and settled in.

About ten minutes later, the movie ended, and Ariel turned on the lights. "Well, hello Derek and Stacey. When did you get in?" Allison asked.

"We came in about 10 minutes ago." Stacey replied, brushing her hair out of her face, inadvertently drawing attention to her left hand.

"How was La Crosse?" Chad asked.

"It was wonderful," Derek replied, subtly attempting to keep his eyes off of Stacey's engagement ring. The ring sparkled in the light, and Stacey fidgeted with it.

"Why so wonderful?" Chad inquired.

"Well, I got to meet all of Stacey's friends. They threw her a going away party, then we had a peaceful picnic by the river until Adam showed up with Nicole and Rusty. Laura and Christian joined us too. Laura tried to get Stacey to tell her everything, which wasn't exactly pleasant, but they took us to a restaurant afterward where we ate lavishly. We ended the day with a trip up to the Bluff and then came home." Derek explained while Stacey sat next to him, continuing to fidget with her ring. Joanna noticed the fidgeting and gasped.

"When did you get that?" Derek laughed, and the rest of the family looked at Joanna, puzzled. "Look at her left hand," Joanna exclaimed. They all turned their attention to Stacey's hand as she lifted it up, smiling. Allison's jaw dropped, and Ariel gasped.

"Why didn't you interrupt the movie to tell us?" Ariel asked, her excitement evident.

"We wanted to see how long it would take you to notice." Derek explained, giving Stacey a hug. The family stood up to join in the excitement, hugging both Stacey and Derek.

"Welcome to the family, Stacey Rosemen," Chad said as he embraced her. They all settled down, and the girls admired the ring.

"Derek, you picked a beautiful ring," Joanna told her brother.

"No..." Derek turned to look at Stacey, brushing her hair behind her ear. "I think I picked a beautiful woman." Stacey blushed at their compliments. As they looked at the clock, it struck ten o'clock at night. Chad reminded the boys that they should be heading home soon. Joanna and Ariel accompanied their boyfriends to their cars to say goodbye. Allison and Chad remained with Stacey and Derek.

"Stacey, have you told your parents?" Allison asked, ensuring that the important people were informed. Stacey explained that Derek had informed her family before proposing.

"Well, we are going to bed. Don't stay up too late," Chad said as he assisted Allison out of the chair. Stacey cuddled up with Derek. He glanced at her left hand, smiling as he gently lifted her chin. He kissed the tip of her nose, and Stacey closed her eyes, a smile playing on her lips as he brushed his lips against the corner of her mouth.

"I love you, Stacey dear," he whispered against her lips. Stacey responded with a kiss. "What am I going to do with you, Stacey Rosemen?" The room was filled with the scent of burning wood, and the dimly lit fireplace created a warm ambiance. Stacey pondered a reply to his question.

"Well, you just agreed to marry me, so I guess that's what you're going to do with me."

"Ha-ha, funny," Derek playfully replied. He gently trapped her in a pretzel hold, making sure not to aggravate any of her injuries, and playfully gave her a wet-willy. Stacey squirmed and attempted to escape. Ariel and Joanna reentered the room, and Derek released Stacey from the hold, acting as if nothing had happened.

"Those were some really long goodbyes, considering you'll see them tomorrow or Sunday," Derek teased his sisters. A blush crept up from their necks to their hairlines.

"We were just giving you more time with your fiancé," Ariel stated. Growing tired and wanting to move, Stacey looked around the room.

"Derek, where did you put the crutches?" He chuckled and pointed to the door. "They're so helpful when they're ten feet away," she said sarcastically, aware that he wanted to carry her to her room. "Could you kindly retrieve those annoying crutches and bring them over here, please?" Derek complied, fetching the crutches and returning them to Stacey. "Thanks, Derek," she said, her smile returning. She leaned on the crutches and grabbed Derek's hand as he walked away. He turned toward her.

"Derek, I apologize for the way I said that. I can't rely on you to carry me all the time. I need to get used to the crutches so when I go to school on Monday, I'll be comfortable using them."

"I understand that, I just like carrying you," he playfully pouted.

"And I like being carried, and eventually I'll be begging you to carry me because I'll be so tired of the crutches." Derek wrapped his arms around her waist. "And please don't walk away from me when you're frustrated with me." He leaned his forehead against hers and apologized. Stacey reached her right arm around his neck and pulled his head down to meet her lips.

"Oh, that's so cute," Joanna remarked just loud enough for them to hear. Derek pulled his lips an inch from Stacey's.

"I'd be quiet if I were you, and I'd also run." Joanna's eyes widened as she hopped off the couch, but Derek caught her and tickled her.

"Mercy, I give up!" Derek laughed, ending the tickle battle. Stacey watched the action as she hobbled out of the room, and Derek followed after the skirmish was over.

"You really don't love your sister, do you?" He shook his head dramatically in a sarcastic manner. Stacey entered her room with Derek at her side. She placed her crutches by her bed, sat on the edge, and removed her knee brace.

"What are you doing?" He sat down next to her and watched as she carefully took off her brace. She handed him the knee brace and then removed the gauze.

"My knee needs some fresh air."

"I didn't know knees had lungs." Stacey laughed.

"You're such a comedian." Derek grabbed his Bible and took her Bible off of her nightstand.

"Where are we?" They looked through their Bibles to find their bookmark. The bookmark was at the end of Judges. They saw the next book was Ruth, a short book. Derek sat next to her on the bed then began reading the book of Ruth. He finished reading it.

"I don't know if I could do that as a woman back then—just offer myself to him, hoping he will help me in my need for a husband." Stacey thought out loud.

"It would be interesting since women couldn't own land. They had to depend on the men in their lives, their relatives. Boaz did the right thing by taking Ruth in as his wife." They closed their Bibles then Stacey grabbed their prayer books.

"Stacey, have your prayers been answered?" Derek asked Stacey.

"Yes, I am engaged to Derek Rysner. Have yours been answered?" She asked while writing in her journal.

"Stacey Rosemen said yes." They checked off their prayers if they were answered then they added a few. "Dear God," Derek started, "May You bless our engagement and our lives together. Please help Stacey heal in every way…"

"God, give us the strength to have You shine through us as we go through our daily lives. We are in Your arms. Amen." They put their Bibles and journals down.

"Goodnight, Stacey," he whispered into her ear as he got out of the bed. She pulled his head back to hers and gave him a kiss.

"Have a sweet dream," she whispered as she scooted away from the headboard to lie down. Derek didn't know what to say after her kiss… he kissed her cheek, tucked her into the blanket and left her alone.

Stacey woke up with a smile on her face as she looked at her left hand. "So it wasn't just a dream," she said to herself as she admired her ring. "Oh, I need to tell Opal," she thought to herself as she grabbed her phone. She dialed Opal's phone number and waited. On the fourth ring, Opal picked up. Stacey caught Opal up on all the happenings of the last week and a half since the last time they had talked. She told her about the move, Aaron, the puppy, and the engagement. In the middle of the conversation, Derek walked in and sat on the bed next to Stacey. She ended the conversation on a happy note, hung up the phone, and relaxed into Derek's arms.

"Just talking about it brings back the memories, doesn't it?" Derek asked, referring to the incident with Aaron.

"Yeah, it's too fresh in my mind; mentioning it brings back the memories," she said. She laid her head on his shoulder to relax and put the memories behind her. Someone knocked on the door. "Come in," Stacey said as Derek sighed. Allison walked in.

"What are your plans for today?" Stacey looked at Derek.

"I think it's going to be a lazy day," Derek answered.

"Well, the girls and I were wondering if you wanted to do a little shopping to calm Ariel down for her performance tonight." Derek raised his eyebrows as Stacey answered.

"That sounds good, but I don't want to be out long because my knee gets sore easily."

"Okay, we will buy some clothes for you that are easier to put on with your brace and everything else."

"All right, just give me half an hour to get cleaned up and I'll be ready."

"You'll be ready before Joanna and Ariel then," Derek commented. Allison laughed as she shook her head and left the room. Derek jumped off the bed, helped her stand up, and gave her a kiss. "Have fun shopping with the girls today, and call me if you need to be rescued." Stacey looked at him suspiciously.

"What are they going to do to me?" she wondered quietly as Derek left the room. She slowly hobbled around the room while getting ready, then she went out to the main area and looked around the room, waiting for the other girls to be ready. She saw a picture on the fireplace mantle of her and Derek on their trip to Northern Wisconsin in the summer; they were in front of a waterfall. Smiling at herself, she turned around to find Derek observing her.

"Do you remember me taking that picture?" Derek asked.

"Yeah, that was a fun family trip." Derek walked up to her and gave her a hug as Ariel and Joanna ran into the room.

"Hey, guys," Ariel announced as they jumped onto the couch. Derek and Stacey smiled as they turned towards the girls. "Stacey, are you ready to shop 'til you drop?"

"I'll drop fast, so yeah, I'm ready." They laughed at her.

"Don't tire her out too much; you want her to be awake during your performance tonight," Derek pointed towards Ariel. She pondered his statement then decided to be nice to Stacey. Derek kissed Stacey's cheek. "Have fun," he whispered into her ear before he disappeared. Stacey raised her eyebrows wondering what she was getting herself into, then she went out to the car.

"Stacey, what do you want to buy today?"

"I think some clothes that will be easier to put on without touching the knee." They nodded their heads in understanding. "What are you girls buying?" They thought for a while.

"I'm buying some cute winter clothes," Joanna said, and Ariel agreed. Stacey looked out the car window to watch the stores, buildings, and cars pass. Looking out at the beautiful clear sky and observing the people walking on the street, she saw the store they were going to. She looked at Allison as she parked the car.

"I thought we were going to go cute winter clothes shopping," Allison shrugged her shoulders.

"The girls wanted to look for bridesmaids' dresses and maybe a dress for you."

"We can look at dresses for the two of you, but I don't want to accidentally trip while trying them on." The girls squealed in excitement, jumping out of the car. Allison grabbed Stacey's crutches and walked around the car to hand them to her. She took the crutches to stand up out of the car, then they followed the girls into the wedding dress store.

About three hours later, the girls had some great ideas for the bridesmaids' dresses, but they wanted to wait until it was a little closer to the wedding. Then they went to do some regular clothes shopping. Ariel and Joanna found some cute pants and shirts, while Stacey found some loose-fitting sweatpants and jeans. Afterward, they went home to relax for the night, while Ariel went to the school to prepare herself for the play.

Walking into the high school to watch the play, Derek showed her to a seat towards the front and then ran into his friends. "Hey Chase, AJ, Dennis, come join us," Stacey suggested as they went to sit down in the second row, talking until the lights went dark. Stacey watched Ariel come out and sing 'Bonjour' from Beauty and the Beast as Belle. "She sings beautifully," Stacey whispered into Derek's ear. He turned his head, and a smile grew on his face with pride for his sister.

"She sings like an angel, like someone else I know," Stacey blushed, then turned her attention back to the play. After the play, Derek rushed up to his sister and gave her a hug while spinning her around. "You did an amazing job, Ariel." She blushed at his compliment and went off to hug her friends and family.

Derek woke up, the sun rays crossing his eyes. The rays were telling him to wake up to the beautiful morning. He covered his face to hide from the sun, but then his alarm clock went off. Slapping the clock, he rolled out of bed and put a shirt on to go out into the living room with his Bible. There, he found Stacey curled up in a blanket with a pad of paper and a pen. He peeked over her shoulder to see plans for the next few years. Leaning over the back of the couch, he kissed her cheek. She turned her head toward him and smiled; then she patted the spot next to her for him to sit.

He sat down and cuddled up with her, sharing the plans for the next few months.

"I start school on Monday, and I still have my physical therapy with Jayne and Dallas, as well as other doctor appointments with Jayne," Derek took the pad of paper from her hands and read the whole list. Then, he set it on the other side of him.

"Derek, may I have my paper back?" He shook his head as he grabbed his Bible and started reading a passage on worrying. Stacey calmed down, listening to his soothing voice reading the Words of God. After he finished reading the verses, he looked over to her.

"I know I need to stop worrying." Derek smiled as he set the book down and held her. Half an hour later, Joanna walked out of her room.

"I thought I heard someone up," she said as she waved and walked toward the kitchen to start breakfast. Derek and Stacey followed her to help her make an exquisite breakfast, consisting of cheesy scrambled eggs with bacon, toast, and milk. Allison and Chad walked in as their kids set the table with all the food ready. They thanked their adult children and sat down to eat. Then Chad stopped them with a prayer.

"Dear God, please help us grow in Christ and trust in You when we are having a hard time relying on You. We thank You for Your strength, love, and our financial security. Bless this food that we are about to eat. In Jesus' name, Amen." They looked up and smiled at him and dug into their food.

"Dad, when are we going to go to the park again?" Ariel asked, wanting more family time.

"After church and lunch, we can go to the zoo because I know that's where you really want to go." Ariel blushed at being read like a book.

"Ariel, I know you want to join your family there, the monkeys. You must miss your family." Derek teased her; she stuck her tongue out at him and threw a piece of toast at him. As the piece hit him on the head, he looked aghast at her, then his face changed from surprise to a playful expression.

"Derek, Ariel, wait until after church so you will have time to pick up the mess," Allison said while putting a bite of food into her mouth. Derek's hand stopped mid-flick and he put the piece of food back on his plate and looked at his mother apologetically. They finished up their breakfast, and together they cleaned up as Allison and Chad headed to the church early since it was his turn to preach. Joanna, Ariel, Derek, and Stacey climbed into Stacey's vehicle and drove to the church after the kitchen was cleaned up. As they walked in, they were greeted by Pastor Jeff.

"Stacey, I know we keep springing this on you, but our worship leader is sick and his backup is out of town. Could you lead today?" Stacey's eyes widened and she wasn't sure if she could, but she heard herself agreeing to lead the singing. Pastor Jeff whisked her off to the sanctuary to do a quick practice with the band. They gave her a handheld microphone and started playing the songs. She felt relieved when she heard familiar songs. The practice went well, and she took a drink of water as they finished the song. Pastor Jeff walked up to her.

"Apparently, you need to become one of our worship leaders."

"I'll think about it, Pastor Jeff, but I would like to settle into school and my other emotions before I commit to something else."

"Chad told me what happened to you this week, so I understand." Stacey grabbed her crutches and took a deep breath.

"Yeah, it will take me a while to get over that." She went back with the band as the church members entered the sanctuary. They huddled into a circle with their arms around each other's shoulders around Stacey, praying for wisdom in words, beautiful singing to honor God with their praise and worship. The band members went out to start the silent hum of music before the service started. Stacey sat down, laying her head into her hands, praying for a calm surrender and peace. Then she felt a calmness settle onto her, and she looked up to see Derek in the doorway.

"I was praying for you and will continue forever. You will praise and honor Him with your voice, as you will also honor me as my wife," he knelt in front of her, taking both of her hands into his. "You have nothing to be afraid of; you have God and I standing with you always." Stacey pulled Derek up as she stood and gave him a huge hug and kiss before she walked out on the stage. Before she started singing, she walked over to her future father-in-law and whispered something in his ear, and he nodded. Then, she greeted everyone and started the worship part of the service. They sang a few songs, had communion, an offering, and one song left before the sermon, then Stacey had the band play softly behind her as she spoke.

"I know that you all want to leave here as soon as possible, but I have something I need to tell you, and Pastor Chad agreed to shorten his sermon so we'll finish at the same time." The congregation laughed as Chad gave her a chair to sit in. "This past week has been tough. I think God decided to test my limits. Quite a few things happened this week, some good, but also some bad. I have a male friend in La Crosse who, in the past few years, has become obsessed with me, very possessive, and he never believed me when I said I had a boyfriend. On my birthday, which was the twenty-first, he tried to kidnap me from the park we were at, but my family and friends caught him. Then, on Tuesday, he successfully kidnapped me and took me to a hotel."

She took a deep breath and felt a comforting hand on her shoulder. "In the hotel, he hurt me and took a sacred thing away from me. I don't want your pity, but I do want your prayers. This hurt me physically and emotionally, and I need prayers to uplift me. God will find a way for me to use this pain, but right now, I need prayers. He has miraculously given me the strength to forgive my friend who brought me here to Madison after she beat me up, and I am working on forgiving the guy who took away my purity. God has also given me a strong Christian man who has proposed to me even in my hardest times. I just wanted to ask you for prayers as Derek and I grow together in Christ and as I seek to forgive my perpetrator." She looked out to see the whole congregation agreeing to pray for her. Chad waved Derek up and laid hands on the two of them.

"Let's pray for them now," the congregation bowed their heads as Chad started, and the band members and other pastors surrounded them. Derek knelt next to her and held her hand as Chad began. "God, we are here to pray for this young woman and young man. We pray that You may be with Stacey as she tries to recover from this pain and that something wonderful may come out of this. And please bless this union that these two have agreed to enter together. In Jesus' name, Amen."

"Amen," the congregation finished as the next song started before the sermon. Stacey sang the song with tears running down her cheeks and Derek singing next to her. When the song was done, Chad kept the two of them up there for his sermon as he brought out small boxes filled with miscellaneous items: rocks, pebbles, sand, and water, along with two peanut butter jars.

"I have these items and my helpers," he said, pointing to Stacey and Derek. "I am going to give each of them a recipe to fill a jar…" he picked up the peanut butter jar.

Pastor Jeff brought out a separating curtain and they started mixing their recipes. When they were done, Chad brought Derek out front but his jar was overflowing. "Derek, how did you make this?"

"Well Dad, I was focusing on my little items first like games, Xbox, play station then I went onto chores, and other things to worry about. Those events are represented by water and sand. Then, the small rocks represent hobbies, interests and friends. Then, these big rocks are God, family and work. Derek carefully picked up his jar, it was overflowing and he had some items left that were supposed to fit into the jar.

"Derek, are you overwhelmed with your life?" He looked at his jar and nodded his head. "Okay, Stacey come out and tell us how everything fit into your jar." She comfortably carried her jar out to him with the cover screwed on top.

"Well, I put God, family and work first, which are the three big rocks then hobbies, interests and friends were put in next. Then, it was chores, and other little things then I poured in the cup of water which is the tiny, non-important things in life such as game boys, Xboxes and play station." She looked at Derek with a smug face.

"So, how is your life going?"

"It is full but since my priorities are straight, I'm content with my life, busy but not overwhelmed." They put their jars on the tables as Chad finished.

"So, you see we need to prioritize our lives so that God is first followed by other major responsibilities, down to tiny, non-important items. If you prioritize like Derek did then you will most likely be overwhelmed. If you do it like Stacey did, it will be a healthier life raring to go on the next adventure. Please think about how you prioritize your life and maybe think about changing it if you feel overwhelmed." The band started softly playing some music in the background as Chad finished then they sang one more song of worship before it was over. People walked up to Stacey saying they would pray for her as they headed for their classes. Derek and Stacey started heading to class when he noticed she didn't have her crutches and she was limping. He stopped her, handed her his Bible and picked her up, carrying her to class. Before they entered the class Joanna showed up with her crutches, which Stacey took to hobble into the room.

Chapter 6

The sun shined through the windows, marking the day as sunny. The light hit Stacey's eyes, waking her up for her first day of school in Madison. Her hands found her covers, pulling them up over her head to block the sun. Then, she heard a knock on the door. The door creaked as someone slowly opened it, trying to sneak in. She peeked over the covers to see Derek putting something on her nightstand. Then, he sat down on the side of her bed and pulled the covers down to see her face. She acted like she was sleeping as she felt his presence, inching closer to her. His lips finally made contact with hers, and she pulled her arms out of the blanket, wrapping them around his neck. He moved back an inch, opening his eyes to see she was awake. Stacey smiled as she pulled him back toward herself, enjoying the wake-up call. Derek sat up and pulled the tray over he had carried in with him. Stacey looked at the tray and saw two fried eggs, two slices of bacon, and two pieces of toast on each of the plates, along with two glasses of milk.

"Breakfast in bed, nice," Stacey said as she situated herself to sit up and had Derek sit across from her. After they were settled, Derek said a prayer over the food and the healthiness of their bodies, and they dug into their food.

"Are you ready for today, Stac?" She finished chewing and swallowed her food before she answered.

"Yeah, I think I'm ready, but I'm going to need a nap when we get home." Derek smiled at her suggestion.

"I wouldn't mind that…" They finished their food in silence and then got ready for school. They left early to get Stacey set up with her classes, locker, and a tour. They finished the tour and went into the commons area in the courtyard.

A few minutes later, they were joined by Derek's friends: Dennis, Chase, and AJ. "How's the knee healing?" Dennis asked as they sat down at the picnic table.

"It's getting better, but I'm still not supposed to walk on it much." They all nodded their heads in understanding as they set up a game of euchre. Stacey watched them play the first game and then started asking questions.

"Why does the nine of hearts win over the queen of clubs?"

"The nine is a trump card; it is part of a certain suit that was picked, which was hearts. So any heart card trumps, or wins, the hand." She nodded her head at Derek's explanation and watched for a while longer, then the bell rang. Derek and Stacey left the boys to clean up the cards as they walked to their first class together. They went to their classes, which almost matched exactly. When they entered their Calculus class, Aunt Addy greeted them with excitement.

"Aunt Addy, you've known Derek the whole time and you never told me." She shrugged her shoulders as she looked at Derek, then gave Stacey a hug. All the classes went on with an introduction of Stacey, and then classes went on as if nothing happened. The last class of the day was Physical Education with Mr. Thompson from La Crosse.

"How's the knee?"

"Slowly but surely healing. What will I be doing in this class?"

"I will need to talk to your physical therapist, but mostly lifting weights with your arms and doing core exercises."

"Yay," she replied sarcastically. "Then Derek will have to carry me out of this place." Mr. Thompson laughed as he started the warm-up for his other students. Stacey went into the weight room and did an arm and core workout.

At the end of the class, Mr. Thompson went to check on her and found her lying on the mats, sprawled out. "Stacey, are you alright?" She lifted her head and started laughing.

"I can get on the floor easily, but getting up is a different story after a workout." His body shook with laughter, and then he squatted down next to her and helped her get up to a chair. A few minutes later, Derek came in, looking for her and smiled when he saw her on the chair, sweaty and red in the face.

"Joanna will get your clothes out of the gym locker," he announced as he lifted her off the chair and carried her to her other locker to get her books. Then they went home. When they got to the house, Allison had a snack waiting for them, and they went into the living room and took a nap on the couch with Wylie.

Mid-November

The sun woke Stacey up from a restless sleep. She had finally given up trying to sleep and had gone to her reading chair to look at the stars. Finally, she fell asleep again, only to be awakened by the sun a few short hours later. What had kept her up all night came back to haunt her. She looked at the clock and saw she was late waking up. She rushed around and got ready in record time. Slowly, she limped out to the kitchen and saw Derek eating some bacon and eggs. Before he felt her presence, she painted a smile onto her face, even though her thoughts were haunting her.

"Stac, you're up," he exclaimed when he noticed her in the doorway.

"Yeah, I didn't sleep well last night." She sat down at the table as Allison brought her food over. The smell made her nauseous, but to hide her discomfort, she acted like she was eating whenever Derek or Allison looked her way. Then, when they left the room, she threw the food away. Just as she was cleaning up, Ariel walked in.

"You know you're supposed to eat that, not throw it away." Stacey smirked at being caught, then limped over to the sink with her plate.

"I'm not feeling well, and I didn't want anyone to know." Ariel just shook her head as she made herself some breakfast. Stacey limped out of the room as fast as she could, as another wave of sickness came over her. She ran into Chad,

"Whoa, Stacey, where are you going in such a hurry?" She moved past him and barely made it to the bathroom in time. He followed her and pulled her hair out of her face. When she was done, he carried her to her bedroom and went in search of Derek. "Stacey isn't going to school today.

She just puked her guts out. I'll stay home and take care of her." Derek tried to argue, wanting to stay with her, but Chad held his ground. Derek went into her room and gave her a kiss on the cheek as she slept. Ariel, Joanna, and Derek left for school. Chad walked into the room a few hours later and saw her moving around her room.

"What are you doing up?"

"I need to talk to Jayne," she announced as she looked for her purse.

"I'll take you."

"You told Derek you were going to watch me, didn't you?" He nodded his head and escorted her to the hospital. They went to Jayne's office and waited for her to arrive.

"Do you know why you were sick this morning?"

"I have a feeling I know why, which is why I'm here." Jayne walked in and looked at Stacey's face.

"Pastor Chad, may Stacey and I have a moment alone?" He stood up from his chair and left the room. "Stacey, why are you here and not at school?"

"I was puking my guts out…can you give me a pregnancy test?" She rushed her question, feeling uncomfortable about the situation.

"When was your last cycle?"

"The eighth of October. I have never been this late. I am usually within a day or so." She looked at her calendar and counted.

"So, it's been about forty days. Let's give you a test." She pulled a home pregnancy test out of her desk drawer. "This is mine, but you need it more than I do, and these are cheaper than the hospital's test." Stacey pulled out five dollars to replace it for Jayne. "Dallas will be coming up soon; we thought you had hurt your knee again. Just go and take the test and bring it out." Stacey went into the bathroom without her crutches and took the test. Before she walked out, she heard Dallas arrive in the office with Jayne. She was waiting for the results to show up when she limped back into the office. The test result showed, 'PREGNANT.' She looked up at Jayne and Dallas, then went limp.

"Stacey!" Jayne yelled as Dallas caught her before she fell to the ground. Chad ran in.

"What's going on?" he asked as he walked in, then he saw Stacey on the floor, out cold.

"She is just overwhelmed. We can't tell you anymore." Stacey started coming to as they were talking, then she handed Jayne the test. "I'm so sorry, Stacey." She rushed back into the bathroom, feeling sick again. She walked out a few minutes later, still not feeling well.

"Stacey, what's wrong?" Chad asked.

"I'm pregnant with Aaron's baby." He opened his mouth to say something, but he didn't know what to say. "Can you take me home?" She walked out the door, and Chad looked at Jayne and Dallas for advice, but they didn't say anything. He ran after Stacey and drove her home. When they arrived, she went directly to her room and locked herself in with Wylie. Cuddling up on her bed, tears ran down her face with anger, fear, and the stress of the future.

Finally, she cried herself to sleep, getting away from the world until she had a nightmare of Aaron trying to get her again. She jerked awake in a cold sweat, barely holding in her scream. She looked at the clock and dropped back onto her pillows, rubbing her head and covering her face. Wylie jumped onto her stomach and walked up to her face, licking it. "Wylie, stop," she said, laughing because his tongue tickled her. "Wylie, how am I going to tell Derek?" she asked while cupping his furry face in her hands. "No reply…" she said to Wylie, "I don't know either." She played with him for a bit longer before she got up, washed her face, and then went out to find Chad. "I'm going to go to the park. I need some fresh air." He was silent for a while, observing her, then decided to go with her. "Chad, you don't need to go. I'm…" He put his finger up to stop her.

"Two things, Derek would kill me if I let you go alone, and I need some fresh air and time to think as well." She agreed and grabbed their coats and a leash for Wylie as they walked out the door. Chad drove to the park, and Stacey went directly to the swings. Wylie stayed with Chad as she pumped her legs to get high in the air. The cool air hit her cheeks and stung her eyes as tears slid down her face. When she got to the highest point, she let the swing move her as she watched the sky, whispering to God,

"Your will be done, Your will be done. I'm in Your arms…" She repeated those words over and over again until the swing stopped. She covered her face as she sobbed, her whole body shaking. She felt something at her feet and peeked through her hands to see Wylie staring up at her with his ears up. She bent down and picked him up in her arms, burying her face in his fur. Then she felt someone lightly push her on the swing. "Chad, how am I supposed to tell your son?" There was silence for a few moments.

"Just tell him, but you need to tell him today." She heard something different in his voice and turned to see tears rolling down his jaw.

"I'm sorry, I…"

"This is not your fault. It does not make you a sinner in God's eyes. He will bless you for what you are going through." Chad stopped pushing her and moved in front of her.

"I just feel so gross, unworthy, impure, and I don't think I deserve your son. He should get a pure, virgin girl, not me." He grabbed her hand and squeezed it.

"Stacey, he sees you as his pure, virgin girl. He knows you didn't want this, he will understand." She stood up and walked away with Wylie. Chad sat down on the swing and watched her slowly limp away and sit on the ground. Then his phone rang.

"Dad, where are you? You're supposed to be at home. Stacey's sick."

"Derek, we both needed fresh air. Come join us at the park just down the road." Minutes later, he showed up and walked up to his dad.

"What's going on?"

"Go ask her, and when she tells you, don't look disgusted or walk away." He looked at his father with worry, then slowly walked up to Stacey.

"Stacey," she looked up with tear-streaked cheeks and buried her face again. "Sweetheart, what's wrong?"

"Derek, if you don't want to be with me any longer, I will understand…" his face looked disappointed, then he remembered his dad's advice and erased his emotions off his face. "Derek, I'm…I'm pregnant with Aaron's baby." He sat down next to her, wrapped his arm around her waist, and used his other hand to turn her face toward his.

"Stacey, I will never leave you. This is not your fault; we will get through this with God. Nothing could make me love you any less; you are my love, my girl, and soon my wife. Nothing could change that." She leaned toward him and kissed him, wanting the pain and hurt to go away.

Feeling safe in the arms of the man of her dreams, Stacey felt comforted. Chad walked up to them, telling them that he was going home. They said goodbye, and then Stacey realized she was getting cold. They went to a coffee shop and bought two cups of hot chocolate before heading home. They laid down on the couch to warm up, and when they fell asleep, Allison set a blanket on top of them. Then, she went to find Chad.

"Why was Stacey sick today?" Chad tried to hide behind his book, but Allison pulled it down. "One of my friends saw you at the hospital with Stacey to visit Jayne, and then you went to the park. She must not be very sick."

"She might be sick for the next four to eight months, depending on how this agrees with her." Allison's jaw dropped as she dropped into the chair across from Chad.

"She's pregnant with Aaron's baby?" He nodded his head.

"It's been a rough day…she was sick this morning, then we went to see Jayne, and they did the test and she fainted. When she woke up, she got sick again, then we came home, and she cried herself to sleep, then woke up with a nightmare. Then, we went to the park; in a way, she looked free as she was swinging high in the air. Then, Derek came, and she told him." Allison let out a deep breath.

"We will make it, but she should tell the congregation since they know the rest of the story." He thought about it.

"The congregation can wait; it's still too fresh, and she needs to tell her family first." They were silent as they thought about what the future would hold. Ariel and Joanna came home hungry after their practices. Stacey woke up to their chatter in the kitchen and held onto Derek, still scared and unsure. She felt a kiss on the back of her neck and melted back into Derek's arms.

"I love you, dear, don't ever forget that." She sat up and turned toward him, putting her finger over his lips when he was going to talk again. She used her finger to trace his jawline, then bent over and kissed his chin and his waiting lips. She put an inch between their lips.

"I love you too, but I will need to hear that more often in the next few months." She whispered against his lips.

"I can do that," he whispered back then closed the space between their lips. They felt Wylie jump onto them and walk toward their faces, giving them kisses. He laid down between them and got comfortable. Derek and Stacey laughed as they pet him. "I think he thinks we were talking about him and we need to give him more love." Stacey smiled and kissed Wylie on the top of his head. He licked her chin, then laid his head down again. A few minutes later, Wylie's head perked up, and he turned to see the family watching them. "Hi Mom, Dad, Ariel, and Joanna. Why don't you join us?" Ariel ran and acted like she was going to jump, but stopped and fell on top of them.

"What's for supper?" Stacey asked as they all sat down in chairs.

"We weren't sure what smells made you feel nauseous, so I don't know," Allison replied.

"I think pizza would be fine," Chad grabbed his coupons, and they planned what they wanted and ordered it.

Stacey woke up feeling nauseous and hot. She opened a window up an inch to cool off. She felt a wave of uneasiness and rushed to her bathroom, throwing up. She relaxed back against the wall waiting for the next wave of sickness to come. A few minutes later it came, and her stomach clenched when nothing came up. A small moan came out as she laid back into the wall again. She slowly stood up to wash her face and brush her teeth before she went back to lay down on the bed. An hour later, she felt someone sit on the bed. She turned towards the person and opened her eyes and screamed. Aaron quickly covered her mouth with his hand and picked her up, carrying her out the window.

As Aaron shut the window, she heard Derek banging on the door and yelling for her. Aaron put tape over her mouth and carried her to his car, stuffing her into the trunk again. Aaron drove off, with no plan in mind. He drove to Wal-Mart and slowly opened the trunk door. Stacey was dead still, so he pulled her out and untied her, then she hit him over the head with a crowbar and ran into the store, hoping to find some help. Just as she spotted a police officer, Aaron caught her and hid behind a shelf, kissing her. The police officer walked over to them to yell at them for making out.

"Sir, this is a public place. You need to be considerate of the families with children." Aaron pulled his lips from Stacey to yell back, but she bolted into the restroom and they followed her. When she arrived in the bathroom, she saw feet in one of the stalls.

"Ma'am, may I borrow your phone. I was kidnapped out of my house." The stall door opened immediately, and the woman handed her the phone. Stacey called Derek, "Derek, I'm at the Wal-Mart we always go to. I don't have time to explain, but I will try to get him to stay here."

"We'll be there in ten minutes, I love you."

"I love you too," she hung up the phone, "Thank-you for the use of your phone." A wave of nausea hit her and she jumped into a stall, throwing up.

"What's going on?" The woman asked Stacey.

"I'm pregnant by the man who kidnapped me, he raped me about a month ago and he won't leave me alone…" she heard a commotion outside the restroom. Stacey grabbed the phone back, "If you want an explanation call me at this number." She added herself as a contact and gave the phone back. "My name is Stacey Rosemen," she extended her hand.

"I'm Debra Dillon and I will be calling you." They shook hands then Stacey walked out to Aaron and the police officer.

"Ma'am, I need to talk to you," she stepped aside with the police officer. "Are you willingly with this man?"

"No, but I'm waiting for back-up because I think he has a gun. Just keep an eye on me and when the other officers come tell them where I am."

"He says your pregnant, is that true?" Stacey's jaw dropped,

"I am but I don't know how he knows because I just found out yesterday."

"I'll agree to let him go until back-up comes but if he does anything I'm onto him." Stacey agreed and walked back to Aaron, her bravery slowly dissipating.

"Okay, Aaron let's go shopping," she announced as she looped her arm into his elbow.

"Hey Aaron, buy her some shoes," he smiled back at the officer and walked away with Stacey on his arm. As soon as they were out of sight Aaron demanded to know what she said to the officer.

"I just told him I felt like throwing up so I ran to the bathroom. Then, he questioned me about my bare feet." She shrugged her shoulders as she led him to the shoe department. Aaron grabbed a pair of flip flops and ordered Stacey to put them on. Sitting down on a bench, she took the tags off and slipped them on her feet while rubbing her knee. "I'm going to be sore tomorrow," she thought to herself as she looked at her knee then

Aaron pulled her up and started walking towards the door. "Aaron, I told the officer we came here to shop so we shouldn't just leave or he'll be suspicious." Aaron groaned as she led him to the clothes section. She picked out a shirt, skirt and a nice sweater. Then, she went to the fitting room and was slowly trying on her clothes when Aaron urgently knocked on the door. She stepped out of the room and was pulled to the front entrance.

"You lied to me, that cop has been following us all over the store," they were almost to the door when Stacey thought of something.

"Aaron, if we go out now, we'll get caught for stealing. We should go check-out then I will leave with you willingly." He complied as Stacey spotted Derek behind a shelf. She took the tags off all of the clothes and handed them to the cashier. Just as the cashier handed Aaron the receipt, the police officer pulled Stacey out of the way as the other officers pointed their guns at him, yelling at him to put his hands up. The officer that pulled Stacey back walked behind Aaron and pulled the gun out from behind Aaron's back and cuffed him while reading him his Miranda rights. They hauled him outside and took a statement from Stacey, Debra, and a few other people.

"Debra, this is my fiancé Derek Rysner. Derek, this is the woman who let me borrow her phone." They shook hands then the police needed to talk to Derek.

"Stacey, how did you stay calm the whole time he was pulling you around?" Stacey was ready to answer her question but her knee was killing her.

"Let's sit down," they walked over to a bench and sat down. "I know Aaron, we went to school together and were friends until he started becoming obsessed with me. He never believed I had a boyfriend until I tore my ACL and moved here for a knee study. He started following me everywhere and about a month ago he kidnapped me out of my room and took me to a hotel. He raped me and somehow he got out of jail to try again. I also had God with me the whole time he was pulling me around the store. God gave me the strength." Stacey saw Derek walking up to her, "I think I have to go but call me and we'll talk again." Debra agreed to call her.

"Stac, we should go, school starts soon." She stood up and started walking then Derek picked her up when he saw her limping. He carried her to his car and drove to school, they were a little late but they were excused and the secretary had an ice bag and a set of crutches ready for her. They went to their first class and the day went on like nothing happened until Calculus with Aunt Addy. It was a work day and Addy called Stacey back to her desk to give her notes.

"Stacey, what went on yesterday and this morning?" Stacey smiled at her aunt's way of getting her back to her desk to talk to her.

"Yesterday, I was sick, and this morning Aaron took me shopping," she pointed to her clothes and smiled.

"How did he get out?" Stacey shrugged her shoulders. "What were you sick from?" Stacey leaned over and whispered the answer in her ear. Addy gasped, which made the whole class look back at them. Addy just smiled at them and gestured for them to turn back around. "Does your mother know?"

"No, I was going to tell her in person, but word is spreading, so I should tell Mom and Dad soon."

"This will break their hearts and Adam's." Addy commented. Tears started welling up in Stacey's eyes, and she brushed them away.

"I'm so scared, and I just feel so gross. I don't want a lot of people to know, but they will eventually find out." Addy pulled Stacey into a hug, and then they focused on the work on the desk. At the end of the day, Derek carried her exhausted body out to the car, and then he went back in for their backpacks.

"Derek," Addy yelled for him. He turned toward her. "How is she really doing with the news?"

"She isn't doing well. She is sick in the morning, and she feels like no one deserves her and that she is unworthy to belong anywhere. This is going to be a tough next few years, but we will make it."

"I know you will. I'll just keep on checking in with her." They smiled at each other with hope as Derek went back to his girl. When he was about to open his car door, his phone rang.

"Derek, I need to check on her knee. Can you come over to the hospital?" Jayne asked while Derek thought for a while.

"Sure, but she just fell asleep." They hung up, and he drove her over to the hospital. Dallas was there waiting, and he parked Derek's car as

Derek carried the sleeping beauty to Jayne. He set her down on the bed, and Jayne checked her knee.

"It seems all right, but it is swollen quite a bit, so she should stay off it for the next few days." She sat down next to Derek. "How is she holding up emotionally?" Derek set his hand over Stacey's and held it.

"Yesterday was rough. She thought I was going to break up with her because of the news. She basically cried the whole morning and partially through the afternoon, according to my dad. Today, she hasn't had much time to think about it because of Aaron this morning, then trying to catch up with school from missing yesterday." They were silent for a few moments, enjoying the silence.

"Derek, how are you holding up?" His eyes welled up with tears.

"I hate that this happened to her, and I just want to take this pain away. I love her, and there is nothing anyone can do about it. We will make it, and we will have this baby because God allowed it." Dallas walked in and set his hands on Derek's shoulders.

"We know exactly what you are going through." Derek looked up at Dallas, confused. "Jayne was raped the same year we were going to get married. We talked about it, and Jayne felt the same way Stacey does: unworthy, undeserving. But I stuck to her because I love her. She became pregnant as well, and he is the light of our life. He is seven years old, and then we have a three-year-old, and we are pregnant again." Derek took some time to digest the new information.

"Does he know that you are not the father?" They both nodded their heads. Stacey woke up a few minutes later.

"Was I dreaming, or did it really happen to you, Jayne?" She asked while sitting up.

"It happened to me as well," they sat there in silence until Stacey said she was hungry. They moved out of the room and went out to eat for supper. Jayne and Stacey went to find seats as the guys ordered.

"Does this feeling of unworthiness and uncleanness go away?" Jayne thought for a while.

"They do slowly go away when you have a wonderful man who gives you compliments every day and shows you his love on a daily basis with little love notes, back rubs, supper, and just doing little things everywhere." Stacey let out a sigh of relief and relaxed. Then, the guys showed up with their drinks and condiments. Derek sat next to Stacey and held her hand while twisting her ring around her finger. They talked for an hour, then Derek and Stacey had to get home to do their homework.

"Thank You for this time and advice," Derek thanked them as they left. In the car, Stacey leaned over the armrest and gave Derek a kiss. He pulled back, "I think we will be fine if you kiss me like that all the time." Stacey's cheeks turned red as he backed out of the parking lot and held her hand.

⸻ ∿◦◖◶◗◦∿ ⸻

Stacey sat down on the hood of Derek's car, waiting for him to come out. The cool air nipped at her cheeks as she pulled her winter jacket in closer to her. He came out laughing at her.

"Why didn't you get in the car, silly?" She raised her eyebrows.

"Cause you never gave me the keys." He patted his pockets and found his keys in his jacket. They laughed as he helped her off the hood and into the car.

"Sorry, I'm a little distracted. Off to your parents' house we go." She kissed his cheek as he pulled out of the parking lot. "Are you ready to tell your parents?" He asked her as he pulled onto the interstate.

"No, I'm not ready to tell them, but they need to know…" they were silent for a while, "And we are coming back tomorrow. I'm leading the songs at church on Sunday and I want to be rested."

"Your mom won't like that." They laughed, then Stacey slept the rest of the way to her parents' house. They arrived around suppertime, surprising her family with the visit.

"What are the two of you doing here?" Laura asked them. Stacey smelled her favorite meal.

"I knew you were making this meal, so we drove up to see you guys and eat." They all laughed as they gave each other hugs, then Stacey saw Nicole's engagement ring and gave her a huge hug. They sat around the table, and Adam said a prayer.

"Dear Lord, thank You for this food that we are about to eat and our surprise dinner guests. Please let us enjoy our time together. Amen." They caught up on each other's lives, and Stacey told them about Aaron's second kidnapping. Then, they were telling stories for hours and they moved into the living room with their dessert.

"Hey, guys, there is a reason why we came up this weekend. We have… well… I have some bad but good news. It's good because we will have another family member, but bad because it is not Derek's." She let them process the information, then she heard her mother gasp and saw Adam get up to pace. Derek felt Stacey squeeze his hand tighter, needing comfort. He wrapped his arm around her, kissing her cheek. She looked up and saw her mom staring at her. Looking away, she saw Adam's face and her father's. Standing up, she limped out of the room, not able to stand their faces of despair, anger, and accusation. Grabbing her jacket, she went out to the porch, swinging on the porch swing with tears rolling down her cheeks.

⸺ ⌇⊶⊶⊷⊷ ⸺

Inside, the family was just staring off at nothing as Adam paced and Derek observed them all. "She needs support in this; she doesn't want to see what I see on your faces right now. She is going to have the baby, and we are going to raise him or her together." After his statement, he left to go find her.

"Mom, you need to stop accusing her of what happened. It wasn't her fault, and if you don't change, we will never see her again. You need to be her mom, not her psychologist." Adam left the room with Nicole.

"Hun, he's right. She didn't do this on purpose, and she just wants to obey God. He gave her this baby, and so she will have it. Don't come out until you understand what we have told you." He squeezed her fingers, then left to find the rest of his family with Stacey out on the porch. When he arrived outside, Stacey saw him, jumped into his arms, and held him tight.

"Daddy," she cried into his neck. He sat down on the porch stairs, holding her.

"Baby girl, I'm so sorry," she felt tears land on her neck as her dad cried with her. Adam held them both, and a few minutes later they took a breath and Stacey went to hold Derek. After their crying subsided, Laura came out with tear-streaked cheeks, and she held Stacey until she had to sit down.

"So, you would be due mid-July," she nodded her head. "So, the wedding would be at the end of August… that's around the same time that Adam and Nicole want to get married." Stacey thought about it for a few minutes, then she whispered into Nicole's ear with an idea. She nodded her head, liking the idea, and they whispered it into their fiancé's ear, and they liked it too.

"We will have a double wedding if the other parents agree." Stacey announced for the four of them. Laura and Christian thought about it and liked the idea. They talked about it for the next few hours until Nicole had to go home. Adam and Derek shared a room, and Stacey had hers to herself.

⁂

The sound of someone cooking in the kitchen woke Stacey up, and then the smell made her run for the bathroom. When she was done, she heard Derek calling her name.

"Stac, are you all right?" She opened the door, letting him in. He brushed her hair out of her face and kissed her forehead. "This is going to be a long first few months." Derek smiled, then she got another whiff of the breakfast food and turned toward the toilet as Derek held her hair back. When she was done, they grabbed jackets and long pants and went outside for fresh air without the smell of eggs. "I guess we forgot to tell them not to make eggs," Derek whispered into her ear as they cuddled on the swing. Stacey laughed softly as they watched the sun rise. A few minutes later, Adam came out.

"What are you doing out here? It's freezing."

"I'd rather be cold than sick…" Adam raised an eyebrow. "The smell of eggs makes me sick," she explained as Derek moved into a more comfortable position. Adam went inside and brought a plate of toast out for them and an extra blanket. "Thanks, Adam," they ate in silence as the cool air made their cheeks rosy and their noses cold. When they were done, Derek carried her into the house, hoping the smell was gone. There was a hint of the eggs, but Stacey just covered her nose with the blanket she was carrying into the house. Derek set her down on the couch and went to look for a few things. Then Christian walked in.

"I'm sorry about the eggs…"

"Dad, it's okay. You didn't know, and I get sick anyway, but the smell of eggs makes it worse." He sat down on the opposite side of the couch, and Stacey laid her head on his lap. Christian helped her arrange the blankets around her, then he brushed his fingers through her hair.

"Stacey, I have missed you a lot." She looked up at him and smiled, "You're my baby girl, and I want to protect you, but you have already been hurt…" he continued running his fingers through her hair.

"Dad, I will live. Though right now it doesn't seem like it. Derek has been wonderful, and so has his whole family. Jayne and Dallas have helped me in numerous ways, and the church has been encouraging us. We have God on our side." She covered her nose again to warm it up. "Where's Mom?"

"She's at the office. For some reason, she still blames you, so Adam and I told her to believe you or leave. She decided to leave for a while." Derek walked back into the room, smiling at what Adam said, then kissed Stacey on the forehead.

"Why are the two of you smiling so much?" Stacey asked, becoming suspicious of the favorite men in her life.

"We were just making plans for our wedding." Adam replied as Stacey cocked an eyebrow.

"And what are these plans?" They looked at each other; Adam answered her.

"We want you to be carried in on a cot by the four groomsmen, then Derek will lift you off and 'heal' you." Stacey started laughing at her brother's description, then when he was done, they were waiting for a reply.

"Ah… No, but thanks for the idea. I think Nicole and I will be planning the wedding." She sat up and pulled Adam onto the couch, playfully torturing him. "You have to say mercy…" she tickled him, and two minutes later he gasped, "Mercy!" They all laughed so hard that tears rolled down their cheeks. "Your arms got stronger," he pouted, then he gave her a hug before Derek sat next to her.

"Is Nicole coming over?" Christian asked him.

"No, she has a study group for school today."

"What do we want to do then?"

"Let's play some board games," Stacey suggested. Adam ran off to find some games, and Christian left to find some snacks. Derek held Stacey as she leaned back into his arms, and she turned to look at him. She reached up her fingers to trace the outline of his jawline. Then she kissed under his chin and his lips. He pulled back a few centimeters, searching her eyes for any anxiety. He brushed her side bangs behind her ear as he kissed the corner of her mouth. She smiled as she sat up and looked at him. He smiled back at her and kissed her hand as Christian walked in with a bowl of chips and salsa, along with a few cups of hot chocolate.

A few minutes later, Adam walked in with Monopoly and a deck of cards. They played a game of Monopoly which took two hours to finish, and then they worked on teaching Stacey how to play euchre. A few hours later, they succeeded.

"Dad, Adam, we have to get going." They looked up at her with sadness as she stood up. Adam gave her a hug, and then her father gave her a hug.

"Be good," Christian whispered into her ear as they pulled apart.

"I will try, Daddy," she replied with her usual response, even though she usually behaved herself. They promised to keep in touch as they went out to their car, knowing they would be seeing each other in less than a week. Stacey drove them home, allowing Derek to sleep.

—⁓⊶∘⊙⊱⊰⊙∘⊶⁓—

Chad and Stacey went to the church early to prepare themselves for the announcement Stacey was going to say. Chad was praying over her when there was a knock on the door. "We're a little busy, can it wait?" Chad asked wanting to comfort Stacey as much as he could before the morning worship. The door opened wide and Stacey gasped when she saw the man.

"You better not be pregnant with Aaron's baby," Aaron's father ordered as he strolled into the office.

"Mr. Jackson, I had no say in the matter. Your son is the one that did this to me. He raped me," she said with tears running down her face.

"You're just saying that now because you freely gave up your virginity and then you realized it was a mistake." He circled around Chad and Stacey.

"Think what you want Mr. Jackson but your son raped me and now I am pregnant. I didn't want this, I didn't want him." She stood up and walked out. He followed her,

"Abort the baby," he yelled at her, she spun around.

"Or what?" she challenged him.

"Or I will do it myself."

"Sir, that's called first-degree murder. Then you could join your son in jail. I will have this baby, and that's that. Live with it," she stormed off as Chad grabbed Mr. Jackson's arm.

"Sir, I think it's time for you to leave," Chad said. Mr. Jackson threw up his hands in surrender and left the building. Chad went to look for Stacey. "Stacey, he left!" he yelled. She slowly crawled out from underneath the pulpit and hobbled towards him, and he held her as she cried. He carried her into his office and laid her down on the couch, sitting on the floor next to her.

"Chad, please don't tell Derek. Mr. Jackson's threats have always been more bark than bite, but he hasn't carried through with any of them," she turned to look at him.

"I'm not keeping this from Derek; he needs to know to keep an eye out for him now. We need to be careful and make sure we don't leave you alone," Stacey buried her head into the couch pillow and yelled with frustration and anger. When she was done screaming, she looked back at Chad.

"Okay, we will tell him, but..." a wave of nausea came over her, and she bolted to the bathroom. After she was done and cleaned up, she went back to the office and saw Chad talking to Derek. She was walking away when she heard her name being called. She stopped and slowly turned around to Chad and Derek.

"Hi Honey," she said as they approached her. Derek shook his head, trying to contain his laughter.

"You are trying to look innocent, but it isn't working. I know what happened, and I know that we are going to keep our eyes on you."

"Oh, but your eyes are on me already," the guys laughed as they headed toward the stage entrance together. They walked out after grabbing their microphones, and the music started. Derek and Stacey walked out hand-in-hand, singing the first worship song. "Good morning, everyone. Hasn't God given us a beautiful morning?" She watched their heads nod in agreement. They sang a few more songs, then Chad came up and laid a hand on her shoulder. Taking a deep breath and slowly exhaling, she started.

"As almost all of you know, less than a month ago, I was kidnapped and hurt by an old friend of mine. Well, I just found out that I am pregnant by this man, and his father wants me to terminate it, but I won't. God allowed me to get pregnant, so I will follow through and have this baby. I will need your prayers, and my family and Derek's family will need your prayers as they support me through this." Chad gave her a hug as they left the stage for the sermon. Derek wrapped his arm around her shoulders, kissed her cheek, and smiled at her as Chad started the sermon. She turned her head toward the front, relaxing into Derek's side.

"God does not give us more than we can handle, and He helps us through all of our trials," Stacey saw him looking into her eyes. "With love and support, anyone can make it through all the storms in life." He smiled at his future daughter-in-law and his son before he continued with his sermon on hope. "Psalm 33:22, 'May Your unfailing love rest upon us, O Lord, even as we put our hope in You.'" He continued his sermon with powerful messages on hope, love, and peace. After the sermon, Stacey and Derek walked up to the center of the stage, singing the last song. Stacey saw the church congregation getting into the music, and she stopped singing to say a prayer in the middle of the song.

"Dear God, please be with everyone in this building and everyone in need of searching You out. And teach them that You are our all in all. You have given us this life, so please help us to honor and praise You with the life You have given us. In Jesus' name, Amen." The background music continued as everyone slowly dispersed to talk and have fellowship. Derek wrapped his arms around Stacey, and then Chad, Ariel, and Joanna joined them in a hug. Slowly, they felt others crowding around them, putting their hands on them in prayer, and then Pastor Jeff said a prayer.

"Dear God, we—as a congregation—pray for this woman and her family. She is a great addition to our worship team, and we pray that she will feel the prayers of Your people when she needs Your comfort most." Stacey was being held up by Derek and Chad as she felt weak and exhausted. "Please keep this young woman safe as there are people who are opposed to her going through with this pregnancy. Please bless this family." Stacey felt a burden being lifted off her shoulders, and Derek slowly went to the ground with her in his arms. The congregation dispersed to their classes, and Chad led his family and Stacey home to rest. Allison and Chad watched their young couple sleep.

"Chad, I have never seen a whole church come together like that to pray for one person… It was like we were all connected, touching each other's shoulders, praying." Chad pulled her in for a hug, rubbing her back.

"God is giving us a miracle through this horrible event. He is bringing our church together, and Stacey may end up counseling raped women because they may feel open to talking to her. There is a reason for every bad thing that God allows; we just have to wait for the good to happen." He kissed the top of her head, then wiped her tears away with the back of his fingers.

The beautiful sunrise woke Stacey as it shone through her skylight while she was sleeping on her reading chair again. Her sanctuary from her nightmares, stretching her body, she prayed. "Dear God, thank You for the support of my family, future family, and the church. They are amazing. Please take the nightmares away." There was a knock on the door. "Thank You for Your love and care," the door opened and Derek walked in slowly. Then he noticed the bed was empty. He paused on the brink of panic. "Derek," she whispered. He turned toward her, smiled, and walked to her, ready to go to school.

"Hey, hun, how are you feeling this morning?" She took a deep breath, taking a moment to assess how she was feeling.

"For now, I'm feeling fine, but it's a come and go sickness." Derek smiled at her sarcasm while sitting on the edge of the chair. Brushing her hair out of her eyes, he leaned down and kissed her cheek. "I should go get ready for school." Derek agreed and moved toward the door to let her get ready. She got ready and was on her way to the kitchen when her phone rang. She answered it to hear her brother's voice.

"How did it go yesterday?"

"It was amazing; they all prayed over us and gave us their blessing. Of course, Aaron's dad threatened to kill the baby if I didn't get an abortion." She heard a sigh over the phone.

"You just can't stay out of trouble," they talked for a few more minutes while Stacey packed her bag for school. Derek walked in and wrapped his arms around her waist.

"Stac, we need to get going."

"Hey Adam, I have to go to school. Stay out of trouble." Adam laughed as they signed off and went to school. When they arrived, they felt the whole school watching them. Mr. Thompson walked up to her.

"I'm sorry, Stacey," he gave her a hug. Then she realized why they were being stared at.

"Word spread fast," they nodded their heads. Derek and Stacey walked through the other students to their lockers. "This is weird," she whispered to Derek as they arrived at their lockers. He kissed her cheek as they headed to their classes.

Chapter 7

The colorful sky woke Derek up as the sun peeked through his blinds. He pulled his pillow over his head to block the sun, then he heard the door creak open. Someone sat on the side of his bed and pulled the blanket down. The person ran their fingernails over his six-pack and started tickling him. He sat up quickly to guard his stomach from being tickled.

"Stacey, stop…please," he said while trying to breathe, laugh, and talk at the same time. She stopped, and he pulled her down next to him.

"Good morning, sweetheart," he kissed her on her temple and got comfortable cuddling with her.

"Derek," she exclaimed, "You need to get ready." She successfully stood up then leaned over to kiss him and walked away before he could grab her. He chased after her but she got away, and he got up.

"How did that go?" Allison asked her when she walked back into the kitchen.

"He didn't want to get up, but I got him up." Allison smiled as Stacey sat at the kitchen table peeling potatoes. About twenty minutes later, Derek walked up behind Stacey and set his hands on her shoulders. He bent down and whispered something in her ear before kissing her cheek.

"Okay, Mom, what is my job for the day?" She put a finger to her chin, pondering his question.

"This year, your job is to keep the fireplace going and to entertain your family and fiancé." He smiled and sat down to help Stacey peel potatoes. When the potatoes were done, Derek whisked Stacey away into the living room. She walked around the room, looking at the pictures while Derek started the fire. A few minutes later, Derek sat back as the fire started to grow. Stacey observed him in his jeans, white t-shirt, and dark blue button-up shirt.

"Derek, did you try to match with me?" He looked at her in her long jean skirt, white camisole, and light-blue button-up shirt.

"Kind of, but you know I love wearing blue." Stacey sat down next to him and leaned into his side until they heard car doors. "Yay, the family has arrived," he jumped up to go greet his cousins, and Stacey slowly followed, adjusting her hair and skirt. "Hello everyone, this is my fiancée Stacey, and this is Joanna's boyfriend Jeremiah and Ariel's boyfriend Kenneth." Derek introduced everyone as they arrived and told stories to keep them entertained until his father was ready to entertain. Stacey went outside to get some fresh air when she noticed that Grandpa West was behind her.

"I heard that you have had an interesting last few months," he said as he offered her a seat on the swing. She sat down nodding her head, "how are you feeling?"

"Right now, I'm fine, but early mornings are rough and some foods don't agree with me." He smiled while looking out and seeing the small snowflakes. "But I guess that's the life of a pregnant woman." Grandpa West nodded his head as he observed her.

"I think you will be a wonderful mother and wife. I can just see it," Stacey smiled then watched the snow fall and cars drive by. "Stacey, this was not your fault. He will help you conquer everything." She turned her head to look into his eyes.

"You must be the pastor," he smiled at being caught and nodded his head. Derek came out looking for her.

"Mom wants you to make your hot chocolate," she stood up and smiled at the men as she went inside.

"Derek, you have picked a wonderful woman who is strong in the Lord."

"Thank you, Grandpa. It means a lot to me. She is the love of my life." They gave each other a hug then went inside to seek the warmth of the fire and hot chocolate. Derek went to the kitchen to help Stacey make hot chocolate for everyone in the house. He snuck up behind her and wrapped his arms around her waist, and she jumped then relaxed back into his chest. Taking a deep breath, she stood up straight, finishing the task she was given. Derek poured the hot water into the cups, then Stacey added her homemade mixture to the cups and mixed them. Derek carried the tray out as Stacey carried the marshmallows for people to add at their leisure.

"Stacey, this is the best hot chocolate I have had," Grandpa West said as he added more marshmallows.

"Thanks, it's a family recipe. It isn't that hard to make." She shrugged her shoulders as she sat down next to Derek with a cup in her hands.

"I would love this recipe," Grandma Rysner announced as she drank more. "I'm not usually a hot chocolate drinker, but this is really good." Stacey blushed under their compliments and agreed to give everyone the recipe. They got the cards out and started playing euchre, which she opted out of to play with the kids. She found some Thanksgiving coloring books and crayons for the younger kids and a board game for the middle-aged kids. She colored with the younger kids while supervising the board game.

An hour later, Derek walked into the room and saw Stacey holding a sleeping little girl in her arms as she colored with the rest of the clan. He sat down with them as Stacey gave him a page to color. They colored for another hour before the parents came to get their kids to get ready for supper. While Stacey and Derek were alone, she leaned back into his chest thinking about the baby in her tummy. Ariel came in to search for them.

"Everyone is about ready to eat," Stacey sat up and rubbed her eyes then went into the bathroom to check her appearance, Derek followed.

"You look beautiful," she smiled at him through the mirror.

"You don't look too bad yourself." Derek held her hand as he led her into the dining room filled with all of his relatives. They split up into two tables and sat down. Then Grandpa West said a prayer.

"Dear God, thank You for this wonderful get-together with everyone that is here. You have blessed us all with a wonderful family, love, and support. Thank You for this food that we are about to eat. In Jesus' name, Amen." The parents made the younger kids' plates before the older kids and adults dove into the food: turkey, ham, mashed potatoes, cheesy veggies, cranberry sauce, stuffing, and corn with grape juice or milk. Stacey put a little on her plate, knowing her stomach didn't feel good. She took a few bites then pushed the rest of her food around on her plate as she listened to their stories.

During the hours around the table, she finally finished the small amount of food that was on her plate and started cleaning up the table as the rest of the family continued talking. Grandpa West stood up to help her.

"Grandpa, you don't need to help. I can manage on my own."

"Stacey, I can tell you aren't feeling well. Either let me help or I'll tell Derek." She gave up her fight, and they cleaned all the dishes together. Stacey washed while Grandpa West dried. When they were almost done, Stacey ran into the bathroom, feeling sick. When he found her, she was washing her face and brushing her teeth. "Are you feeling any better?" She raised her hand and made a small hand motion, indicating "a little bit." "Okay, now you need to either go lay down in your room or on the couch." She didn't argue and headed towards her room, with him following her and talking to her as she fell asleep. After she had fallen asleep, he tucked her in and closed the door behind him to rejoin his family. Half an hour later, Derek started looking around for Stacey.

"Has anyone seen Stacey lately?"

"Have you lost your future bride already?" Grandpa West teased him.

"That's funny, but seriously, have you seen Stacey?"

"The last time I saw her, she was sleeping in her bed," Grandpa West replied, and Derek stood up and ran to her room. "Why is he in such a hurry?"

"Every time she was kidnapped, she was in her room alone," Chad explained to his father-in-law.

"I thought her kidnapper was in jail," Grandpa Rysner stated.

"He is in jail, but his father doesn't want her to have the baby, so we are being cautious." Grandpa West entered her room to make sure she was all right. When he walked in, he saw Derek sitting on the side of the bed watching her sleep.

"Derek, I'm sorry, I didn't know. She's the one who picked the room instead of the couch." Derek looked at his grandpa.

"Papa, it's all right. I'm just mad at myself for not noticing that she wasn't feeling well and that she disappeared."

"She hid it well. I only noticed because I was keeping an extra eye on her." They sat by her and quietly talked until she woke up. She stretched her arms and saw the man of her dreams and his grandpa.

"Hey sweetie, how are you feeling?" He knelt next to the bed and held her hand.

"I'm feeling better," she sat up and got off the bed, giving Derek a hug. They went out to the living room to rejoin their family and played more games and told more stories until ten o'clock. Then, the families left to go home. Derek carried the sleeping Stacey to her room and laid her under her blankets. Then, he knelt down next to the bed and prayed.

"Dear God, please help Stacey stay healthy as this baby grows inside of her. And please keep her safe as Aaron's father comes after her. And please help us grow stronger as a couple." Derek felt a hand on his head and looked up to see Stacey awake. "In Jesus' name, Amen." Stacey moved over on the bed and patted the spot next to her. He laid down next to her as she rested her head on his shoulder and fell back to sleep. Derek stayed awake for a while and eventually slipped out of her arms to go to his own bed. On his way there, he ran into Chad.

"Hey bud, how are you holding up?" Derek shrugged his shoulders with an exhausted sigh.

"I know she's trying to take care of herself so she doesn't wear out our help, but it's exhausting to keep an eye on her and still enjoy the company." Chad laid his hand on Derek's shoulder.

"You're not the only one who can watch over her, so don't exhaust yourself. Grandpa West took care of her today, and her family will probably take care of her tomorrow." Derek pulled his dad in for a hug and squeezed him.

"Thanks, Dad, for everything." They went their separate ways, each offering prayers for Stacey's good health and safety.

⁓⁓∘∘⟨⟩∘∘⟨⟩∘∘⟩⟨⁓⁓

Stacey's phone went off early in the morning, waking her up so they could start packing and head to her grandparents' house, which was about an hour north of Madison. She moved cautiously around her room, mindful of not overexerting herself. After her shower, she went into Derek's room and slowly pulled the covers down, then placed a snowball — collected from outside — on his bare chest. His eyes popped open and he grabbed the snow, playfully throwing it at Stacey.

"You couldn't find a gentler way to wake me up?" Stacey laughed as his feigned annoyance turned into amusement.

"But it's so much fun," she teased. He jumped out of bed, grabbed her, and playfully tossed her onto the bed, pinning her down. He leaned in to kiss her and then released her arms. Stacey wrapped her arms around his neck and playfully pressed her cold hands against his shoulder blades. He recoiled in surprise, and Stacey grinned mischievously as she hopped off the bed. "Derek, we should get going, so go shower and change."

He pulled her in for a hug and a quick kiss before she left the room. Stacey returned to her own room, put on her knee brace over her jeans, and packed an extra set of clothes. Waiting in the living room, she saw Derek emerge, freshly showered and dressed in blue jeans, a white t-shirt, and a dark green button-up shirt. "We're matching again," she pointed out, and Derek smiled, walking over to her. He pulled her out of her chair and into a warm embrace.

"I'm sorry I didn't keep an eye on you last night," Derek said, a hint of concern in his voice.

"Derek, I could have told you, but I wanted you to enjoy your time with your family without worrying about me. If I really need your attention, I know I can get it. Today, you can relax because my family will be pampering me." Derek smiled at her request to ease up on the fussing. He picked up her bag and guided her to his vehicle, placing the bag in the back. They drove for about an hour to reach her grandparents' house.

Upon arrival, they were the first to get there. Grandma Adams came out with her arms wide open. Stacey rushed into her embrace, feeling the warmth of a long-awaited hug. "Hello, Grandma," Stacey whispered, cherishing the embrace. "It's been a while." Her grandmother nodded, tears of joy in her eyes.

"Hun, your dad's mom called. She won't be coming today." Stacey nodded, understanding that her other grandmother wouldn't be attending.

"Thanks, Grandma but I knew this was going to happen. She hasn't been staying in touch." They walked into the house leaving Derek and Grandpa alone.

"How has she been doing?" Derek thought for a second while retrieving their bags from the car.

"She tries to keep her sickness to herself. She doesn't feel like she should bother us with how she is feeling because the baby isn't mine. And she doesn't like being babied." Grandpa laughed at his description of his granddaughter.

"That sounds like her, even when her other grandmother was keeping her sick she didn't say much." They set the bags inside the porch and then went back out for a walk. Grandpa continued talking to Derek about Stacey. "She has always been independent only wanting to depend on the ones she loves when she has to. But I can tell she loves you because she is relying on you, so you shouldn't worry about anything." Derek smiled at how well he got read.

"Thank you, Grandpa, she is such a wonderful woman but strong-willed." They smiled at each other continuing their talk. They looked up at the kitchen window to see Stacey watching them, they waved and she waved back.

⎯⎯∿∘⊙☙◑☙◐☙∘∿⎯⎯

"Grandma, I wonder what they are talking about…" She let the curtain fall back into place and helped her grandma clean the kitchen.

"They are probably talking about you; your grandpa has been very worried about you. Every night he prays for you before we go to bed and he has the church praying for you as well." Stacey sat down on the bar stool, stirring the cup of hot chocolate she made.

"Grandma, I'm doing all right, right now. The morning sickness and nausea are the only things I'm battling right now. I'm blocking out the rest so I may enjoy life but my nightmares have come back with no surrender…" she sipped on her hot chocolate. "Derek and his family have been wonderful as have my doctor and her husband, who is my physical therapist." She sat down next to Stacey, setting her hand on Stacey's, "Mom hasn't taken it very well, she…"

"She doesn't understand how to separate her career job from being a mom." Stacey nodded her head in agreement. A few minutes later, Derek and Grandpa walked in laughing, carrying in some firewood. They set down the firewood and joined their women at the island to drink hot chocolate. Derek laid his cold hands on Stacey's neck which made her jump then she relaxed as he massaged her neck and shoulders. Stacey nibbled on some graham crackers while sipping on some hot chocolate. Derek heard some car doors close and told Stacey. She walked to the door to greet her family, Adam ran to her and gave her a bear hug then Nicole came and gave her a gentle hug.

"So, I heard that Grandma Rosemen isn't coming…" Adam nodded his head. "Do you know why?"

"Dad had a fight with her about you, she is blaming Dad for your pregnancy because he wouldn't let her stay with you." Stacey laughed as her mom and dad came and hugged her. Then, they all went in to greet Grandma and Grandpa Adams. The rest of the family started arriving. Aunt Addy walked in as her four-year-old ran in.

"Stacey!" he ran into her arms and she spun him around kissing his chubby cheeks. "Stacey, come visit us," the adults smiled as the other kids crowded around Stacey wanting to play games.

"Let's get all bundled up and go play in the fresh snow." The parents bundled up their youngins as the teenagers got themselves ready. They went out and started making snow forts for a snowball fight. When the forts were ready, Stacey split up the group into teams, trying to keep the ages equal. Stacey and Adam lead one team while Nicole and Derek lead the other. The snowball fight began—the kids were throwing gently so no one would get hurt. The little ones made the snowballs for the older ones and the game was becoming intense when Stacey saw that the little ones were starting to get cold. She stood up to call a timeout when a snowball hit her in the face.

All bodies stopped moving as she wiped the snow off her face and looked for the one who threw the ball. She saw Nicole pointing to Derek and she grabbed a snowball and pelted it at him, which he dodged. He ran at her and gently tackled her into the snow. He was rolled onto his back as Stacey grabbed a handful of snow and smashed it onto Derek's face. While he was still in shock, Stacey got up and ran towards the house calling a timeout, pulling the younger kids with her. They were all laughing as they took their outerwear off and went inside to the fireplace. Derek was still on the ground when he saw Adam above him.

"Did that just happen?" He asked Adam as he helped him up.

"Oh yeah," Adam started laughing then Derek joined him. "My sister knows how to get even or ahead." They went inside with a plan to get back at Stacey. As they walked into the living room, Stacey kept her eyes on them suspiciously; she saw water dripping from their hands.

"Oh no, you don't," she harshly whispered as she ran into the kitchen. They slowly followed her and then saw that she had the sprayer from the sink aimed and ready. They dropped the snowballs throwing up their hands in surrender; she thought for a second then decided to spray them anyways. They came after her and grabbed the sprayer getting the three of them soaked. Then, they finally all surrendered and saw the whole family watching them. They sheepishly smiled at the family as water dripped everywhere. Stacey started wiping up the water when Derek stopped her and told her to change into dry clothes. She slipped into a pair of sweatpants, a t-shirt, and a sweatshirt before she went back into the living room.

They had cleaned up the whole kitchen and were telling stories when she arrived. She went over to Derek—hoping he didn't have anything— and sat down in front of him with an ice pack for her knee. They were snacking on food waiting for the turkey to be done. Christian and Derek were in an intense conversation about football when they noticed that Stacey had fallen asleep on Derek. Christian looked at her with tears welling up in his eyes.

"Christian, umm…I mean Dad, she is all right, right now. She doesn't like people feeling bad for her but she still needs to be watched over."

He nodded his head in agreement,

"I'm glad she found you, the two of you make a perfect match…" They observed Stacey for a while longer then they joined in with the other conversations. A few hours later, Grandma started giving orders so everything would be done at the same time, which left Derek and the sleeping Stacey alone by the fireplace. Derek whispered into her ear,

"I love you Stacey Rosemen," she smiled and turned onto her side.

"I love you too Derek Rysner," she looked up at him with her hand on his chest as he bent his neck down to kiss her.

"Ooo…" they heard as they kissed then looked up to see Adam and Nicole in front of them. Stacey shook her head as she slowly stood up with Adam's help. Derek carried her into the dining room to eat.

"Are you going to eat more today?" Stacey shrugged her shoulders, not sure how her stomach was feeling. Her mother sat down next to her and they were all ready to eat. Grandpa told them to bow their heads,

"Dear God, thank You for this wonderful gathering of families and that this may continue as we all grow old. Please be with those that couldn't make it tonight. And please bless this food in front of us and let it nourish our bodies like You nourish our souls, Amen." They all raised their heads and started passing the food around. Stacey was about to give herself a small serving of food when her mother plopped a huge serving of mashed potatoes, turkey, and corn on her plate. Stacey's eyes bulged out as she tried to contain her frustration, she grabbed Derek's hand and squeezed it. During the dinner, when her mother wasn't looking, Derek gradually stole half of the food off Stacey's plate, which her father saw. She looked up at her dad and smirked as he shook his head with laughter. After everyone was done, they cleaned up the table while the guys went to go find a football game on TV. The ladies made Stacey sit down and watch as they cleaned everything so she went in with the boys. After a while, she got bored with the games. She went to go find the youngsters, they were sleeping and she decided to join them.

An hour later, she felt a little body jump on her and she looked up. "Hey monster, what are you doing on top of me?" He pointed toward his mother; she quietly moved out of the room and joined Aunt Addy in the kitchen. She sat down on a stool, holding Addy's baby girl, while Addy played with her hair.

"How far along are you?"

"Almost two months but it feels longer than that," she smiled, enjoying the head massage.

"How has your mother taken this?"

"I don't know, she won't talk to me anymore. You know we were never that close then this happened and we have grown farther apart..." She thought about her situation and wanted to change the subject. "Aunt Addy, will you sing at our wedding?"

"Yeah, and I will probably be singing at Adam's as well." Stacey scrunched up her face in confusion.

"Dad didn't tell you?" Addy became confused as she shook her head. "We are doing a double wedding. The four of us are going to get married on the same day to make it financially easier on everyone." She thought about the idea and agreed it would be easier. "Personally, I wouldn't mind eloping then just having a party later but I think our parents would kill us," she commented as she saw Derek in the doorway.

"Yeah they would kill you," she stated as she finished Stacey's hair. Derek walked in, wrapped his arms around Stacey, and kissed her cheek. They talked for a few more hours then, Addy and her family had to leave, slowly all the families except for Stacey's left.

"Grandpa, is the pond frozen over?" He looked shocked at her question and then responded.

"Yes, but it's too dark tonight…you can go tomorrow." They all started heading for bed, Stacey and Nicole shared a bed.

"I want this year to be over with," Nicole whined. Stacey giggled,

"I know what you mean," they talked about the wedding and came up with a few more plans before they fell asleep.

The smell of eggs assailed the house, making Stacey sick to her stomach. She sprinted to the bathroom making it just in time. When she was done, she covered her face with her sweatshirt and grabbed her jacket on the way out the door. She found her ice skates in the shed and slipped them on. They were testing her knee's stability but she skated around the pond. Favoring her right knee she spun on it, pulling her arms in to go faster. She stopped when her stomach started protesting. She looked up and saw Grandpa watching her. She motioned for him to join her to talk to him; he joined her by the ice.

"How is your knee holding up?"

"It will be sore tonight but I'm not using it very much."

"You are still skating beautifully," Stacey smiled. "How long has it been since you skated?"

"It has been since I fell through the ice and got sick." Her grandpa grabbed his skates and joined her on the pond.

"What made you decide to skate again?"

"I'm getting pretty good at getting over my fears right now so I decided to add another one… and I can't stand the smell of eggs." He smiled as he skated with her on the pond, then she saw Derek on the porch watching them. When he saw her stop, he started walking toward them with two cups of some sort of hot drink. He stopped by the pond and waited for them to join him. They skated over to him and he handed them the drinks, one was coffee and the other was hot chocolate.

"Derek, there is an extra pair of skates in the shed that should fit you…if you want to join us," Grandpa suggested as he sat down on a bench. Derek jogged over to the shed and found Adam's skates and carried them out to Stacey. He sat down to put them on then Stacey helped him stand up. He was unsteady on his skates then Stacey took a sip of her hot chocolate before helping him skate around. She went backward pulling him along, he let go after the third lap and was going on his own. Stacey sat down to rest her knee and enjoy her drink. A few minutes later, Adam joined her on the bench,

"So, you let him wear my skates?"

"Is there a problem with that?"

"No, but I wanted to skate with Nicole."

"Wear Mom and Dad's skates, I'm not going back in until the smell is gone." Adam smiled as he ran to the shed, grabbing the skates.

"You can tell Mom doesn't talk to you much, she's the one who made the eggs." Stacey laughed then stood up pulling Adam on the pond with her. They danced together on the ice, a routine they made up years ago, then Stacey tried to do the same with Derek. He tripped over his skates and fell, pulling Stacey down with him. They were laughing so hard they couldn't get up. Adam came over and helped them up as Nicole was putting her skates on. They all skated around as Grandpa watched them fall, pick on each other, and cuddle. Christian walked out and joined them.

Inside

"Mom," Laura looked at her mother, "I don't get it. I made this delicious breakfast and Stacey hasn't come to eat it."

"Laura, the smell of eggs makes her sick. She was throwing up in the bathroom before she bolted out of here." Laura sat down on the stool feeling defeated.

"Mom, I don't know how to talk to my daughter," she buried her face in her hands. Her mother walked over to her and put her hand on her shoulder.

"Just ask her how the pregnancy is and how she's feeling or how her day is and don't overthink her answer. She is being very strong for what has happened to her but she doesn't need anyone accusing her of doing something wrong." Laura sat up and looked her mother in the eyes.

"I have heard many stories like hers from my clients but they had wanted to have sex then decided later that they didn't. Her situation is similar because he was a friend." Her mother put up a hand to stop her.

"But it's different because he kidnapped her out of the Rysners' house and tied her up until they arrived at the hotel where she made a scene and the receptionist called the police. She didn't want anything to do with Aaron. He has been following her for the last few years and wouldn't leave her alone. When she moved and he noticed that she was dating someone else, he went crazy and decided that he needed her no matter what." Laura was in shock with her jaw dropped.

"How do you know all of this?"

"Laura, I listen…" Laura tried to interrupt. "I know, you get paid to listen but you don't take the advice that you give other parents. Keep your mind open and let them talk without interruptions. Stacey is doing well with her fiancé and his family; there isn't much else that can be done. Jayne and her husband have been helping her physically and emotionally." Laura's eyebrows raised then looked lost and unsure. "Just remember the advice you give to the parents you counsel and remember that she didn't entice Aaron on purpose." Laura moved away from the window and grabbed her coat on the way out the door. She walked down to the pond and sat next to her husband.

"Christian, I'm sorry for the way I have been acting. She does need just a mom, not a psychologist and that's what I need to do."

"I'm glad you realized that but you need to tell Stacey not me." He called Stacey over and left them alone.

"Stacey, I'm sorry for the way I have been acting. I guess I haven't been listening to you over the past few years. I didn't know all the facts so I drew a conclusion that was wrong for you but what I have seen in my counseling. I want to work harder at listening to you and I want to be more involved in your life. And I'm sorry about the eggs." Tears were rolling down both of their cheeks.

"Thanks, Mom, this means a lot to me." They gave each other a hug then Laura caught up with Stacey's life until they were shivering. They went inside to warm up by the fire and Derek checked their phones for messages to find one from his mother.

"Hey Derek, we were just wondering when the two of you were coming home. Love ya, Mom." He called her back,

"Mom, we are going to head out soon, we just got in from ice skating. We will warm up and then come home." Derek hung up the phone after they talked a few minutes longer. "Hey babe, we should head out, Mom has something planned for us." He sat down next to her to warm her up then half an hour later they packed up his car.

"Don't be strangers," Christian whispered into her ear as he hugged her, she smiled as she headed to everyone else. Everyone got their share of hugs then they drove off.

"So, are there plans tonight or did you use that as an excuse to leave?"

"We do have plans tonight…" Stacey waited for him to tell her the plans, "to lie around, doing nothing." She smiled as she held his hand. He picked up her hand and kissed the back of it.

⸎

Stacey woke up early to Wylie whining, she patted the spot next to her and he jumped up onto her bed, licking her face. "What's wrong Wylie?" He looked at the window and started growling; Stacey followed his stare and saw someone duck their head. She slipped out of her bed and went into the living room holding Wylie. Turning the TV on softly, she closed her eyes while petting Wylie until she felt his body go tense. Her eyes shot open when something piqued her interest on the news. She turned the volume up,

"We have some breaking news this morning; some inmates have escaped from jail, if you see any of the following people, call the police immediately." Stacey looked at the mugshots and recognized Aaron. "They were getting transported to the new jail when they broke out of custody. Three policemen were shot, one was killed. The police are not commenting right now but they are looking for the men who broke out of custody…"

the news continued. Stacey was frozen in her spot holding Wylie. He started barking frantically when there was a knock on the door. Derek ran out to them and headed towards the door,

"Derek, don't," she yelled, all motion and noise stopped. He looked out the window and saw Aaron Jackson on their front porch. He ran back to Stacey and carried her into his sisters' room.

"Joanna, call the police, Aaron is outside our door." She called the police as Derek went to go wake his dad up. They all stood guard as they waited for the police to show up. Minutes later, which felt like hours, the police showed up and found Aaron by a window looking for Stacey. They arrested him and took statements from all of the family members. After Stacey's statement, she asked to talk to him. The police officer looked at his partner and they agreed. Stacey walked out to the police cruiser and sat sideways in the passenger seat looking back at Aaron.

"Aaron, I don't understand what you want. You just keep digging yourself into a deeper hole."

"You have my baby inside you so you belong to me." Stacey shook her head,

"I don't belong to anyone but Derek has my heart. This baby will be mine and you will not get custody or any privileges to see him or her." Aaron's head drooped in disappointment, "Please leave me alone and let me live my life. I forgive you for what you did to me but I don't ever want to see you again." She stood up out of the police cruiser and walked with her head up until she was behind closed doors. She ran to the bathroom and threw up. After she cleaned up, she went into her room and got ready for school. She walked out to the living room to find everyone sitting on the couches staring at her. "I'm going to school; I don't want to miss anymore." She walked out of the house and drove herself to school.

"Did the police officer say that she forgave him?" Allison asked Chad as they continued sitting there in shock. He nodded his head slowly as he stood up.

"If you don't want to go to school you don't have to," he announced then went into his office. They scrambled to get ready and went to school. Allison joined Chad in his office, sitting across from him.

"How could she do that? He just keeps coming after her and she forgives him with an open heart." Chad walked around his desk and knelt in front of Allison.

"God decided to give her the strength to forgive him and the grace to do it for God. We'll see that Stacey can make it and how He'll provide for her." Allison bent down and held her husband; he stood up with her and held her.

—⁓∘⚬⟶⚬∘⟵⚬∘⁓—

School

Stacey walked into the school alone and saw everyone staring at her then she saw Chase and Dennis walking up to her. "We heard on the news that Aaron was free so we all thought you would have stayed home."

"The police caught him already so I'm here to learn." They were impressed and talked to her as she went to her locker and first class. Two minutes before class started Derek ran into the room, hoping to be on time. He kissed her cheek and then sat down at the desk next to her.

"Stacey, can we talk later?"

"Derek…" she took a deep breath, "There isn't much to talk about. I felt God push me to talk to Aaron and I did, feeling compelled to forgive him, so I did." The bell rang before he could reply. The class went by slowly as Derek played with his pen, wiggled in his chair, and tapped his feet. Finally, the bell rang, he pulled Stacey into an empty room.

"What's going on Stacey? You're not talking to me and you seem distant." She avoided his eyes until he held her chin to look at him.

"I need some time alone, after school, I'm going to go to physical therapy alone and go eat alone. I have some things to think about and I need to do it alone." She jerked her chin out of his hold and walked out of the room.

"God, please be with her as she struggles with her thoughts and feelings. She needs Your guidance," Derek continued praying for her throughout the day, leaving her alone. At the end of the day, he was waiting for her by her car.

"Derek, I said I wanted to be alone," he put his hands up in surrender.

"I know, I just wanted to say goodbye and let you know that if you want some company, I would gladly join you." He gave her a hug and a kiss on her temple before she could protest and walked away. She watched him until he was out of sight then she got into her car and called Jayne.

"Jayne, can we cancel today?"

"We can cancel but we are going to talk, come over to our house." Stacey agreed and drove to Jayne's house. When she arrived, Jayne's mother greeted her at the door and offered her a cup of tea which Stacey politely declined. She sat down on the couch waiting for Jayne to show up. About ten minutes later, Jayne walked in with her kids.

"Honey, can you go join Grandma in the kitchen?" The little three-year-old ran to the kitchen. "Stacey, I want you to meet my son, Robert." Tears rolled down Stacey's cheeks.

"My friends call me Robbie," he offered his hand and she shook it. He wiped the tears off her cheeks, looking at her. "Did someone hurt you like they hurt my mommy?" She nodded her head; Robbie hugged her and she clung to him. A few minutes later, Stacey let go of him and Jayne told him to join his sister in the kitchen. Tears were rolling down her cheeks in a torrent as Jayne joined her on the couch and hugged her.

"How do you get over this shame, this pain, and this hurt?"

"Stacey, it takes time with lots of love and support, which you have, and a belief that God will be with you always." Dallas walked in and turned the TV on, they were talking about Aaron.

"Aaron Jackson was caught this morning at Pastor Chad Rysner's house. After they caught him, they brought him to the jail but he fought them and was shot during the struggle…" there was a pause as the newswoman touched her ear. "We just got an update that he died in the ICU after his surgery." Jayne turned the TV off and watched Stacey's reaction.

"I didn't want him to die, I just didn't want him around me," she stood up and started pacing. Her phone startled her when it vibrated in her pocket. "Hello?"

"Stacey, some reporters want a comment from you. Would you be willing to do that?" Chad asked her, not sure what her reaction would be.

"Are they at the house?"

"Yeah, they have been here all afternoon, waiting for you to come home."

"I'm on my way…" she hung up and looked at Jayne. "I guess I'm leaving," Jayne looked at Dallas and they nodded their heads.

"We'll go with you," they packed their kids in their car and Dallas drove her over with Jayne following them. When they arrived, the news crews crowded around her.

"Can you give me some space; I'll talk to all of you at once and answer questions." They made a pathway to the front porch where she stood.

"What were your thoughts when you heard that Aaron Jackson died?" She took a moment to organize her thoughts.

"I felt sorry that his life had to end that way and that his father will now be grieving for his only son and family member left."

"Did you know Aaron personally?"

"Yes, we went to school together and were good friends until he hurt me." They asked a load of more questions before Chad intervened and ended the questioning. Stacey went inside and Robbie cuddled up with her.

"Is the bad man dead?" He asked Stacey.

"Yes, the bad man is dead but I didn't want that for him, I just wanted him to leave me alone," she explained to him. He looked up at her and cuddled closer with her, they fell asleep on the couch. Derek sat across from them, happy to see a smile on her face but sad that he wasn't the one putting the smile on her face. Dallas walked up to him,

"Let's go walk and talk," Derek stood up and left with Dallas. "Life right now may be harder than before, she outwardly forgave Aaron but daily she will need to remember that. The baby is growing strong in her but she's still not sure about it. She will need you to be strong for her but know when to back off. This kind of hurt is complicated especially when there is a baby involved. One day she may be fine and another she may be devastated." Derek took in all the advice while walking slowly with Dallas.

"I want to give her space but Mr. Jackson threatened her and now that his son is dead, he may come after her with a stronger force. I just don't know what to do." The chilly air was silent as they both tried to come up with a solution.

"I think you are going to have to let God do the protecting and let Stacey do what she wants unless it harms the baby." Derek agreed as they approached the house. He told Dallas to go in and he made another round around the block. He watched the breeze move the snow across the sidewalk and the brittle branches bend against the winds. God gave him a beautiful life, family, and the woman of his dreams and he wouldn't let that go. He jogged back to the house against the cold breeze, determined to be the best fiancé he knew how and show her his love. He walked into the house to find total silence, he looked around to see Stacey and Robbie were still napping then he found his family in the basement reading, doing puzzles, and doing homework. Jayne and Dallas were gone but their little girl was still there putting puzzles together with Ariel. Everyone looked up at him with a somber look.

"What's going on with you guys?"

"We don't want to wake Stacey…" they whispered to him. He shook his head as he walked up the stairs to make plans for the future in his room.

A few hours later, Stacey woke up and lay still until Robbie woke up.

"Do you want to go see where everyone is?" He eagerly nodded his head and stood up with her. They found Derek in his room with loads of papers around him. "Hey Hun, what are you doing?" His head snapped around then he smiled.

"I'm just working on some plans for us. When I get done, I'll show you." She leaned against the doorway, trying to sneak a peek of the papers around him. "So, how was the nap?" he asked Robbie,

"It was refreshing, Mister Derek," he smiled up at Derek then up at Stacey. "When are you and Mister Derek getting married?"

"At the end of August, why do you want to know?" He shrugged his shoulders and smiled mischievously as he ran off to go find the rest of the people in the house. "Derek," he looked up at her, "Robbie is the baby Jayne had after she was raped." He carefully climbed off the bed without messing up his papers and enveloped her in his arms.

"He's a great kid Stac, ours will grow up the way Robbie has." Derek brushed her bangs out of her eyes and rubbed his thumb across her cheek.

"Derek, he knows that Jayne was raped…well hurt by another man and that he isn't biologically Dallas'." She hid her face in his shoulder.

"When we need help, we'll get some tips from Jayne and Dallas." Derek picked her up and moved her back into the living room. They cuddled on the couch until his family came up the stairs and turned the TV on to watch a movie.

———⁓⁓◦◦~◦~◦◦⁓⁓———

The morning sun shone through the window announcing a beautifully sunny day. The light poured onto the bed making light lines on Stacey's face right onto her eyes. She rolled over and tried to go back to sleep but Wylie was jumping all over her. "Fine, I'll get up," he jumped on top of her chest and started licking her face. Laughing, she pushed him off and jumped out of the bed. She went into her bathroom and looked in the mirror, "Wow, I look horrible." She touched her cheeks, which had thinned out and she saw the dark circles under her eyes. "It's time for me to get back to normal…well as normal as I can get." She washed her face then put a light layer of makeup on and went out to the kitchen to eat breakfast. She was eating her toast when she felt strong hands on her shoulders; she looked up to see Derek and smiled. "Good morning, Derek,"

"Good morning, sweetheart," he kissed her then made himself a bowl of cereal. They left for school and acted as normal as possible. At school, Chase walked up to them.

"Stacey, you're looking better not as tired and you're smiling." She beamed him another smile then laughed,

"I just decided that I'm not going to sulk anymore and live life to the fullest no matter the rollercoaster ride it may be." They went to their first class and everyone seemed to notice the difference in her.

After school, Stacey's phone rang, "Hey Stacey, I was just thinking about you and praying for you then I decided to call you."

"Hey Opal, thanks,"

"I saw the news about Aaron and that you are pregnant?"

"Yeah, I'm sorry for not calling to tell you that. Life has been hectic."

"Oh, I understand but I want to come see you sometime soon and when is the wedding?"

"You can come anytime you like and the wedding is in August." There was a moment of silence on the line,

"I'll come after Christmas but before New Year's," they agreed to talk more often and that they would see each other in a month. They talked for a while longer, then they hung up.

"She seems to be a wonderful friend," Derek said after she set her phone down.

"She is," they drove home and did their homework together.

Chapter 8

Mid-December

Stacey sat at the piano, looking at the music and waiting for her cue. When Allison pointed to her, she started playing and singing some Christmas songs with the little kids from the church. Derek was the male leader and Stacey was the female. After the music was done, she walked over to the group and started the script for the play. They all had their lines memorized and the rehearsal went smoothly. After the rehearsal, Stacey, Derek, Allison, and Chad took the six kids out to eat at a fast-food restaurant. They all fit into a corner booth with an extra chair.

"Stacey, when is the baby coming?" One of the little girls asked.

"The baby is coming mid-July." The little girls became excited and the boys talked about baseball as they waited for the food to show up. Derek and Chad carried the ketchup and drinks over and handed them out as the food began to arrive. The table was silent besides the crinkling of wrappers and sipping of drinks while they ate their food. Stacey finished her food first and started ripping the free ice cream coupons off the bags and taking orders from the kids. She went up and ordered the ice creams. While the workers were working on her order, Debra Dillon walked up to her.

"Stacey?" Debra asked,

"Yeah," she turned and recognized her. "Hey Debra, how have you been?" She hugged her, excited to see her.

"I've been busy, I'm sorry I never called you."

"It's fine, I've been busy as well," her ice cream order came up. "Why don't you order your food then we can talk." Debra looked at the huge tray of ice cream. "You won't take me away from anything. We're just feeding some of the kids from church, we had rehearsal tonight." Debra agreed and Stacey went to hand out the ice cream and inform Derek of what was going on. She picked a small booth and sat down with her ice cream, waiting for Debra to join her.

"Isn't that your beau over there?" Stacey nodded her head. "So, I saw that your attacker died…" Stacey slowly nodded her head not sure where the conversation was going. "Did you mean what you said during the press conference?"

"Yeah, I wasn't overjoyed that he was dead, and I didn't want him dead. I couldn't wish that upon anybody." Debra looked puzzled as Stacey explained her reasoning. "God is ruler over all and He loves us all and I try to show His love through me." Debra ate silently for a few minutes.

"I couldn't do that, he deserves to die." Stacey slowly processed the new information and thought of a way to reply.

By the way you said that, either you or a close friend has been hurt in the same way I have been." Debra nodded her head.

"It happened to be just like two weeks before you banged on my stall door for my phone. I was eager to help because I wanted someone to be there to help me but no one was around…" she took a bite of her burger and a sip of her drink before she continued. "I was just walking from my car to my apartment when I was grabbed." Her voice went down to a whisper, "The guy had his hands all over me, pulling at my clothes, ripping them. He did what he grabbed me to do and left with one last kiss." Stacey looked at Debra with a look of understanding and sorrow.

"Did you know the man or was it a stranger?" Debra closed her eyes trying to picture the man in her head.

"I recognize him but I can't put a name to his face." Stacey finished her ice cream and set it to the side as she reached across the table to comfort her. "After I met you, I have wished that I had told someone and not kept it to myself. My boyfriend broke up with me because he couldn't understand the changes in me. My life has gone upside down since that night." There was a pause as Derek walked up to them.

"Stacey, we're going to drop the kids off then I will bring the car back and Dad will drive me home," he gave her a kiss and the spare keys as he left with the kids and his parents. After he left, Stacey focused her attention back on Debra.

"I just have no motivation anymore, no reason to live."

"Debra, I want you to live and God wants you to live. He gave you this life to live and He has a reason for you to live." Debra pushed her tray away and buried her face in her hands. Stacey moved over to Debra's side of the table and put her arm around Debra's shoulders. "Are you going to visit family for Christmas?" Debra nodded her head. "Are they supportive of you?" Again, she nodded her head. "Then I think you need to tell your family. What's helping me the most are love and support, you need to tell them." She looked up at Stacey with tears rolling down her cheeks, leaving black streaks from her mascara.

"Can we talk more often?" Stacey nodded her head, offering Debra a napkin.

"Call me, whenever you need to talk, you have my number?" Debra nodded her head then left to go clean up her face and came back, looking refreshed. She sat down and they talked about lighter topics until the restaurant closed. They said their goodbyes and left for home. Stacey arrived back at the house to find Derek sleeping on the couch, waiting for her. She bent down and kissed him then whispered into his ear,

"I'm home." Derek opened his eyes and smiled at her as he pulled her down to cuddle with him.

"How was your talk with Debra?"

"Umm…needed, she went through a similar experience as I did and she's been keeping it to herself." She cuddled up more into his arms wanting comfort.

"So, you are probably going to be a counselor for raped victims, is that God's blessing?" Stacey thought about his statement and took a deep breath.

"Yeah, that sounds like something God would do." She sat up and started moving away when Derek stopped her.

"Where are you going?"

"Derek, it's been a long day and we have the play tomorrow. I need to go to bed," he sat up next to her and held her.

"I love you, Stacey,"

"I love you too." She kissed him goodnight before she went to her room to sleep. She went directly to her reading chair, hoping she wouldn't have a nightmare.

Chaos and noise are what Pastor Chad found as Stacey and Derek tried to get the kids ready for their play. Finally, Allison whistled and the whole place went silent. She gave them a pep talk before they started then they all headed to their spots ready for it to begin. Derek stood behind Stacey as she started playing a song and singing then he joined her with his guitar and baritone voice. They were welcoming the entire congregation to the celebration of Jesus' birth. The kids walked on after the song was over as if they were on their way to Sunday School. They walked up to Derek and Stacey, greeting them before they sat down.

"Does anyone know what's going on this week?" Stacey asked with enthusiasm.

"It's Christmas," the kids yelled in unison, Derek and Stacey nodded their heads.

"What happens at Christmas time?" Derek asked. One of the kids raised his hand,

"We get lots and lots of presents," all the adults smiled.

"Yeah, but why do we have Christmas?" The kids thought about the question then a little girl stood up looking at the audience.

"We have Christmas because this is a celebration of Jesus Christ's birth. He was born unto this world to save us." She looked at Stacey for approval and sat down with a huge smile. They walked through the whole story of Jesus' birthday with all the songs that had been created for Christmas. After the program, the whole cast bowed at the applause then they went to their families and cleaned up. The parents of the children gloated over them, praising them. Then, they all headed to the dining area and ate a feast created by all the hands at the church. As they ate lunch, people of the congregation praised Stacey and Derek for their participation in the play.

"You guys were wonderful even with all the mishaps," Ariel said as she stole a cookie from Derek.

"Since you gave us a compliment, I won't do anything to you for stealing my cookie." She smirked while taking a bite of the cookie. They all visited with the people of the church, having barely enough time to eat. The parishioners started leaving to go home, leaving the Rysner family, Stacey, and Pastor Jeff's family left to clean up. Stacey walked back to the worship hall and saw someone in a pew. She stepped closer and recognized Debra, she was crying. Stacey walked up to her and cleared her throat. Debra's head snapped up then she relaxed when she saw Stacey. Stacey slid into the pew and rubbed Debra's back.

"Hey girl, what's going on in that mind of yours?" Debra looked up at her and hid her face in Stacey's shoulder. Stacey brushed Debra's hair with her fingers. "Do you want to talk about it?" She felt Debra's head move and released her hold.

"I want the peace that you have and I know this is where you find it. Please help me," she laid her head on Stacey's shoulder.

"I will help you as much as I can." Stacey saw Chad walk up and then paused when he saw the two of them and sat down in the pew in front of them. He turned in the pew facing the girls. "Debra, I'd like for you to meet my pastor and future father-in-law." She wiped her face and then turned to Chad. "Debra, this is Pastor Chad Rysner, and Chad, this is Debra Dillon." They shook hands,

"So, I heard you helped our Stacey out when Aaron kidnapped her," she shifted uncomfortably in the pew. "Thank you," he looked her in the eyes as she smiled.

"It was my pleasure," she looked at Stacey. "She has become more of a help to me than I was to her." Chad smiled at the pair.

"Well, I think we are heading home, Debra if you would like to join us you are more than welcome," Chad offered then went on his way. Debra agreed to join them and Stacey drove with her over to the house. When they walked in, they saw Allison lying on the couch,

"I think we can call that a success," Allison announced to Stacey, "Thank you for all the work you did," Stacey smiled and then introduced Allison to Debra. Everyone joined them in the living room to play a game.

———∽∽∽∽∽———

The door opened allowing a pool of hot air into the room. Stacey released her grip from her comforter as her room warmed up from the fireplace in the living room. Stacey opened her eyes when she felt her bed shift and she looked up to see Derek trying to sneak on the bed next to her.

"Derek, what are you doing?"

"I want to cuddle with you…" he pulled the blanket over him and lay next to her. "You're freezing," she smiled as she put her cold feet on his legs. He jumped back and then cuddled up again trying to warm her feet up.

"What time do we have to leave today?" Derek thought for a few minutes enjoying the feel of her in his arms.

"We should probably leave as soon as we are ready," Stacey pushed up off the bed only to be pulled back down.

"You know, we can't get ready if we don't get up." He nodded his head still holding onto her then she called Wylie. He bounded onto the bed and attacked Derek's face with kisses, making him release his hold on Stacey. She jumped off the bed and into the bathroom before he could catch her. They were ready in record time and on their way to La Crosse for the Rosemen and Adam's family party. When they arrived, Grandma Rosemen met them out on the porch. Stacey walked into her arms accepting her grandma's love.

"How are you feeling Stacey?"

"I'm feeling better, Grandma…" She stepped out of the embrace and wrapped her arm around Derek's waist. "Grandma, you remember Derek, right?" She nodded her head as they shook hands.

"I think we've met a few times," Derek agreed as Adam and Nicole came out hugging them and pulling them into the house. They sat down on the couch getting comfortable while waiting for the rest of the family to show up. All of her aunts, uncles, and cousins from both sides of the family walked in ready to party and visit.

"Addy, where's my little monster?" Stacey asked, knowing that he was hiding and giggling behind Addy.

"Oh, I don't know," she answered while acting like she was looking for him. Stacey stood up and snuck around Addy's legs and grabbed him, surprising a squeal out him. She spun around with him while kissing his baby cheeks.

"Stacey, you scared me," he whispered while looking into her eyes, being serious.

"I know my little monster, I'm sorry." He hugged her and then got down to play with Adam. The adults laid out a board game and started playing while catching up on each other's lives. The kids were quietly playing when Stacey went to go check on them.

"It's a little too quiet in here, what's going on?" They all pointed to Ben, Stacey's little monster. She looked at him and saw what they did to him. Her eyes grew as she tried to keep a straight face. "Why are there marker marks on Ben's face?"

"We were bored," one of the children answered.

"Ahh, Addy," she yelled, "You might want to come here." The whole family came tromping in and they all gasped as they saw the little guy's face. Adam and Derek covered their faces so the kids wouldn't know they were laughing. Addy knelt to Ben's level and tried to wipe the marks off but they wouldn't come off. Stacey saw that some of the markers were permanent.

"Hey monster, let's go wash your face off," Stacey suggested as the parents tried to figure out what to do. He went with Stacey to the bathroom and she set him on the counter. "Why did you let them color on your face?" He turned his face away from her.

"They said it would make my mommy happy." Stacey's shoulders slumped as she thought about what her younger cousins did to Ben. She set a washcloth underneath warm water and then wiped his face. Some of the marker came off but the black stayed on which was the permanent marker.

"Grandma," Stacey yelled out, a few seconds later she walked in. "What takes permanent marker off?" She looked through the medicine cabinet and pulled out fingernail polish remover. Stacey found a cotton ball and wiped the marker off being as gentle as she could. About fifteen minutes later, there was barely a trace of the marker on his face. They walked out to the living room to see the four kids involved sitting on the couch with somber faces. Addy looked at Ben's face,

"Now that's the cute, adorable face I like to see," Ben ran into her arms and they all had a chat about drawing on people. After the kids apologized, they all went on playing games, and then mid-afternoon they all gathered in the living room to open presents. Nicole, Adam, Stacey, and Derek sat next to each other as couples, waiting for the younger children to pass out the presents. Adam and Stacey were shaking the presents, trying to guess what was in the wrappings. Derek laughed at the two of them and sat back to watch.

When all the presents were passed out, the younger children took turns opening presents. Ben got a play-dough set from Stacey and Derek. After he was done opening his presents, he sat with Stacey and Derek as they opened the presents. The two couples got presents of cookware, baking equipment, decorations, and money to help out with the wedding. Stacey opened her present from Derek; it was a beautiful silver heart necklace with a heart-shaped diamond in the middle. She turned her head to look at him, smiled then kissed him. Stacey handed a present to Derek, he opened it to find a silver mechanical watch. He took it out of the box and tried it on; it fit him perfectly and comfortably. He leaned forward to kiss the side of her face.

"Thanks, Stacey," she leaned back onto his chest and watched the rest of her family open their presents. After all the presents were opened, they realized they were hungry. They all gathered in the kitchen to pray and grab food, the kids stayed in the kitchen with Nicole and Stacey as chaperones. The rest of the family went to watch the football game. When the game was over, Derek and Stacey packed up their vehicle and said goodbye to the family before they drove to Madison. When they arrived at the house, all the lights were out so they snuck into the house and went to their separate rooms.

The smell of food rolled into the room as Derek carried a tray of food in. "Good Morning Stacey," she rolled toward the side of the bed and smiled as he set the tray on the bed and kissed her awake.

"Derek," he bent down to kiss her again, "When are we opening presents?"

"We will open presents once all of us have eaten breakfast." He set the tray over her lap and they quickly ate their French toast together. When they were done, Derek carried the tray back to the kitchen and went back to carry Stacey into the living room. He saw her rubbing her knee and went into the kitchen to grab an ice pack. He handed her the ice pack as he sat down behind her, leaning on the couch. The girls came in as Allison and Chad slowly walked in with their coffee. They saw the ice pack on Stacey's knee,

"How's the knee?" Stacey rubbed it,

"It's a little stiff today but it is always stiff in the morning." They smiled at her as they settled into their spots and the girls distributed the gifts. They each opened a present at a time. Ariel opened her present first; it was a music player big enough to hold all of her music. She screamed in excitement then started opening the packaging and trying to set it up right away. Joanna was next; she stood up next to her huge box and opened it. As she saw the items inside, she jumped up and down covering her mouth in surprise. When she calmed down, she pulled out a brand-new paint set, charcoal pencils, and three canvases.

"Thank you so much, Mom and Dad," she bounded over to them to hug them when they shook their heads and pointed to Derek and Stacey.

"They bought the presents that are under the tree, we are paying for a day together." Both girls jumped up and gave Stacey and Derek hugs. Derek laughed at the girls as he stood up to open his huge present from Stacey. He took the wrapping off and opened the box to find bubble wrap and another box. He opened that box to find another. He smiled and shook his head as he continued through four more boxes. He was about to give up when he opened a little box with a gift card to his favorite store.

"Stac, that was a lot of work to find this little thing," he tried to say with anger in his voice but everyone was laughing so hard, he couldn't keep a straight face. Stacey finally settled down when she saw Derek jumping onto her. He pinned her down, "I hope you had fun wrapping that," she smiled as she nodded her head. "Thanks, Stac," he released her arms as he leaned down to kiss her. She put her hands on his jaw and held him, enjoying the kiss. Then, they broke it up and it was Stacey's turn to open her present -- it was in the shape of a ball. She started unwrapping it and realized it was going to take a while. Derek had used newspapers, paper towels, dishcloths, and one of his shirts to disguise a gift card to her favorite clothing store. Everyone was laughing again,

"Great minds think alike," Stacey announced while looking at Derek. After all the presents in the living room were opened Allison led them into the dining room to find sweaters and skirts. The skirts were long enough to hit their calves and different color plaids, and the sweaters complimented the color of the skirts. The boys including Jeremiah and Kenny—who showed up right on time—had complimentary clothes.

"We decided to make a day of it today. We have plans to go ice skating, go out to dinner and enjoy the day." They all rushed out to change and start the day with the family. Stacey put her knee brace on as she got ready then went out to find the boys ready and fur hats waiting for them along with new dress coats. The boys stood up when she walked in and Derek greeted her with a kiss. They sat back down to wait for everyone else and Stacey sat on Derek's lap and Wylie joined them.

"Hey Wylie," Kenny said as he pet him. Wylie jumped into Kenny's lap, enjoying the attention of an old friend. Wylie started playing tug-o-war with Kenny when Ariel and Joanna walked in. He froze in his play with Wylie and Wylie pulled the toy out of Kenny's hand. Both boys stood up and greeted their girls with a kiss on her cheek. Allison and Chad came out and they all packed into two vehicles.

"Stacey, I forgot to ask you earlier, how are you and the baby feeling?" Jeremiah asked as Derek followed his parents.

"I'm doing better, the morning sickness is gone. The baby is growing normally and at a steady pace."

"Do you still go to Physical Therapy?"

"Yeah, I go in once a week and get it checked out. It still gets stiff from overdoing it but for the most part, I can do almost anything." Derek gave her a knowing look, "Okay, I lied, I can't go running and a few other activities yet but in moderation I can do most things." There was a pause,

"That's a pretty fast recovery," they all nodded as Derek pulled into the parking lot. They got out of the car and went to the ice skate rental store. They rented ice skates for those who didn't have their own then they went to the benches to put them on. Stacey was the first one with her skates on and she did a few laps, spinning, twirling, and going backward before the rest of the clan joined her. Derek wrapped his right arm behind her back and held her left hand as they skated in sync. As the afternoon went on, they switched partners, had coffee or hot chocolate breaks, and enjoyed each other's company. As the Christmas music played in the background, the last song was announced. Stacey and Derek walked to the ice and started dancing on the ice. People cleared the ice to watch them gracefully spin along with the song. Derek and Stacey only noticed each other as the music continued. When the song finished, they stopped and stared into each other's eyes as their faces grew nearer. Finally, their lips met and their passion was shown to the whole world. Their kiss was interrupted when they heard clapping and cheers. They smiled at each other as they turned towards the crowd and bowed. They skated over to the edge of the pond, took their skates off, and put their boots on. Derek carried Stacey to the car and the rest followed with their skates.

"Derek, where did you learn to skate like that?" Joanna asked him as they climbed into the car. Derek pointed to Stacey and started driving. Joanna's jaw dropped. "Stacey, where did you learn?"

"I used to train with my grandpa in the wintertime until I fell through the ice one year and Thanksgiving this year was my first time back on and I showed Derek how to do that." She shrugged her shoulders and turned the heat up to get warm. They sang along to Christmas Carols as they drove to dinner.

⸏⸏⸏⸏⸏⸏

Stacey felt the bed move as if someone was lying down, so she turned around to see who it was and screamed with delight. She grabbed the person in for a hug. "Opal, when did you get in?"

"I got in last night after you went to bed but we didn't want to disturb you, so I slept in Derek's room as he slept on the couch." Stacey lay there watching her friend.

"I've missed you, girl." They started talking to catch up with each other's lives then they heard a knock on the door. Derek walked in,

"It would probably be a good idea to get ready while you talk," he suggested. Stacey looked at the clock and her eyes grew then she shooed him out of the room as they scrambled to get ready. They were ready in record time and on their way to the church. Derek and Stacey rushed into the sanctuary to get ready for worship. Pastor Jeff prayed over them before the service started and they walked out, Derek with his guitar and Stacey with the microphone. Derek sat on a stool and Stacey stood nearby leaning on the grand piano. The lights dimmed down and the parishioners settled down as Derek started strumming the guitar.

"Good morning everyone," she sang out, softly. They all sang it back to her, then she started singing the welcome song. Everyone greeted each other as they sang the song then the worship began. Pastor Chad walked up during the song before the sermon and sang with Derek and Stacey. After the song, Derek went to the side playing music and softly singing, leaving Stacey alone with Chad.

"Stacey, what have you got there?" Stacey looked at the huge piece of cardboard in her hand.

"I'm not sure Chad," she continued to examine the object in her hand. "It must be a puzzle of sorts." Pastor Chad nodded his head to confirm her assessment of the huge object.

"Let's put it together…" They laid out the pieces showing the audience the back of each piece and saying one word.

"Faith,"

"Courage,"

"Love,"

"Mankind,"

"Trinity…" the words went on as they put the whole thing together. When they were done, they used a pulley system to lift the giant puzzle they had just put together. The whole audience gasped at the painted picture of Jesus as a baby and then a graphic picture of Jesus on the cross. There was a verse at the bottom.

"For God so loved the world that He gave His one and only Son, that whoever believes in Him shall not perish but have everlasting life. John 3:16." Stacey read then she joined Derek singing softly as Chad continued.

"I don't know about you but this picture hit me. Jesus came to the Earth as an innocent baby to be killed as an innocent man. His whole purpose in life was to teach us and die for us. Every one of our sins is a hit from the whip or a deeper hit from the nails. He is not dead but alive to live for us and be there for us." A crowd of people started gathering and kneeling up in the front. The music intensified as the drummer and bass player joined them, Chad pulled out a knife. There was a huge gasp heard from the audience.

"Lust," he yelled as he stabbed the picture of baby Jesus. He pulled the knife out of the picture

"Hate," he stabbed the picture again. People screamed as he continued to yell out sin and stab or rip the picture until it fell to the floor. The music slowed down as Chad composed himself. Stacey continued for him.

"All of our sins that we do cuts Jesus which hurts God but He has enough love for us that He will give us a clean slate, if we ask for it." Chad pulled up the same picture but without the holes. The parishioners gasped with amazement and Derek started a new song. The whole congregation joined in as the Pastors, Elders, and Leaders walked around and prayed for anyone who needed it. Stacey walked around singing when she saw Opal on her knees, rocking. She turned her microphone off as she approached her best friend. She sat down beside her and wrapped her arms around her. "Hey girl," Stacey whispered into Opal's ear to let her know who it was. Opal turned into Stacey's arms and held on for dear life.

"I have fallen from His arms and I didn't know until today." She buried her face into Stacey's shoulder.

"Then today would be the best day to get back into His arms." Opal agreed and prayed for forgiveness, mercy, and love. After her prayer, they stood up and Stacey hugged her before she turned her microphone on and started singing again. They sang until everyone who wanted prayer received prayer. A lot of people walked out with a refreshed feeling of hope and their spirits were high. Stacey sat down on the edge of the stage as people talked to her. Derek joined her and saw that she was exhausted. He made up an excuse to steal her away and took her to his father's office.

"What did you do that for?"

"Stacey, you are exhausted, just watching out for you." He shrugged his shoulders, scared of how she was going to react. She took a deep breath and then leaned against him,

"Thanks," Derek wrapped his arms around his exhausted fiancé, then lifted her and carried her to their vehicle. He called Opal to tell her his plan and she agreed to tell everyone and he took Stacey home to rest.

A few hours later, Opal walked into Stacey's room as she woke up. She joined Stacey on the bed, "I approve of your man." She declared as Stacey smiled.

"I'm glad you approve," they laid down continuing to catch up on each other's lives. Joanna and Ariel joined them a while later. "What's up, girls?" They sat down on the bed,

"Are we doing anything tonight?" The girls looked down then Stacey remembered.

"Your boys are gone, aren't they?" The girls smiled at being caught,

"Since we had them yesterday, they have to hang out with their families today." They spread out on Stacey's bed and started talking about the wedding plans. Stacey called Nicole to ask about a few of the plans when she walked in.

"I didn't know you were coming today," she shrugged her shoulders as she joined the girls on the bed. "Nicole, this is my friend Opal, and Opal, this is Adam's fiancée, Nicole." They shook hands greeting each other.

"So, you were asking me about wedding plans." All the girls smiled as Stacey grabbed a notebook, pen, and her calendar. They talked about the wedding for a few hours then Stacey realized that the boys weren't around.

"So, Nicole, where are you hiding the boys?"

"Derek and Adam wanted to go skiing so I am here to distract you. They went with a few of Derek's friends." Stacey smiled, knowing that Derek has been waiting to go skiing but didn't want to leave her out. "They should be back in an hour or so," Nicole announced then they continued the plans. Stacey heard a car drive up and all the girls went out to greet the boys. The boys took their winter coats, hats, and gloves off and walked into the living room. Adam, Derek, Dennis, Chase, and AJ sat down by the fireplace. Adam and Derek put their cold hands on Nicole and Stacey making yelps come out of them. Stacey realized that Opal didn't know anyone.

"Opal, these are Derek's friends Dennis, Chase, and AJ, boys this is my best friend, Opal." They all shook hands with her then Derek brought out the new Pictionary game. Before they started, Dennis and AJ left because they had family coming. They partnered up, and Chase and Opal ended up being partners for the game because Joanna and Ariel were expecting their boys to join them soon. Opal and Chase felt awkward at first then as the game progressed, they started beating all the other couples. Allison walked in carrying a tray full of soup bowls and crackers. They paused the game to eat and settled in as they watched a movie. Stacey, Derek, Adam, and Nicole got the couch. Chase and Opal got the loveseat as the other two couples got the floor. Opal sat as far away as she could on the love seat from Chase but as the movie progressed, they ended up holding hands. At midnight, Allison kicked Chase, Jeremiah, and Kenny out and the girls went to their rooms.

"Opal, do I see a smile on your face?" Stacey teased Opal which made her smile grow wider.

"He is really nice," she retorted back as she jumped on the bed and buried her face into her pillow. Stacey joined her on the bed as Nicole sat on the reading chair.

"We'll talk about it tomorrow, good-night ladies."

Stacey woke up when she felt someone brush her hair out of her face. She opened her eyes and saw Derek standing over her. "Hey babe, come join me in the living room," he whispered to not wake the other girls up. She nodded her head and he lifted her out of the bed, carrying her into the living room. They lay on the couch and talked until they fell asleep again. A few minutes later, Joanna walked out and found the two of them sleeping. She retrieved her sketch pad and pencils and then started drawing the two of them sleeping peacefully on the couch. She noticed when Stacey started waking up and left them to finish her drawing from memory. Stacey woke up feeling safe in Derek's arms.

"Dear God, it has been a beautiful, wonderful last few days. Seeing Your people fall on their knees for You and giving their lives over to You. I'm not sure what You have planned for my life but it is Yours to run. Thank You for this wonderful fiancé, family and friends. I am in Your arms." She set her hand over Derek's hand on her expanding stomach and interlocked her fingers with his. Suddenly she felt Derek nuzzle his nose in her neck and kissed it. "Hey Derek,"

"Hey sweetheart," he pulled her in closer, wrapping his arms around her. "How are you and the baby feeling?"

"I'm starting to feel the stretching but the morning sickness is gone. I am starting to crave foods but I'm doing wonderful." Opal walked out and saw the two of them.

"Aw, you guys are cute," she looked at Stacey. "I was wondering where you went, now I see that Derek stole you." They all smiled, Allison walked in,

"What do you want for breakfast?"

"We can make our own, Allison," Stacey said, "You've done a lot in the last few days, just relax today." Allison smiled as she walked back into the kitchen.

"I will bet you anything that my mom will not relax today." Stacey thought about what she could get out of the bet.

"Okay, I'll bet you an hour-long back massage."

"Deal," Opal laughed as she watched them interact. Allison walked out of the kitchen.

"Derek, I'm going to do some pleasure shopping and get the back massage Stacey gave me. Make sure you are a good host." Stacey kept a straight face as Allison walked out the door.

"You set me up," Derek yelled jokingly, Stacey laughed.

"I bought her the back massage a month ago for everything she has done for me. I guess she decided to use it today." Derek sat up and tickled Stacey,

"You still set me up."

"So, what are you making me for breakfast?" she asked with puppy eyes, he shook his head at her and tried to hold back a smile. Opal helped Stacey stand up then Derek went into the kitchen and the girls sat down.

"I wish I had what you have," Opal whispered as she watched Derek leave the room.

"What did you think of Chase last night?" Opal's smile grew,

"He seems really nice and sweet," she was staring out the window daydreaming.

"Come back girl," Stacey waved her hand in front of Opal's face. She shook her head and smiled again. "What's going on in that head of yours?"

"I'm going to not get ahead of myself and think that there might be something there when there really isn't."

"Good idea," Derek walked in carrying three plates of French toast and they sat down to watch a movie. Adam and Nicole left to go home as Joanna and Ariel grabbed their breakfast before they joined them for the movie. Chad came home and started a fire in the fireplace.

"How was work?" Derek asked his father.

"Even during the holidays, people need help."

"Are we working at the soup kitchen tonight?"

"Yeah, we were hoping the two of you would provide some entertainment." Stacey ran all the Christmas songs through her head. "You don't have to if you're not up to it." Stacey thought about it and then replied.

"I can for part of the night but not the whole night." Chad smiled as he called a few people and set up a time to practice for a few hours. Then, Stacey, Derek, and Opal got ready to go to the church. They drove to the church and set up the stage for the performance. A few of the band members showed up—one of them being Chase. They made a list of the songs and found basic sheet music for all of the songs. And they practiced all of the songs once before they took a break. Derek led Stacey to some chairs and had her sit down. Chase and Opal joined them and they planned out the order of the music and when to have just background music. The church ladies came in and started setting up the tables and finished up the food preparations. Stacey stood up, helping the ladies when Derek whisked her to Chad's office.

"Stacey, you don't need to overdo it. Agreeing to sing is enough for you today."

"I just wanted to help them," she said as she dropped onto the couch, feeling defeated.

"Jayne wants you to take it easy," he sat down next to her and brushed her hair out of her face.

"That is easier said than done," she leaned into his chest and closed her eyes in relief. A few minutes later, Chad walked in.

"Is everything all right?"

"I'm keeping her from getting exhausted," Chad nodded his head knowing how hard it is for Stacey to be inactive.

"Are the two of you ready to sing?" He asked as he sat down in front of them.

"Yeah Chad, the baby and my knee are wearing me out. We will make it with God's strength." Stacey reached her arm out and pulled Derek's head over so she could kiss him. Then they huddled together and Chad prayed with them before they went out to start the dinner. Stacey sat down on a stool with her microphone and got everyone's attention before the dinner was served.

"Hello everyone, we are glad that all of you could make it," Stacey saw Debra in the crowd. "First, the food will be served then we will be singing some Christmas songs and some new songs. You may mingle amongst yourselves and enjoy the food." Chad walked out and said a prayer then the serving began. Stacey slipped off the platform and hugged Debra. "I'm glad you could make it girl." Debra smiled then Stacey went back to sing. Stacey observed everyone as she sang and was very pleased with everyone's interactions with each other. About an hour later, Stacey took over the piano as everyone else grabbed something to eat. Opal went up to Stacey,

"Hey girl, let me play for a while, you need a break."

"Okay, I'll give you a chance to impress Chase," Opal blushed as they transitioned into an old duet they used to play and then Stacey got up as the song ended while Opal continued playing. Stacey joined the line and mingled as she waited in line. Chase walked up to her.

"Wow, she can play," he whispered to Stacey.

"She has been playing since she was six years old. It comes easy to her," Chase couldn't take his eyes off Opal. "Ask her out," Stacey suggested. Chase's head whipped around to see if Stacey was serious. She nodded her head as she went to go sit down. Chase followed her and sat down next to her.

"Do you really think so?" Stacey looked from Chase to Opal then back to Chase and nodded her head. He smiled as he thought about a few things. Then Derek came over and interrupted his thoughts.

"Chase, we should head up and start a few songs then Stacey, you can join us." They all agreed and left Stacey at the table to eat. Chase took over the piano, letting Opal get up and enjoy the music. The boys sang a few songs they wrote then Stacey joined them again to finish off the night. For the last song, the band left the stage except for Stacey and Derek.

"This is the last song of the night, feel free to leave, dance, or talk." Derek started strumming his guitar and Stacey joined in with the piano. Chase walked up to Opal and tapped her shoulder and she turned around to face him.

"Will you give me the honor of a dance?" He asked as he held out his hand and she accepted by putting her hand in his. They walked out to the dance floor and started slow dancing. Opal caught Stacey's eye, she winked at her and smiled. The song ended but Stacey continued playing the piano because she didn't want to see Opal's happiness go away. After a few minutes, they realized no one else was dancing and they awkwardly separated to help clean up. Stacey finished the song and went over to hug Derek.

"Give this to Chase," Derek looked at the piece of paper and smiled. He walked over to Chase and handed him the piece of paper, Chase looked puzzled.

"It's Opal's number, give her a call tonight." Chase nodded his head as he put the number into his phone and continued cleaning up the room. Derek went back to Stacey and smiled at their conspiracy. As he observed his fiancé, he whisked her into his dad's office. "Are you feeling all right?" Derek asked watching her eyes.

"I'm a little worn out but I can make it." Derek thought for a few seconds as he gently brushed her hair out of her eyes, kissed her forehead, and led her back out to the main area. When the whole church was picked up, they all went home and dropped onto the couch. "Hey Derek, you still owe me a backrub," Stacey announced as he walked in with a bowl of popcorn. He sat behind her and gave her a back rub while watching a movie. Opal was intently watching the movie when her phone rang and she unconsciously answered it. When she heard who it was her eyes grew as large as saucepans and she looked at Stacey with a smile. After a few minutes, Opal stood up and left the room to talk.

"I think that was a successful set-up," Derek whispered into Stacey's ear then kissed her cheek. She snuggled back into his chest and fell asleep watching the movie. An hour later, Opal ran back into the room excited and talking one hundred words a minute, which woke Stacey up.

"Sorry, I woke you, Stacey." Stacey smiled as she observed Opal's body language, she was happy and excited. "When did you give him my number?"

"I had Derek give it to him when we were cleaning up."

"Thanks," Opal sat down on the floor by Stacey. "He asked me out on a date. Do you mind that I go out when I came here to visit you?"

"That's fine Opal, I want you to go." Opal hugged her then they decided to go to bed. Opal walked ahead of them as Derek carried Stacey into the room. "Good night Derek," he leaned down to kiss her and then stood up to leave. "So, what did the two of you talk about?"

"We talked about our families' funny stories and our favorite things to do." Opal went into the bathroom and changed into a pair of sweatpants and a tank top.

"Are you excited for your date tomorrow?" Opal nodded her head as she jumped onto the bed.

"I can't believe he likes me back. Are you paying him to go out with me?" Stacey looked at her appalled.

"No, I am not paying him to go out with you. He came up to me and asked me questions about you so I answered them and he couldn't keep his eyes off of you." Opal lay under the comforter and covered her face with it as she smiled with excitement.

Chapter 9

Stacey woke up feeling refreshed and pain-free for the first time in months. She looked out her window and saw a fresh layer of snow. As she watched the snowflakes fall, she curled into a ball in her window chair. As the snowflakes fell, she reflected on the last few months and everything that went on in those months.

"God, You have given me the strength to make it through this last year and I know You will be with Derek and me through this next year. We have so much to plan for and a future of a child to think of. Please be with us and guide us." She laid her head against the window frame when she heard the door open. Wylie ran in and jumped onto Stacey's lap as Derek slowly followed behind.

"You have a peaceful look on your face, my dear," Derek commented as he held her chin with his hand, looking deep into her eyes.

"God gave me peace this morning and I am pain-free for the moment." Derek wrapped his arms around her and kissed the top of her head.

"I'm glad to hear that my dear," Stacey sat back against the wall and became transfixed on the snowflakes falling on the ground again. "What are our plans for today?"

"Well, the only thing I can think of is keeping Opal calm before her date."

"I heard that Stacey Rosemen," Opal called out from the bed, Derek and Stacey laughed as they went out to the kitchen.

Eleven o'clock at night

Opal snuck into the house hoping not to disturb anyone when she heard someone call her name from the living room. She walked in there to find Stacey and Derek watching a movie quietly. "You didn't need to stay up for me." she quietly commented.

"We didn't stay up for you. We are watching a movie while cuddling. Do you have a problem with that?"

"No," she replied as the credits began to roll across the screen. Stacey extended her arms out for assistance and Opal helped her up as she went into the bedroom. Stacey said good night to Derek and then headed for bed.

"Opal, you look disappointed. Did the night go alright?" Opal let her hair down slowly and then smiled.

"It was wonderful," she turned around with a face filled with delight. "It was more than I could have ever dreamed." Opal jumped onto the bed and hugged Stacey. "Thank you, we both needed the encouragement for both of us to date."

"You're welcome," they settled down and Opal told Stacey about her night ice skating, dinner, and hot tub. Then they fell asleep with smiles on their faces.

Chase knocked on the Rysner's door early in the morning, and Stacey greeted him. "So, what makes you risk dealing with grouchy people to be here this early in the morning?" His face became red.

"I think, I would risk grouchy people to see the beautiful young lady you're hiding in the house." She let him in and showed him to her room where Opal was still sleeping.

"Don't do anything that I wouldn't do," Derek said to Chase as he held Stacey and nuzzled his nose into her neck. Chase smiled as he walked into the room. He sat down on the edge of the bed and brushed her bangs off of her face. She moved her face into the heat of his hand as the pad of his thumb brushed her cheek. Her eyes opened with a smile on her face then she saw Chase.

"Hey Chase," he leaned down and kissed her cheek. "How did you get in here?" he smiled as he pointed towards the window, and her jaw dropped.

"I'm kidding, Stacey let me in." He knelt beside the bed and kissed her hand. "I think Derek and I have plans for you girls so I'll let you get ready." He stood up, brushed his fingers gently down the side of her face before he left the room. He joined Derek in the kitchen, "She looks so peaceful when she's sleeping." Derek chuckled as he handed him a plate of eggs. Stacey walked in and sat down at the table as Derek set a plate of toast in front of her.

"What, no eggs for your girl?" Stacey laughed as she played with her toast.

"Well, less than a month ago, she couldn't even stand the smell of eggs without getting sick. This is a grand achievement," he raised his plate of eggs and smiled. Opal walked in and stole Chase's plate. He chased her around the table then caught her and spun her around.

"Chase Ebert put her down," Chad ordered. Chase put her down and threw his hands up then he saw the smile on Chad's face. Everyone started laughing as they all sat down and enjoyed their breakfast.

"So, Derek what are our plans for today?"

"We are going to go shopping, movie, dinner, and…cuddling." They laughed at how Derek said the last part, quiet and reserved.

"Sounds good babe, let the day begin," they piled into Stacey's vehicle. They arrived at the mall and started walking around hand-in-hand.

"So, boys what are we shopping for?" Stacey asked.

"We are shopping for anything and everything," Derek responded as he guided them to a clothing store. They arrived at the women's area, Stacey turned towards Derek to see if she could figure out his plan but he wasn't giving any hints. Opal pulled Stacey to the dresses and they picked up a few to try on. Derek and Chase hung out outside the dressing rooms expecting a fashion show. Stacey put on the first dress which was skin-tight. Opal looked at her and smiled.

"I didn't see your baby bump until now," Stacey placed her hand over her tummy and smiled.

"Derek likes spanning his hand over it and feeling the growth. We just started noticing it." Opal put her hand on Stacey's stomach and kissed it before they went out to show the boys. They walked out, hips swinging and arms moving.

"Wow," Derek said as Chase's jaw dropped.

"Those look like you're going to Cinderella's Ball," Chase commented then he noticed Stacey's baby bump. "How far along are you?"

"I'm just over three months but I'm showing a little." Chase looked at Derek and saw his face.

"I think you're going to be a cute pregnant lady," Derek shot a look at Chase then smiled when he saw that he was teasing.

"Thanks, Chase," the girls went back in to try on another dress.

"Yeah, this dress made Derek speechless so not until later." Opal laughed as they put on some winter dresses. The dress was long-sleeved just off the shoulders and flared out at the hips and stops in the middle of the calves. Opal's dress was neck high, low back, ¾ sleeves, and flares at the hips down to her calves. Stacey's was maroon with black ribbon and Opal's was dark blue with black ribbon. They walked out to the boys.

"Beautiful, just beautiful," Chase said as he saw them walking out, Derek turned around and smiled. He walked up to her and hugged her.

"You look amazing and I like the baby bump," he kissed her forehead. They tried on a few more dresses then they went to the men's area. The girls picked out a few outfits for the guys and they modeled for the girls. After a few more outfits, they went to a jewelry store. Chase and Opal went off to look on their own then Stacey got her ring cleaned and tried on other jewelry.

"When is the wedding?" The jeweler asked.

"At the end of August," Derek answered with his arm around her waist. Derek found charms for the bracelet he bought her for her birthday. He picked out a heart charm and bought it for her, adding to the bracelet. Chase and Opal joined them with a new necklace for Opal.

"Let's go to the next store before we break the boys' bank." Stacey got her ring back and interlaced her fingers with her man. He led them to a bookstore,

"We might still break your guys' bank at this store," Opal commented as she followed them in. Chase smiled at her and let her go in front of him, letting her have the lead. Derek watched them leave and led Stacey to the children's department. They played with the books that have noise, the touch books, and stuffed animals.

"Derek, do you want a girl or a boy?"

"Either one would be nice, a girl would be just as adorable as you and a boy would be fun to play with." Derek wrapped his arms around her stomach and kissed her neck as they read one of the stories together. When the story was done, Stacey put it back on the shelf and led Derek to the game area. They found a few mind games and a puzzle to buy when Chase and Opal found them.

"Let's buy these then go to the movie," Chase suggested, knowing the plans for the day.

Everyone agreed as they bought their merchandise and went out to the car. They walked into the movie theater and bought popcorn, soda, and candy. The previews of the movies started as they climbed into the chairs. During the movie, Derek twisted Stacey's engagement ring around her finger and had his other hand around her shoulders. Chase sat the same way Derek did, with one arm around her shoulders and the other hand holding Opal's hand.

After the movie, they went back to Rysner's house and played the new game Derek bought. At midnight, Chad kicked Chase out of the house and sent everyone to bed. "Stacey, I had a wonderful day. Thank you for introducing me to Chase, he is wonderful." Stacey smiled at her as she lay under the blankets.

"Well, we will have some more fun at his New Year's Eve Party," Stacey declared as they settled in for the night.

Opal opened her eyes to a stream of sunlight that landed across her face. She rolled over and covered her face with a pillow. "Opal, it's time to wake up." She heard from underneath her pillow. Ignoring the voice, she buried her face into her pillow and bed so her dream wouldn't go away. Finally, she felt a body on her, trying to wake her up. "Opal, it is twelve o'clock in the afternoon." Stacey's voice was finally heard, Opal turned in the bed letting the pillow fall off her head.

"Why did you ruin my wonderful dream?" Opal whined as Stacey got off of the bed.

"One reason is that I didn't know you were having a wonderful dream and two, Chase's party starts in a few hours. I thought you would want a few hours to get ready." Opal smiled as she thought of Stacey's reasoning and thanked her as she got up. A while later she appeared in the living room.

"Now, look who's up and about this afternoon," Derek teased as she plopped onto the couch. "What time did Chase drop you off last night?" Opal's face turned red as she answered.

"About two o'clock this morning," Derek's jaw dropped as Stacey walked in.

"Did you hear what time this young lady came home last night?" He asked Stacey, she smiled as she nodded her head.

"I heard her come in and I looked at the clock." Derek shook his head in disbelief watching Opal's reaction. Her face turned to the color of a cherry at Derek's teasing. They all cleaned up the house while Allison was at the store then they got ready to go to Chase's parents' house. When they arrived, Joanna and Ariel ran up to their boyfriends and went inside. Chase walked out of the house to greet them.

"So Chase, how late did you sleep in today?" Derek asked to tease him.

"Mom woke me up at 10 o'clock, why?" Chase asked innocently.

"Well, this young lady," Derek set his arm around her shoulders, "slept in until noon because someone kept her out until really early this morning." Chase glanced at Opal then looked Derek in the eyes.

"Is there a problem with that?"

"No, but I know this friend who would rather go to bed than watch a movie with his buddies, then stays up all night and part of the morning with this beautiful girl." Chase's face became red.

"Derek," he turned his head to look at Stacey, "At least he has his priorities right," she commented in a sarcastic tone. Opal held Derek back as he tried to get at Stacey. Derek got free from Opal and caught Stacey and jumped into a pile of snow, being careful to not hurt her, the knee or the baby. "Derek, the snow is cold," Stacey whined as he held her down.

"I think cold is part of the definition of snow," Stacey tried to keep a straight face as he stood up and pulled her out of the snow.

"Derek, my pants are wet now." He brushed the snow off of her then carried her into the house. Chase grabbed a pair of his sweatpants and gave them to her. "Now, he is a gentleman," Stacey said trying to act annoyed.

She went into the bathroom and smiled to herself, knowing Derek was falling for her angry act. She changed into the sweatpants and replaced her knee-brace on her knee. She walked out limping with the huge pair of pants on and threw the wet pants at Derek. He caught them and her as she walked away.

"Stacey girl, I'm sorry you got wet. We were just playing around." Stacey stared at his chest, "Are you hurt at all?" She looked up at him and smirked,

"You worry too much my dear fiancé," his jaw dropped off to the side, surprised.

"You girl, should be an actress," she looked at his chest playing with the collar of his shirt.

"No, I only act around you to keep you on your toes." She tipped her head back as Derek leaned in to kiss her. "But you did jostle my knee so I am going to sit down," she said against his lips. He leaned down and lifted her, carrying her to the sofa. Opal sat down next to Stacey and pulled Stacey's leg up to elevate it. "So, what are the plans for tonight?" Stacey asked Chase as everyone sat down in the great room.

"We have a few games we can play." The group of peers spread out to different rooms playing games. After one full set of a card game, Stacey stood up to stretch her leg and was looking out the front window when she saw her brother walk up. She rushed to the front door and jumped into his arms as he entered.

"I missed you too sis," Adam spun around and set her down gently.

"Where's Nicole?" Adam spun around looking for her.

"I don't know…I lost her." Stacey laughed as she saw Nicole walk up the sidewalk and enter the house.

"Sorry, I was on the phone with my mother." Nicole hugged Stacey and saw that she was favoring her good leg. "Let's have you sit down," Adam picked her up and carried her into the kitchen to grab some snacks.

"How are Mom and Dad?" Stacey asked even though she just saw them a few days before.

"They are doing great, they miss you being home but they are getting used to it. They say it is slowly preparing them for next year when we are both gone." Stacey took a bite of a chocolate covered strawberry and smiled.

"Mom was not ready for me to be gone next year; I can't imagine what she is like now with me gone a year early." Nicole looked at Adam giving him a look.

"She is being a bit overprotective and possessive of me." Stacey looked at Nicole and she pinched her index and thumb together trying to look through them. Then she rolled her eyes and shook her head.

"So, you're saying I should visit more often?" Nicole and Adam aggressively nodded their heads. Stacey pursed her lips together and leaned back into Derek's chest when she smelled his cologne. Adam smiled seeing his sister content with her man. "Oh boy," Stacey whispered when she saw someone outside through the kitchen window. Adam's head turned to see Aaron's father outside the kitchen window.

"Derek, take her into the living room," Adam ordered him as he pushed Nicole into the other room. He went out to talk to the man in the yard. "Mr. Jackson, I'm going to ask you to leave. You are not welcome here," Adam stared him down expecting a physical fight but his shoulders slumped as he walked away, peacefully. Adam walked back into the house being tackled by Stacey.

"Adam, don't ever do that again. Let the police handle him, I don't want anyone else to get hurt." Stacey buried her head into his chest and screamed. "I thought this was all over but I guess not." She turned into Derek's arms as Adam held Nicole. A few minutes later, Opal and Chase joined them and saw their somber faces.

"What's going on in here?" Chase looked at each of their faces, wanting answers.

"Aaron, the guy that hurt Stacey, his father made an appearance and didn't look too happy." Adam answered as Nicole held him tighter. "Mr. Jackson threatened Stacey a few months ago, so it gave us a scare to see him. But he did leave when I asked him to." Adam tried to make the last part seem positive. Chase walked over to Stacey and Derek, giving her a hug and Derek a shoulder squeeze.

"Okay, let's get some smiles on these faces and go join the party." Chase suggested as he grabbed a cookie and led the way to the fun and games. Stacey relaxed into Derek's arms as the games proceeded and the night went by. Stacey watched as Chase and Opal interacted, seeing they were both tired and becoming hyper from lack of sleep. Around 11:58, everyone crowded into the great room for the countdown with the windows from floor to the ceiling of the second floor to see the fireworks. Stacey stood up to see out the window and Derek hugged her from behind, nuzzling his nose into her neck. There was a minute left of the old year.

"A new year with my future wife, a baby on the way and a new adventure," Derek whispered into her ear. "I'm excited." As the countdown began Stacey turned into his arms.

"I love you Derek Rysner."

"I love you too Stacey Rosemen soon to be Stacey Rysner." They heard the countdown: 3, 2, 1 and Stacey jumped up into his arms and kissed him as the fireworks went off. "Happy New Year, my darling," Stacey smiled as he set her back down to the ground. Everyone was giving hugs starting the New Year with happiness, love, and friendship.

New Years Day

People started leaving as the morning of the New Year went by. They were all still up at five o'clock in the morning, exhausted. "I suppose I should start cleaning up and surprise my parents by having this all cleaned up." Chase stood up to clean up and they all pitched in. Within an hour, the house looked as clean as it had before the party started. They all crashed on the floor or couch while watching a movie. They were all asleep within 10 minutes of the movie, cuddling with their significant others. Stacey heard footsteps on the stairs and looked up to see Chase's parents. They saw Stacey awake and walked over to talk to her.

"When did you guys clean up this place?"

"We just finished not twenty minutes ago. We thought that since you provided a safe, non-alcoholic place to party that we should clean up, so you would do it again." Chase's mother smiled as she motioned Stacey into the kitchen. Stacey gently crawled out of Derek's arms and went into the kitchen. Mrs. Ebert put water on the stove to boil then sat at the counter with Stacey.

"I'm so glad Chase met your friend Opal. He has been so happy and helpful around the house. Thank you for introducing them, we have had a blast getting to know her." Stacey smiled as Mrs. Ebert made her a cup of hot chocolate.

"I didn't think they would get together. I was just having Opal join all the festivities and they noticed each other. I just encouraged it." Stacey sipped on her drink and warmed up her hands around the cup.

"Well, thanks…" She took a sip of her hot chocolate. "How's the pregnancy treating you?" Mrs. Ebert asked as the nurse in her came out.

"The first month was rough, with morning sickness and nausea every morning. My doctor has been very helpful emotionally and physically."

"Your doctor is Jayne Dolan, right?" Stacey nodded her head. "She had a rough year that year and she is the perfect person to help you. Did you know that she had the same knee injury before she was raped?"

"Yeah, she was going through physical therapy with Dallas. That's how they met then she was raped and became pregnant with Robbie."

"So, they told you the whole story?"

"Yeah, Jayne has been counseling me and Dallas is counseling Derek, so he knows how to be supportive without hovering." Mrs. Ebert smiled.

"When is your first ultrasound?"

"January 26th, I'm still unsure about this and raising the baby but Derek is super excited which makes me excited. Aaron's father is mad at me and he showed up last night and then left when Adam went to go talk to him. Mr. Jackson has been threatening me ever since Aaron raped me. He blames me for Aaron's mistakes then when Aaron died, his father disappeared. We thought he had just given up on me but I guess he was waiting for us to put our guard down." Stacey heard Adam crying out and she rushed to him and held his hand.

"Stacey, what's going on?" Mrs. Ebert asked as Adam settled on the couch holding Stacey's hand.

"Ever since we were little, anytime anything bad would happen to me Adam would have a nightmare. Even a threat triggers them. If he senses my presence he calms and goes back to sleep."

"Wow, that's weird."

"The doctors say it's a twin thing…"

"Wait, you're twins?"

"Yeah," Stacey unlocked Adam's death grip and stretched her hand. Mrs. Ebert smiled and left the twins alone. A few minutes later, Adam woke up startled then saw Stacey and relaxed. Adam turned on the couch and watched Stacey play solitaire.

"Stacey, why was Mr. Jackson here if he didn't want to do anything to you?" Stacey took a deep breath as she put an Ace on the top right of the table.

"I think he wanted to see if I was showing or not. He might come after me later but now he is probably thinking of Aaron and the baby growing inside me." She continued playing the game avoiding eye contact with Adam.

"Stac, look at me," she looked up and saw concern on his face. "Please be careful, I want you around for a long time."

"The feeling is mutual," Stacey finished the game and then found a spot to sleep for a while. Around noon, Stacey woke up disorientated and then remembered where she was. She slipped into the bathroom to fix her hair; she re-braided it off to the side and went out to find everyone else. Derek saw her coming and stood up to greet her.

"Good morning darling," he kissed her forehead while hugging her. "Do you want some food?"

"No, I think I ate too much last night and this morning." She saw Mrs. Ebert's head twist around and study her.

"Are you sure? I make wonderful waffles." Mrs. Ebert asked, sensing that Stacey wasn't telling the truth.

"I'm sure Mrs. Ebert. I think we should head home anyways. We need to get rested up for church tomorrow and school the next day." Derek agreed as he told his sisters to get ready. Mrs. Ebert pulled Stacey aside.

"Are you feeling okay?"

"I'm just tired and the junk food from last night is not being friendly with the baby." Mrs. Ebert smiled as she remembered her pregnancies.

"Eat a bowl of soup with some crackers; it should help you feel better." Stacey agreed as Derek escorted her out the door. Opal stayed with Chase and his family for the rest of the day as Stacey slept through the whole day and night.

—⁓⦿⁓⦿⁓—

Stacey woke up to her alarm clock, "I must have slept through the night." She thought to herself as she got up and went into the bathroom to take a shower. When she walked out, she saw Opal sitting on the bed dressed and packed to leave.

"Hey Stac, I'm sorry I didn't spend more time with you."

"You don't need to apologize, I'm glad the two of you connected. We'll see each other more this summer." Stacey walked over to her friend, hugging her.

"Stac, you found a wonderful man. He is everything you ever wanted. He loves you and will do anything for you; don't forget that. And thanks for introducing me to Chase, he is wonderful." They hugged each other again and then carried her suitcases to her car. Chase took the suitcases from Stacey and helped Opal pack her car. Opal walked up to Stacey for one last hug.

"Call me when you get home," Stacey told Opal.

"I will," Opal replied as she moved to hug Derek. "Take care of her Derek, she is going to need it," she whispered into his ear and he agreed as Opal moved to her car and Chase. He kissed her goodbye and gave her a hug before he let her get in the car. Then, she drove off. Stacey walked back into the house and finished getting ready for church. Stacey went to the church with Chad early to get some quiet time before worship. As she was sitting in one of the rooms alone, she heard someone at the door; she looked up to see Mr. Jackson.

"You didn't abort the baby like I asked you to." Stacey was too shocked to respond. "I will give you another month to abort that thing before I'll do it myself."

"Mr. Jackson, don't you want someone to remember your son by?"

"I don't need anything to remember my son. That thing inside you is…is…," he paused to think, "Needs to disappear."

"Your son wanted this baby, why don't you?" He started pacing then Stacey saw the gun on his side.

"That thing and you killed my son," Stacey heard people beginning to arrive.

"Church starts soon; you might want to leave if you want to be a free man." He froze and then looked at Stacey.

"One month," he warned her before he left. Stacey curled up in a ball in the corner of the couch and prayed for peace. As she was praying,

Derek walked in and rubbed her shoulders. She jumped and looked up to see Derek over her.

"Derek, I didn't hear you walk in." He stayed behind her and leaned down as Stacey lay down on the couch. He kissed her upside down, then sat down on the edge of the couch.

"You were deep in thought…are you ready for this morning?"

"Yeah, go get my microphone set up, I'll be there in a few minutes." Stacey calmed herself and followed Derek to the stage. Chad walked up behind her as she grabbed her microphone. He tapped her shoulder; she jumped as a squeal came out of her mouth.

"So, are you going to tell me who visited you this morning?"

"Since you're asking, I suspect you know." He nodded his head and pulled Stacey into his office to find Jeremiah's father, Detective Kent.

"What did he say to you?" Detective Kent dug into the problem. Stacey looked at Chad and asked him to leave.

"He told me I had one month to abort the baby or he would do it for me," the detective's mouth opened.

"And you didn't call the police?"

"No, it would have just made him angrier." Stacey sat down at Chad's desk feeling defeated.

"Do you know why he is giving you a month?" She shrugged her shoulders. "Do you think he will follow through?" Stacey stood up when she saw the clock.

"Mr. Jackson has been sending me e-mail threats for the last two months. I have to go, service starts soon and I don't want to have to explain why I'm late." Detective Kent grabbed her arm,

"Call me the next time he contacts you in any way," he handed her his card and she agreed and went out to the stage to start the service. After the service, Stacey went back to the room she was in earlier; she had left her Bible there. On top of her Bible was an abortion brochure, which she crumpled up and threw away. Derek found her in the room,

"What are you doing in here again?" She spun around and walked to him.

"I forgot my Bible in here earlier today." She wrapped her arm around his waist and turned him towards the hallway. He set his arm on her waist and went to say goodbye to friends and fellow worshippers. Adam and Nicole were the last ones out of the sanctuary.

"I miss you leading worship at our church in La Crosse," Nicole said as she hugged her.

"Yeah, we miss you in La Crosse," Adam confirmed while hugging her too. "We want to take the two of you out for lunch before we head back to La Crosse." Stacey looked at Derek and he agreed as he found their jackets and informed his dad. They met at an Italian restaurant and Stacey ate breadsticks and salad, making herself so full she could barely eat a bite of her main course. Nicole and Stacey talked about the wedding while the guys talked about sports. Stacey boxed up her main dish and got a few more breadsticks to go. Adam paid for them then they said goodbye by the cars.

"Be careful sis," Adam whispered during their hug.

"We'll keep in contact and continue making plans as the school year goes on," Nicole promised as they hugged. They got into the car and drove away. Stacey and Derek got into their car and drove home.

"What do you want to do, my dear?" Stacey turned her body to look at him when he parked the car, and she answered him.

"I want to cuddle with you," his smile grew, "but I need to tell you about something that happened this morning." Derek's smile disappeared and became a concerned frown. "This morning, I had an unwanted visitor. Mr. Jackson came into the room I was praying in." Stacey watched Derek's jaw clench and slowly relax. "He says I have a month to have an abortion before he will do it himself." Derek got out of the car looking upset, he opened Stacey's door.

"I wish you would have told me earlier when you jumped when I touched your shoulders." Stacey turned her legs to step out of the car. Derek lifted her and carried her into the house. "Did you tell the police?"

"Yeah, your dad saw Mr. Jackson leave and he got Jeremiah's dad to take a report." Derek's eyes darkened when he heard that his dad knew about it. "He didn't want you to worry during the service. Don't yell at him, I wasn't going to tell anyone so you can yell at me." Derek set her down and began to pace, Stacey went into the living room and sat down. Derek followed her and started scolding her with his finger but he couldn't figure out what to say.

"Derek, don't yell at her," Chad said as he walked into the room. "At least she told you, she could've kept it a secret." Derek glared at his father.

"She was planning on keeping it a secret until you figured it out," Derek yelled at his father. Stacey stood up and walked out of the room, locking herself in her bedroom.

"It doesn't matter if she was going to keep it a secret or not. She told you and you need to comfort her not be angry at her. She doesn't need any more stress." Chad quietly lectured him; he dropped into a chair and dropped his head into his hands in defeat.

"Dad, I just want to protect her but I can't protect her if I don't know what's going on." Chad sat down next to Derek and rubbed his shoulder.

"Let her tell you in her own time. She believes she is protecting us from worrying if we don't know. She won't do anything to harm the baby or herself." Derek took a moment to compose himself then he went to Stacey's bedroom door and knocked. There wasn't an answer.

"Stac, please yell back just so I know you're in there and alive." He heard movement by the door and he had hope that she was going to open the door. He waited but nothing happened. "Stacey," he said loud enough for her to hear.

"Go away Derek," she responded, he leaned against the wall and slid down it in relief, frustration, and weariness.

"Stacey, I'm sorry I yelled at you. I just want to protect you and I can't do that if I don't know about the threats." He set his head into his hands hoping Stacey was listening. "Please unlock the door so we can talk," he stayed quiet and waited half an hour then Stacey finally came out.

"This is not going to make you happy but you asked for it," she motioned him into her room and handed him all the e-mails she had received from Mr. Jackson. He read half of them and then put them on her bed. Then, she handed him a journal that had a few entries of Mr. Jackson's confrontations and threats. Stacey went and sat on her reading chair, waiting for Derek's reaction. A few minutes later, Derek slowly walked to her with a somber expression on his face. He sat down next to her with his elbows on his knees staring at the floor.

"I wish you would have told me," he whispered. Stacey leaned forward while slipping her hand underneath his elbow to hold his hand. He held her hand with both of his,

"I should have told you, I just didn't want to worry you anymore. You have enough to worry about." Derek turned his body to look at her.

"You have as much to worry about if not more; it's my job to worry about you, my dear. I signed up for worrying when I asked you to marry me." He cupped her face with his hands, brushing her cheeks with his thumbs. Stacey's eyes closed, loving the moment. A few seconds later, she could feel Derek's hot breath against her lips. She leaned into his body closing the distance between their lips. She pushed him back an inch and put her forehead against his.

"I'm glad you signed up to worry about me," Derek's smile grew then they lay on the chair to discuss their plans for the next few weeks.

Stacey groaned as her alarm clock consistently beeped, not wanting to reach her arm out of the warm blanket, she listened to it go off. Finally, she quickly reached her arm out and slapped the clock to turn the noise off. She wrapped herself in her blanket and walked into the bathroom, jumping into the hot shower. After the shower, she dried off and wrapped up in the blanket again to go to her walk-in closet. She put a sweater and jeans on then walked out to the kitchen after putting her knee brace on over her jeans.

"Why is it so cold?" Stacey asked Chad as he greeted her in the kitchen.

"It is cold because it is winter and the electricity went out last night and just came back on a few hours ago." Derek walked into the kitchen shivering.

"Why was my shower freezing?" He asked his dad.

"Stacey took the last of the hot water that was stored in the tank." Then he explained how the electricity was out. Derek put his cold hands underneath Stacey's shirt on her back.

"Derek," she squealed while jumping away from him. He smiled as Chad handed him a cup of steaming hot chocolate. He wrapped his hands around the cup as his sisters walked in shivering as well. Chad explained the situation again then they all ran off to school hoping it was warmer there. Chase ran up to them from outside,

"It's cold outside,"

"It's cold in our house too," Chase raised an eyebrow. "Our electricity went out last night," Derek explained.

"I think you're the only house that did, Dennis didn't say anything about a power outage and he is your neighbor." Stacey's eyes grew as her mind went wild with ideas on how it happened. Derek looked at her and she knew he was thinking the same thing. "Is something going on?" Chase asked as he saw their faces.

"Aaron's father has been threatening Stacey and he might have cut our electricity," Derek explained while wrapping his arm protectively around Stacey's waist. Chase's mouth stood agape as he remembered New Year's Eve.

"What is he threatening?"

"He's threatening to kill the baby, in any way possible." Derek pulled Stacey in closer and kissed the top of her head.

"Do the police know?" Stacey nodded her head.

"Mr. Jackson has been sending me threatening e-mails and I gave them access to my account. I told them everything he has said and done." Chase seemed content with her answer as they arrived at their first class. Stacey concentrated on the classes and was able to forget her problems for the day. At the end of the day, she went to physical therapy with Derek as her escort.

"Hey Jayne, Dallas," Stacey greeted them. The boys left the girls alone as Jayne did a simple check-up on her knee and the baby.

"How's everything feeling?"

"My knee is sore but functioning and the baby doesn't like sugary foods," Stacey complained with a pout. Jayne laughed.

"The baby is making you eat healthy?" Jayne asked in a sarcastic tone. Stacey nodded her head trying to keep the pout on her face but burst out laughing. Jayne finished the check-up declaring Stacey and the baby as healthy as can be. Then Stacey went into the torture room with Dallas, stretching, bending, and exercising her knee. Jayne and Dallas walked them to the entrance of the hospital.

"Keep stretching that knee," Dallas ordered her then Jayne hugged her.

"Keep up the good work and be careful." They waved as Derek and Stacey walked out the door.

"She will be fine," Dallas whispered to his wife. Jayne looked up at him with her forehead scrunched up. "Aaron's father has been threatening Stacey. He wants the baby dead." Jayne's eyes grew to the size of golf balls.

He pulled her in for a hug, "When is it the mark of the fourth month?" Jayne looked at her schedule.

"We have an ultrasound appointment on the 26th, so that would be 16 weeks." Dallas nodded his head as he guided her back to her office.

Rysner's house

"Dad, can I talk to you for a moment?" Chad motioned him in as he finished his call.

"What's up, son?"

"Did you know that we were the only house on the block that lost power?" Chad slowly nodded his head.

"I suspected that but wasn't sure until I called the electric company. They came by and checked it out and they saw that someone tampered with it. When I woke up this morning freezing, I checked the furnace and noticed there wasn't any electricity. I checked the fuse boxes and the electricity wouldn't turn on so I called Kenny's father and he did a temporary fix until he could come back with the proper equipment." Derek slumped back against the chair.

"Okay, we'll watch Stacey more carefully and not leave her alone." Chad thought about saying something but saw Derek's determination and let him be.

Chapter 10

Derek ran into the room and jumped onto the bed. Stacey pulled the covers over her head, groaning. "Stacey, aren't you excited?" She pulled the blanket down just enough to see Derek's excitement and smiled underneath the covers.

"What would I be excited about?" She asked while still underneath the covers.

"We get to see the baby today," he replied, hoping Stacey was as excited as he was. Stacey heard the uncertainty in his voice and let him see the huge smile on her face.

"We have made it through the month without any mishaps except the electricity. Maybe Mr. Jackson decided to leave you alone." Derek whispered as he pulled her out of the bed.

"He said a month from the first of the month so we have a few days to go," Stacey replied trying not to get her hopes up. Derek set his hand over Stacey's expanding stomach, so excited to be a daddy. "We still have school to go to so leave, I need to get ready." Derek kissed her and then her stomach as he ran out the door. "Oh God, please help me be as excited as him." She prayed as she got ready. As the day went on, she got more excited watching Derek skip around smiling.

"So, I hear that you get to see the baby today," Chase whispered to her as they watched Derek run around. She laughed as she turned to talk to Chase.

"Yeah, Jayne wants me to see the baby so she scheduled an early ultrasound," Chase observed her as emotions ran across her face.

"You still don't want it to be true," Stacey whipped her head back to look at him.

"Jayne says when I see the baby I won't care who the father is. She says I will fall in love more than I am... How did you know?"

"The way you said it, you should have said, 'I'm too excited to wait to see the baby so we scheduled an earlier ultrasound.'"

"I hope Derek doesn't find out and seeing the baby makes me want him or her more." Chase moved behind her and rubbed her shoulders to help her relax. The bell rang and they went back to class.

Hospital

Jayne put gel on her stomach warning her that it would be cold. Derek held her hand and kissed it as he waited for Jayne to start. Jayne turned the monitor on and found the baby right away. "The baby's heartbeat is strong, normal growth, but I can't tell the gender, the baby has decided to be uncooperative." Stacey looked at the monitor, kissed her fingers, and touched the monitor. Tears ran down her cheeks as she smiled,

"Hey baby, Mommy is here for you," Derek stood up and kissed Stacey's forehead. Jayne finished the visual examination and printed the pictures out. She handed them to Stacey while she wiped the gel off of her stomach. Derek kissed Stacey's baby bump before she could pull her shirt back down. Jayne let them be alone.

"Stacey, I love you. I know having this baby scares you but I will be there the whole way through it." Derek promised as he laid his hand on her stomach and kissed her, rubbing his thumb over her tummy. After the kiss, he helped her up and they walked out with a smile on each of their faces. As they arrived home, Derek grabbed the pictures and ran into the house to show his family. He was showing his mom when his dad asked him a question.

"I see the baby but where is the mother of this baby?" Derek's eyes grew as he set the pictures down and ran out to get Stacey, she was on the steps.

"I'm sorry," Stacey laughed as he walked in with her. The whole family was laughing when they entered together.

"I see who's more important in this family," Stacey teased Derek. He shrugged his shoulders and smiled. "Chad, may I use your scanner? I want to e-mail Mom and Dad." He nodded his head and helped her scan the pictures in and send them. Minutes later, she got a call from Adam,

"The baby is a little squished and dark and…"

"Adam be nice, it's a little dark where the baby is growing and I'm stretched out enough right now." She replied as Derek walked into the room. She talked to her whole family and then called Opal and talked to her for a while. Derek brought her a cup of chocolate milk as she hung up the phone.

"So, your family is coming down this weekend?" Stacey nodded her head as she sat forward on the couch to stretch her lower back. Derek sat next to her and had her turn so he could massage her back. Chad walked in,

"You're going to regret giving her back massages now then she'll expect them all the time." He teased as Stacey enjoyed the back rub.

"If he knows what's good for him, he'll continue giving them," Allison yelled from the kitchen making them all laugh.

February

"Well, today we are going to be extra cautious," Derek declared as they walked out of the house.

"We don't even know what to be cautious of or if he's going to do it today." Stacey reasoned with him. They arrived at school and all of his friends were watching out for her. They went through the whole day with no mishaps. At the end of the day,

"I don't know if I can go through another day of that." Stacey looked at him.

"A day of what? Nothing happened," Stacey replied relaxed.

"Exactly but worrying about if something might happen." Stacey moved behind him and massaged his shoulders and neck.

"You know God says not to worry," Derek smiled as he relaxed against Stacey.

"I think I've heard that before." Stacey moved to the side and kissed him. Derek pulled Stacey onto his lap and put his hand behind her neck to pull her in for a deeper kiss. Stacey pushed against his chest to get some air.

"I'll be fine," she whispered while she brushed her thumb across his jawline. She kissed him one more time before she laid her head on his shoulder and set her hand on her growing baby.

Mid-February

Stacey woke up early, excited for date night. She showered and put some clean sweats on, "God, why do I feel compelled to be close to Derek right now? Is something going to happen to him?" She went to his bedroom door. "I give You my life as I spend time with my fiancé." She lightly knocked on his door and walked in. She found him lying on his stomach, blanket down to his lower back. Slowly, she crawled onto his bed and started massaging his back. As she started, Derek looked at the clock,

"Stacey, it is five o'clock in the morning on a Saturday," Derek announced in a growl even though he was enjoying his back rub. Stacey rubbed his shoulders then moved down to his shoulder blades and quickly tickled his sides. His body jumped and then relaxed when she stopped.

"Derek, let's go to the living room, start a fire in the fireplace, and cuddle." He turned around to look at Stacey and saw puppy eyes and a pout. He agreed as he got off the bed, grabbed a sweatshirt and a few pillows. He handed everything to Stacey then lifted her off the bed and carried her into the living room. Derek started a fire in the fireplace and he laid down on his stomach as Stacey continued the back massage.

"So Stacey, why are we up so early this morning?"

"I just felt like being close to you, you have come earlier in the morning just to cuddle with me."

"True," Derek turned onto his side and Stacey lay down, facing the fire with Derek behind her. Derek put his sweatshirt on and arranged the pillows and blankets to be comfortable. As he laid down again, he draped his hand over her side spanning it over her baby belly.

"What are the plans for today?" Stacey asked Derek as she interlaced her fingers with his over her belly.

"Relaxing like this for a majority of it then I'm taking you out to dinner."

"Where are we going?" Derek chuckled.

"That's a surprise my darling," Stacey smiled then nestled into his arms and pillows, closing her eyes. Derek stayed awake watching the flames flicker light across her face and reflecting on the last four months. "God, please continue to keep the three of us safe. Thank You for this wonderful reminder of love, I love her so much." An hour later, Derek heard someone approach them.

"I thought I heard the two of you up," Chad whispered when he saw Derek awake.

"We were quiet, how did you know it was us?"

"The fire, the girls don't like starting the fire." Derek smiled and pulled Stacey closer. "Who woke up who?" Derek showed Chad with his eyes that it was Stacey. "That's a first; it's usually you waking her up. I wonder what made her want to wake you up."

"She said she wanted to be close. I don't care, I got a nice back rub out of it and I'm cuddling with my favorite person." Chad smiled then left them alone to go study in his office. Gradually, the rest of Derek's family woke up and moved around quietly to let Stacey sleep. A few hours later, Stacey stretched against Derek and nestled back into his arms.

"Hmm…I like waking up next to you." Stacey whispered as she turned to face him. "Huh, this baby puts space between us and I'm only 19 weeks along." Derek smiled and wrapped his arms around her, not minding the space knowing the results.

"Well, we will just have to cuddle now and then make up for what we miss while you're further along in the pregnancy."

"I don't think we'll miss much cuddling because we both like it too much." His smile grew before Stacey kissed him,

"The two of you are making me sick," Joanna said as she entered the room.

"It's not like you can say much," Derek retorted, Joanna's face became red.

"Okay, it's time to get up, the floor and my back are arguing." Derek laughed as he helped Stacey up off the floor. She walked into the kitchen and Allison served pancakes in the shape of hearts with strawberries on top. "That's cute," Stacey complimented Allison as she sat down at the table to eat them. Stacey stole the strawberries off of Derek's pancakes and drank her hot chocolate in peace.

"Stac, you're eating all of my healthy food, Mom's not going to be too happy." Stacey's eyebrow rose,

"I'm sure you hate the fact that your fruit disappeared." Chad laughed while he listened to their friendly banter.

"What are your plans for today?" Chad interrupted them.

"Derek's not telling me," Stacey replied avoiding eye contact with her chin up as Derek tried to keep a straight face.

"Well, then if it is a surprise, I won't ask any more questions to ruin the surprise." Chad smiled at Stacey then stood up to put the dishes in the sink then squeezed Derek's shoulder on his way to his study. Derek cleaned up the kitchen then they went in to watch a few movies before their date.

"We should probably start getting ready," Derek announced when the last movie ended. Stacey took a quick shower to freshen up then put on a dress she had tried on when they had a double date with Opal and Chase. She put on the maroon long-sleeved, off the shoulders, dress that goes down to her calves. Some black ribbons outlined the dress and tied in the back. She braided her hair off to the side, put dangling earrings in, and put the necklace she got at Christmas on. She walked out to Derek in a pair of black flats and a shawl. "Wow, you look amazing," Derek said as he walked up to her and kissed the top of her head.

"You don't look too bad yourself, mister." She replied as she adjusted the collar of his shirt. Derek helped her put her coat on then put on his own as they said their goodbyes and got into Stacey's vehicle. "So, what are we doing tonight?" Derek held her hand and kissed the back of it while staying quiet. When Derek slowed down the car, Stacey looked up to see the restaurant she had always dreamed of going to since it opened. She turned her head to look at Derek and saw his smile grow a mile wide as he put the car in park. He got out of the car and opened the door to help her out of the car. Derek gave his keys to the valet and placed Stacey's hand in the crook of his elbow, escorting her into the restaurant.

"We are here for the Rysner reservation," Derek announced to the host. The host showed them to their seat.

"Derek, this is amazing," Stacey whispered as she opened the menu. He was about to reply when their waiter came to take their drink orders.

"What would the two of you like to drink?"

"Do you have any sparkling grape juice?" The waiter hesitated before he nodded his head, trying to compose himself from them requesting non-alcoholic drinks. He walked away without telling them the specials. Stacey smirked at Derek over the menu and then figured out what she wanted to eat. Stacey told Derek what she was going to order and then talked until the waiter came back with the grape juice in a bottle wrapped up in a towel and chilled in an ice bucket.

"Do you know what you would like to order?" He asked as he poured the juice into wine glasses.

"Yeah, I would like the tenderloin steak with a baked potato and green beans. And she would like the bacon-wrapped tenderloin tips with mashed potatoes and green beans." The waiter looked at Stacey to confirm the order then he took the menus away. The live background music was some of Stacey's favorite love songs. Stacey sat back in the chair listening to the music and relaxed. Derek reached his hand across the table and Stacey held it, watching the candlelight flicker across his face.

"I love you," Stacey mouthed, he smiled as he mouthed it back. The waiter came back with their entrees. As the waiter set the plate down, he saw Stacey's pregnant belly and almost dropped the plate. After he set the plate down, he smiled,

"I hope you enjoy the meal," Stacey smiled at him before he left. They bowed their heads and said a prayer over the food then dug in. At the first bite, Stacey sighed as it melted in her mouth.

"This tastes as good as I thought it would," Derek nodded his head in agreement. Stacey savored every bite as she listened to the live music and observed Derek.

"I'm glad you're enjoying this, I have been planning it for a while." Stacey ate her last bite. "Do you want to dance?" She nodded her head as she put the napkin back on the table. They stood up to dance.

"Thank you, Derek," Stacey whispered into his ear while they danced.

"You're welcome my love," when the song ended they went back to the table to find dessert on the table.

"Oh, chocolate," Stacey whispered as they sat down. Derek chuckled as they both ate the rich chocolate cheesecake. The waiter brought the bill and Derek paid with cash, which surprised the waiter again. Derek left a tip as they walked out smiling. When their vehicle pulled up, they got in and drove off. "That was amazing Derek, thanks."

"You're worth it…" Stacey held his hand, brushing her thumb along his. "I think we flustered the waiter," Stacey laughed thinking the same thing.

"He almost dropped my plate on me when he saw my baby bump." He moved his hand to put his hand on her expanding belly. Then, he pulled his hand back to kiss her hand. He saw a set of lights out of the corner of his eye coming right for them.

"Stacey!!" He yelled as he tried to turn the vehicle. Stacey saw the lights coming at her and turned to look at Derek as the car hit her side of the vehicle. The impact of the car moved them to the other side of the street in the line of more cars. One more car hit the front of the vehicle. When the impacts subsided, Derek reached for Stacey and panicked when he saw her face. "Stacey," he tapped her cheek. "Stacey, wake up please," her eyes fluttered. Derek pulled his cell phone out of his pocket and called the police. They arrived within seconds, as people had started to move the car back so they could get to Stacey.

When the EMTs arrived, Stacey was moaning, "She's pregnant," Derek informed them as they got her door open. Derek held her hand as they checked her over then they got her out and into the ambulance. Derek was stuck in the vehicle from the second impact. The firefighters cut Derek out and put him on the stretcher and into another ambulance. "How's Stacey?" He repeatedly asked as the paramedics bandaged up his leg and head. They never answered him then they arrived at the hospital. "Let me see Stacey," he yelled trying to get off the stretcher. The nurses held him down and gave him a sedative as they sewed up his leg and head.

Stacey's ambulance

She woke up in pain, "What's going on?"

"You were in…" she screamed in pain. The paramedics checked for the baby's heartbeat but they couldn't find one. "Stacey, can you tell me what hurts?"

"My stomach, it feels…" she groaned in pain, "Like someone is stabbing it and twisting the knife…inside of me." The paramedics tried to keep their fear and concern off of their faces. They arrived at the hospital and they rushed her into an operating room. The nurses rushed an ultrasound machine in and checked the baby. They couldn't find the baby's heartbeat.

"The baby is…" Stacey screamed and they checked underneath her dress and found a mess of blood coming out. Stacey saw their faces and started crying as the contractions continued to come. They hooked up an IV and gave her some medicine to help her deliver the baby. Not long afterwards, the pain was gone and Stacey realized what happened as they gave her the baby. "No…." she cried as she held her baby tight. "I'm sorry baby girl," she whispered. They cleaned everyone up, stitched up a few other cuts Stacey had, and moved Stacey to a room where she still held her baby with tears running down her face. A little while later, with her permission, she handed the nurse her baby and cried as they carried her baby out. Jayne came in to see how she was doing and to finish checking for injuries.

"I'm sorry Stacey," she whispered as she hugged her. Stacey clung to her.

"Me too…" Jayne held her for a while then Stacey turned over and curled up in a ball. Jayne left the room to give her some space.

⁓⁓∽◦◖∾◯◉◉⦶◯◦∾◗∾⁓⁓

Chad and Allison showed up at the hospital after they got a call from the police. "Where are they?" The nurse showed them to each of their rooms. Jayne met them there before they entered the rooms.

"Let's sit down," they went and sat down in the waiting room. "Derek is in good condition. His leg was cut up and he has a cut on his head." They took a breath of relief; Jayne took a deep breath and then finished her report "And Stacey lost the baby." Allison turned into Chad's arms and cried. "They are both sleeping; Derek wouldn't calm down when the doctors wouldn't let him see her. Stacey just fell asleep after delivering the baby and the emotional drain of the loss." Jayne wiped the tears from her cheeks. "Dallas and I will sit with the two of you. We can sit with either one of them or we can mismatch but someone needs to be there when they wake up."

"I think you ladies should sit with Stacey and Dallas and I can sit with Derek," Chad decided for everyone. They all agreed and went to their rooms. A few hours later, Stacey's family showed up as did Jeremiah's father, Detective Kent.

"I'm sorry to bother you but we would like you to keep an eye out for Mr. Jackson. The initial car that hit them is registered to him. He fled the scene seemingly unharmed but we are out there looking for him." Chad stared at him with his mouth wide open.

"He said he was going to terminate the pregnancy," Chad whispered, Christian stared at him like he lost his mind. "Stacey never told you?" Chad asked him, Christian shook his head confused. "Aaron's father has been threatening Stacey ever since he figured out she was pregnant. He said she had a month to terminate it or he would but he is two weeks later than he said." Christian stood up rubbing the back of his neck.

"He was late because he has been in jail," Christian announced while pacing. "He received his second DUI and they kept him in jail." Detective Kent took notes and then left them with an officer to keep an eye out for Mr. Jackson. They went into the rooms to watch over Stacey and Derek. Derek was the first one to wake up and saw Adam reading in the chair next to his bed.

"Tell me she's okay," Derek ordered as he sat up. Adam stood up and pushed Derek back against the bed.

"Stacey is fine but she lost the baby," Adam said slowly. Derek covered his face with his hands,

"Ouch," he growled when he hit his stitches. "I want to go see her," Adam agreed as he went to go find a nurse to help him. They found Derek a wheelchair and wheeled him to her room. Everyone cleared out to let Derek be with her alone. He kissed the back of her hand and prayed,

"We lost the baby," Stacey whispered to him. He jerked his head up,

"I know, baby."

"So, how are you?"

"My leg is cut up and my head has stitches but that's about it," she brushed the side of his face.

"Do you think you can manage to get up here and cuddle with me?"

"I think I can manage," Stacey turned onto her side facing him as he gently crawled onto the bed. Derek cradled her head against his chest as she cried. She had finally fallen asleep when Jayne came to check on her.

"She was up?" Derek nodded his head as tears rolled down his face. "She had to deliver the baby. The baby had died from the accident. The contractions had started already and the doctors gave her medicine to help the process. She was awake when they delivered the baby and she was able to hold her before they took her away." Derek looked up at Jayne as his tears started again.

"The baby was a girl?" He asked softly, she nodded her head slowly. Derek kissed the top of Stacey's head and closed his eyes. He fell asleep holding the love of his life in his arms.

⁓⊷⊶❀⊷⊶⁓

Stacey woke up startled from a nightmare then she relaxed as she felt Derek's arms around her. She looked at Derek's face and kissed his chin then nestled her head into his chest, feeling empty and in pain. Derek shifted then he kissed the top of her head. "Derek," she whispered, "Did you hear the gender of the baby?" He moved his head to look into her eyes.

"The baby was a girl," tears rolled down her face. Derek brushed her hair out of her face. "Hey girl," he kissed the tears off her face and pulled her in for a hug. Christian and Laura walked in and squeezed her shoulder. Derek moved to get off the bed when Stacey clung to him.

"Please," she begged him to stay on the bed, and he did. She turned around so she could see her family and friends.

"Baby girl, I'm sorry," her father whispered as he kissed her forehead and held her hand. Stacey looked up to see her mother by the wall watching. A few minutes later, Jayne and Mrs. Ebert came in to check on them.

"Stacey, I would like to examine you and Mrs. Ebert needs to clean Derek's wound. Do you think you can part for fifteen minutes or so?" They all waited for a reply. "Derek will just be on the other side of the curtain." Stacey nodded her head then her parents left and Derek moved to the other bed with Mrs. Ebert. Jayne did a full body exam then helped her take a shower and put a fresh hospital gown on. When they got back to the bed, Jayne put Stacey's knee brace on, "It's swollen you should stay off it for a few days." Stacey looked over to where Derek was supposed to be. "He wanted a shower so Dallas came in and took him. He should be back soon." Just as Jayne finished informing her the guys arrived back. Derek was using a pair of crutches. He sat down on the bed next to her placing his arm around her waist. Laura and Christian walked in,

"You two need some rest. We will come get you in the morning if they release you." Stacey looked at Jayne.

"Since you just delivered a baby, we would like to monitor you overnight, especially with the blood loss and head injury. And Derek has a concussion too. He will be in the bed next to you." Stacey laid back on the bed and closed her eyes. Everyone but Derek left.

"Do you want to talk about it?" Derek asked quietly. She shook her head. "Are you going to talk at all?" She shook her head. He sighed as he looked at the love of his life. "Dear God, we need Your peace and comfort as we mourn the loss of our child. We were so excited to meet her and we will miss her much. Please help Stacey physically and emotionally as this is a lot to take. Your loving children, we are in Your arms." Stacey grabbed his hand and squeezed it. "Can you talk to me? It doesn't have to be…"

"They let me hold her for about an hour before they took her away." Derek gave her a small smile. "She was so small, barely bigger than my hands, but so beautiful." Tears streaked down her face.

"I'm glad you were able to hold her. I wish I could have been there with you. I'm sorry you had to go through that on your own." Stacey wiped the tears off his face.

"If you could have been, I know you would have been." She whispered. "I want to try to sleep." She shifted on the bed and rolled onto her side. Derek looked at her and decided to let her be by herself for a little bit. He moved over to his bed and tried to fall asleep.

⸺⁓⁓⁓⁓⸺

The next morning, Stacey woke up and looked over at Derek in his bed. "God, I need some help getting out of this dark place. Please help me heal both physically and emotionally." She whispered as she got up and moved to Derek's bed.

"Hey babe," he said when he woke up at her touch.

"Can I cuddle?" He moved over and she slipped in. "We really never get much sleep, in hospitals, do we?" He chuckled.

"They are just making sure we are ok and if we need any help," Derek said as he remembered all the check-ins throughout the night. "How are you feeling?"

"Sad, sore, tired," she listed off.

"Me too." They cuddled until Stacey's parents showed up.

"Okay kids, let's get you ready to go home," They packed up all their stuff and got dressed then got their discharge instructions. Then, Stacey and Derek grabbed their crutches and limped out of the hospital to the waiting car. When they arrived at the house, Adam came out to greet them,

"Stacey," he helped her out of the car and carried her into the house. Derek slowly followed, careful not to slip on the ice. Adam went out to help him and they came in laughing as Adam had fallen on the ice. Derek dropped onto the couch next to Stacey and set his crutches down next to hers.

"Adam, can you get me an ice pack and some pain meds?" Stacey asked him,

"Can you get me some too?" Derek asked as well. Adam chuckled as he went to retrieve the items.

"We make a pair, don't we?" Stacey teased as they cuddled on the couch with their legs elevated. Derek's body shook with laughter.

"I think we are a cute pair," Stacey raised an eyebrow, "An injured one at least." Adam brought in their requested items and a tray full of food.

"Thanks, Adam, can you put a movie in now?" He walked over to put a movie in.

"Am I going to be your slave?"

"Just until you leave," she retorted as he sat on the chair next to their couch. The Rysner family arrived home and joined them in the living room. They all relaxed until the Rosemen's had to leave.

"Call me," Adam whispered as he hugged her. Stacey stood up to give her mom and dad a hug.

"I love you, Daddy," he kissed her forehead then went out to the car with Adam. "Mom, goodbye," Laura brushed her bangs out of her eyes.

"This is probably for the best," she said as she looked at Stacey's stomach.

"Don't even start with me Mom, I loved that little girl as much as any mother should." Stacey limped to her room as Laura reached for her then stomped out to the car, insulted.

"What did you say to her this time?" Christian asked as he drove off.

"I just said that it was probably for the best,"

"Laura!"

"Mom!" Christian and Adam yelled at the same time.

"Laura, no matter how she became pregnant, the baby was hers. She fell in love with the baby and she is grieving for the baby she lost." Christian stared out at the road as he drove.

"Mom, you should know better than to say losing a baby is better. You've counseled women who have had miscarriages or lost babies before. I can't believe you said that to her." Adam put his headphones on and turned his music on.

Rysner house

Derek grabbed his crutches and went into Stacey's room. He found her on her bed, crying. "Stac," she peeked out of her arms and moved for him to join her. He curled up around her and held her as she grieved for the lost baby. "Your mom was wrong," he whispered into her ear. "It isn't better that we lost her, it is a shame that we did." Stacey turned to face him,

"Thanks, Derek, I know you were excited about the baby."

"We can always have another one. I'm just glad I didn't lose you." Stacey fell asleep in his arms then he slipped out after putting a big teddy bear in her arms.

"Derek," he turned around to Stacey's voice. "I love you."

"I love you too," he closed the door behind him and went to his father's office. He dropped into the seat across from his father.

"How are you feeling?" Chad asked.

"Physically, I'll live but emotionally will be a little harder for the both of us." Chad observed his son, "Her mother isn't helping much either." Chad nodded his head as he went behind him and massaged his shoulders.

"I heard about that," Chad replied. "Stacey isn't very close with her mother, is she?" Derek shook his head. "I think there is something that Laura is hiding." Derek looked at the clock.

"I think I should head to bed to rest, we didn't get much sleep last night. We are going to decide in the morning if we are going to school or not." Chad nodded his head as he helped Derek stand up and watched him leave his office.

"God, thank You for protecting those kids in the accident, please continue to protect them from harm."

⸺⁓⦾⦾⦾⁓⸺

Stacey woke up and squeezed the big teddy bear and stretched. She limped into her bathroom to freshen up and went to Derek's room. "Happy Valentine's Day," she whispered into his ear as she massaged his shoulder. He turned around and pulled her into his arms.

"Hey sweetie, so are we up to going to school?" Stacey twisted her finger in his hair.

"I think it would be a good distraction," she watched his hair twist as her finger twirled it.

"Okay, I'll get up and get ready for school." He kissed her and rubbed the back of her neck. She held onto him, "Stac, getting up requires getting up." She kissed him one more time then stood up and went to the kitchen to eat. Chad walked in, carrying her crutches.

"You're supposed to be using these," he handed them to her then carried her bowl of cereal to the table for her. Joanna walked in

"So, I guess it's my car today," she teased.

"Yeah, I guess so, you've been draining our gas tanks long enough." Chad laughed at Stacey's reply as Derek crutched in.

"So, what is everyone laughing about?"

"Everyone is not laughing, just Dad," Joanna replied as she flipped the eggs in the frying pan. After breakfast, they piled into Joanna's car and went to school. Joanna and Ariel helped Derek and Stacey out of the car with their crutches. Chase, Kenny, and Jeremiah greeted them as they entered the school.

"The two of you are matching with injuries except for the leg that is injured," Chase commented as they walked to their first class.

"Ugh, these crutches make for slow going," Derek complained as they finally made it to class. Stacey laughed.

"This is what I have been doing on and off for the last few months." The day started with smiles.

⁓⁓⌀⌀⌀⌀⌀⌀⁓⁓

At lunch, Aunt Addy found Stacy in the Cafeteria and hugged her. "I'm sorry girl," Addison whispered. "I'm surprised you are here." Stacey shrugged her shoulders. Addison sat down with them and ate lunch with them. "Come visit, Ben wants to see you." Stacey smiled as she agreed.

"I wouldn't mind holding your little girl either, she is such a peanut." They made plans for her to visit them that night. Derek held Stacey's hand as they waited for the bell to ring. The day went on as if nothing happened then they went home. They ate a snack then Stacey drove them over to Aunt Addison's house. Addison made it home just minutes before they got there. Ben saw Stacey walk in and he ran into her arms.

"Stacey, I missed you!" He kissed her and nestled his head into her neck.

"I missed you too, monster," she stood there holding him until he wanted down.

"Do you want to color with me?"

"Sure, why don't you go get your colors and bring them to me?" He ran off as Addy, Stacey, and Derek went into the family room.

"When I picked him up and told him you were coming over, he almost jumped out of his car seat." Stacey sat on the floor beneath the coffee table where they would be coloring.

"Where's your peanut?" Addy pointed to the playpen. She was quietly playing with her blanket. Ben ran in and sat on her lap as he opened his coloring book and crayons. Stacey colored with him until his dad came home and he ran to greet him. Stacey moved up to the couch as Addy got her baby out of the playpen and handed her to Stacey. Derek wrapped his arm around her shoulders as she sat back with the baby. Addy left them to go finish dinner,

"She is so cute," he whispered as she grasped his finger with a death grip. Stacey held her and let tears run down her cheeks freely. Addy came in a few minutes later, she announced that supper was ready and carried the baby into the kitchen. After supper, Stacey sat at the counter as Addy did the dishes.

"Thank you for having me over, holding your little peanut was therapeutic…" she snacked on some cashews, "I can't believe I lost her. It's so surreal; it is still hard to believe and the physical effects of delivery are not fun either." Addison moved around the counter and held her.

"You will make it girl and after you marry your man, you can try again." Stacey turned back to the counter as Addison sat down next to her. "Your dad called me and told me what your mom said yesterday." Stacey looked at her aunt, "He wanted me to check on you." Stacey laid her head on her arms,

"Did something happen to her, similar to my situation?" There was a pause then Stacey looked up at her aunt and saw shock on her face.

"Yes, she was raped and she gave the baby up for adoption. She didn't want anyone to know about it. Your father met her a few months after the baby was born and helped her get her life back." Stacey's jaw dropped.

"How do you know this?"

"I helped your father get your mother's attention and helped her through her emotional meltdowns until they got married." Rubbing her eyes, Stacey took a deep breath in and let it out.

"It's getting late, I think we should head out," Stacey stood up and hugged Addison before she went to go find Derek. As they were putting their coats on Addy carried her baby to Stacey so she could kiss her then Ben hugged her.

"Aunt Addy, thanks for telling me," Addison nodded her head as Stacey and Derek went out to their car. When they arrived home, Stacey called her mother.

"Hello,"

"Mom, I talked to Aunt Addy, why didn't you tell me what happened to you when you were younger?" A sigh was heard over the phone.

"I didn't think it would ever come up and I didn't think I would react as emotionally to it when it happened to you." Stacey rolled onto her stomach while thinking about what to say to her mother.

"The next time we see each other we should talk then there wouldn't be as much tension." Her mother agreed as they ended the phone call.

Laura listened to the radio as she drove to talk to her daughter. "I can't believe she figured it out and asked Addison about it. I never wanted to talk about this ever again but she deserves answers." Madison came into view as she became nervous about talking to her daughter. She saw the park where they were supposed to meet at and turned toward it. Laura saw Stacey sitting in the gazebo, waiting for her. After a deep breath, she opened the door and walked to her daughter. Stacey saw her coming and waved at her.

"Hey Mom," Stacey stood up to hug her then led her to the bench. "Mom, can you tell me what happened?" Snow fell around the gazebo. Laura reached out to catch a few snowflakes.

"It was a cold winter night; I was at a party with friends. We were having a sleepover after the guys left at midnight. I didn't have the energy to stay awake—the night before was long and I didn't get much sleep. So, I went into one of the rooms to take a nap and I locked the door. When I woke up, I was exposed and my best guy friend was on top of me with his hands all over me. I tried to scream out but the music was too loud for anyone to hear. When he was finished with me, he stood up, readjusted his clothes, and threw a blanket over me. As soon as he was out the door, I grabbed my clothes and ran. I went back to my apartment and cried my eyes out. For summer vacation, I did a summer job and didn't go home. I didn't go home until the baby was born then I gave him up for adoption. My parents still don't know." Stacey scooted closer to her and wiped the tears off of her cheeks.

"You regret something, what is it?" Laura shot a look at Stacey then looked down at her hands.

"I regret not telling my parents and giving him up." Stacey held her hand and Laura grasped it.

"Mom, I think we should go get a cup of hot chocolate, you're freezing." Stacey led her mother to her mother's car and she drove them to a coffee shop. Inside they found a secluded table to talk at and Stacey went to order their drinks and a few muffins. When she sat down again, she squeezed her mother's hand. They sat quietly while drinking and eating their food and warming up.

"Stac, you would be an excellent psychologist or counselor. You have made me feel so much better than any psychologist has ever made me feel." Stacey blushed as she took a drink. "What are you going to college for?"

"I didn't have a plan because I was just going to stay home with the baby. So now, that's what I'm going to think about." They talked for a few more hours then Laura dropped Stacey off to the car in the park.

"Thanks for listening to me," Laura said as she hugged her.

"Thanks for telling me Mom," She got out of the car and went to Derek's car to find Mr. Jackson leaning against it. "Mr. Jackson, the baby is gone; can you please leave me alone?"

"I know the baby is gone but my grief isn't," Stacey slipped her phone out of her pocket and called Detective Kent secretly. "I don't know how to make this pain go away."

"Pain doesn't just disappear. It has to be talked through," she motioned for him to go sit at the gazebo. "Mr. Jackson, I don't know what you want from me but I will listen to what you have to say." He sat down on the bench and fidgeted with his coat. Stacey noticed the grey hairs and wrinkles that weren't there before.

"My son loved you and you just threw his feelings to the side. He protected you from all the bad guys then you go behind his back and start dating Derek. Aaron was heartbroken; he laid around the house moping so I told him to do something about it. The next thing I knew, he was in jail for raping you. Then…then…he was dead. I started drinking and hated you then I found out you were pregnant. I couldn't even think about Aaron's baby here when he wasn't so I hit you with my car and the baby is gone." Stacey saw Detective Kent slowly approaching the gazebo.

"I'm sorry about how everything came out to be but I didn't kill your son…" she tried to stay calm. "You killed my baby girl," his jaw dropped as she whispered the gender.

"The baby was a girl?" Tears ran down his face as he asked the question. Detective Kent walked up and arrested Mr. Jackson. As they were walking past her, he paused, "Stacey, I'm so sorry for killing your baby." Detective Kent escorted Mr. Jackson to his squad car and Stacey slowly followed.

"You did a wonderful job, Stacey," she smiled then went off to Derek's car and drove home. As she arrived, Derek greeted her and she told him everything.

Stacey woke up feeling refreshed from a nap for the first time in a month. She grabbed her planner and looked at the plans she had. The wedding date, "The only reason it's so late in the summer is because of the baby." She wrote down plans she had and some things she wanted to do then she went out to find Derek awake on the sofa.

"What are you doing?" Derek asked Stacey as she sat down next to him.

"Oh, I just started thinking about our plans and was wondering if we could move the wedding up." Derek looked into her eyes and realized she was serious. "We only planned the wedding so late because of the baby."

"Let's talk to Adam and Nicole to see what they say," Stacey's eyes lightened up as Derek pulled out his cell phone and called Adam then did a three-way call with Nicole. They told them what they were thinking and Adam and Nicole were thrilled. Stacey and Nicole talked to decide when they were going to get together then said their good-byes. Derek watched Stacey and saw more thinking going on. "What else are you thinking about?" Stacey looked at him

"I want to find my mom's son," Derek smiled as he kissed her temple.

"I will help you in any way that I can." They started researching and looking for Laura's first baby.

Chapter 11

The sun was shining on the beautiful May Day, the sky had minimal clouds and everything was blooming. The checkered blanket was filled with food as were all the other blankets around. Children were running around screaming, yelling, and playing. Stacey laid back against Derek, watching the activities from afar for the church gathering. They were ready to nap when they saw Detective Kent walk up to them.

"Hello Detective Kent, isn't today a beautiful day?" Stacey asked as he sat down with them.

"Stacey, we found him and he wants to meet you and your family." Her eyes widened and her jaw dropped. "He would like to meet you at the Family Café," Stacey nodded her head speechless. "He says he has been searching for his biological mother for the last five years. He wants to meet all of you but you can decide when and how."

"When does he want to meet me?" Detective Kent stole a grape off of Stacey's plate.

"Any time after tomorrow," Stacey pulled out her calendar and looked to see what she had open.

"Friday after school works for me," he took note of the time and laid back on the blanket. The children gathered around Pastor Jeff as he started telling a story. The parents sat back, enjoying the story as much as the kids.

"Stacey, it's time to go perform," she sat up and pulled Derek up.

"Sorry, we have to leave Detective but come enjoy the show." Derek pulled her away then they walked onto the stage together. "We are glad that all of you could join us to celebrate the ending of the school year."

The kids yelled in excitement, "So, we are going to sing for a few hours to worship the Lord who gave us this wonderful school year." Chase started the count in and the worship began.

The sun was out and shining on Stacey's face, "You look nervous," Stacey turned her face from the sun to look at her fiancé.

"I'm just excited but scared of what he'll think of me," Derek pulled her off the picnic table into his arms.

"He will see the amazing woman you are and wish he was around years ago." He kissed her and then hugged her. A car horn honked and they turned to see Detective Kent waiting for her. Derek walked her to the car, "Thanks for escorting her to meet him, please get her back by five." Detective Kent raised his hand in acknowledgment as he drove off. He parked the car at the Family Café. Before Stacey opened the door, the detective informed her of how they were going to proceed.

"I'm going to introduce the two of you then sit at a separate table until it is time to go."

"Why couldn't I come alone?"

"Derek wanted to bring you but he has to help set up for the concert so he asked me to come just to make him feel better about this until you guys get a chance to get to know him." Stacey got out of the car and waited for Detective Kent to come next to her. They walked in together and Stacey recognized him—he was a darker version of Adam. "Stacey, this is your brother, Todd Shust. Todd, this is your sister, Stacey Rosemen." Stacey reached out her hand to give him a handshake when he hugged her.

"I can't believe I found my family. I've been looking for my mom for the last five years, now I found my sister." Stacey was too shocked to say anything. Detective Kent left them alone, Todd motioned for her to sit down. "So, tell me about your life," Todd started.

"Well, Mom and Dad have been married twenty years. Mom's a psychologist and Dad is a computer programmer. After they were married for a year, they found out they were pregnant and were even more surprised that it was twins. Mom had Adam and me, my brother and I are very close." The world around them didn't seem to exist and everything became quiet as they talked. "Where did you grow up and what do you do for a living?"

"I'm a doctor and I grew up in California." Stacey was shocked.

"What brings you to Wisconsin then?"

"You and your family, I took the next few weeks off to get to know my mom and her family." Stacey was still surprised when she saw Detective Kent stand up.

"Okay, I have to go but if you follow us, I will introduce you to our family." He agreed as he followed Detective Kent's car back to the school. "Thanks, Detective, I'll see you at the concert tonight," she waved at him as he drove off then Todd caught up with her. He followed her into the High School, "Derek," Stacey yelled when she saw him down the hallway. He turned around and jogged to her, kissing her as he met her. "Derek, this is my brother Todd Shust, Todd this is my fiancé, Derek Rysner." The two men shook hands then they rushed off to make it to dinner. "I'm going to go warn Mom," Stacey walked ahead of them to their table.

"How long have you known Stacey?" Todd asked Derek as they slowly walked behind Stacey.

"We have been friends since we were five," Derek showed him the way to their table after they lost sight of Stacey. Laura saw him and covered her mouth,

"Mom, I would like to introduce you to Todd Shust, your son." Laura rushed up to him and hugged him. Adam's mouth stood open as he looked at Stacey. She sat down next to him and briefly explained as their mother cried over her long-lost son. The restaurant continued to work around them as they held each other. Finally, they sat down and talked. An hour later, Derek and Stacey had to leave,

"Give him a ride to the concert; we have to go get ready." They rushed out the door, "Your mom got her wishes, the whole family knows and she is back together with her son." Stacey's smile widened as she thought of their future.

"We only have a few weeks until graduation and then our wedding; it has turned out to be a wonderful year despite the sad things that happened." Derek held her hand and kissed the back of it. They rushed to the stage to practice then the concert started and Todd was able to watch them. Stacey and Derek were in a Jazz group with Chase, AJ, Dennis, and Joanna plus a few other girls. They sang classic jazz songs, a few pop songs, acapella songs, and a goodbye song—it was their last year singing together. They sang their goodbye song and bowed before they left the stage. The group went into a group hug as they entered backstage; their teacher joined them and then pushed them back on the stage for an encore. The audience was standing up clapping and cheering.

"I guess we can sing one more song," Chase exclaimed as AJ started the vocal percussion. They finished off the concert with a bang and sang as they headed to the back of the audience and left on the last note. The audience came out with hugs and congratulations. Todd found Stacey among the crowd,

"Stacey, you were amazing," she blushed as she was pushed around by the crowd.

"Thanks, Todd, I'm glad you could come to watch."

"I would like to come to more of your events," the crowd started to disperse as Stacey talked to Todd.

"Adam and Nicole have a concert Monday night. In a week, Derek and I graduate. A week after that, Adam and Nicole graduate. Then the four of us have our double wedding a few weeks later, which you are invited to as well."

"Why is there another concert on Monday?"

"Mom, Dad, and Adam live in La Crosse. I live here because of my knee injury; they are doing a knee injury study and I am participating in so… I moved in with Derek's family. So, you will have two of every event except the wedding." The crowd was gone and Stacey's family was waiting for them.

"Todd, how long are you around for?" Laura asked.

"A few weeks,"

"Do you have a place to stay?" He shook his head, "Come stay with us," Laura walked up to him and hugged him.

"I would love to come stay with you,"

"Adam and Nicole are staying for the weekend so if you want you can stay here with them and come back when they do or you can come with Christian and me today." They all waited for his answer.

"Since I won't see Stacey in a while, I'll stay here for the weekend and come home to you when Adam and Nicole go back." Laura hugged him and said goodbye to all of her kids. Then, all the kids went home to Rysner's house.

———⁓⦿⦿⦿⁓———

A cool breeze lifted the curtains as the birds chirped their morning song. Stacey heard the glorious noise and listened to God's wonder. The creak of the door made Stacey open her eyes, it was Todd. "Good Morning Todd," he walked in.

"I hope I didn't wake you, I just wanted to check on you." She turned in the bed to sit up and get out.

"You didn't wake me, the birds did," Stacey answered in a whisper to avoid waking Nicole. She walked out to the kitchen with him.

"I see the scars on your knee, when did you get injured and how did it happen?" Stacey started preparations for breakfast and then sat across from her brother.

"It was in October, one of my friends tried to start a fight with me but I ran…into the road in front of a moving car." The toaster went off and Stacey went to retrieve her toast and put jelly on it. "After that accident, I moved here with the Rysners for the knee study, which led to a series of other events." For the next hour, Stacey told Todd about the whole last year. When she finished, he sat back in his chair amazed. He was still speechless when Derek and Adam walked in. They greeted each other then, Derek sat down next to Stacey and kissed her cheek.

"She told you about our adventurous year, didn't she?" Derek asked the shell-shocked man. He slowly nodded his head and then sipped on his coffee. "She's a strong woman, and I love her for it," Stacey smiled as she turned to Derek, kissing him. Adam noticed that Nicole wasn't up and snuck into Stacey's room. He climbed under the covers and curled up with her, kissing the back of her neck. The breeze hit Nicole's face and she turned into the warmth of Adam. She woke up wide-eyed and shook her head with laughter.

"Adam, you scared me." He joined in her laughter and held her even tighter.

"What do you think of my brother?" She thought for a few seconds before she answered.

"He seems nice and he wants to be included in this family."

"I just can't believe Mom never told me."

"From what I hear, Stacey had to pry the story out of your mother." Adam looked at his beautiful fiancé.

"You do wonders to me, did you know that?" She enthusiastically nodded her head. Adam laughed then tickle attacked her, she screamed for help with laughter in her voice. Stacey ran in and attacked her brother and the girls were winning. Derek and Todd stayed back as they watched. Adam finally surrendered and settled on the bed with his two favorite girls. Derek and Todd joined them on the bed.

"Since you ladies won't let Adam or I escort you, why don't you let Todd take you." Stacey looked at Todd to see if he wanted to go.

"Where would I be taking you?"

"We have our last wedding dress fitting today," Nicole answered. Todd's face lightened up.

"Sure, I'll take you. Then, I can treat you to lunch." The girls agreed and then kicked the boys out so they could get ready. Todd walked out to the car with a girl on each arm. "So, who's in the wedding party?"

"We are each just having one person stand up with us but Derek's sisters and Nicole's sisters are getting cute bridesmaid dresses and walking down the aisle. They all have their dresses, we are here today to try on our dresses for the last time then we get to take them home." Stacey explained as they arrived at the dress shop. The girls went into the dressing room and came out with their dresses on. Stacey's was a tube top with some lace going over her shoulders then it goes down into a bell at the bottom. The midsection was embroidered with a sash. Nicole's was a halter top ending like a bell at the bottom. It had some embroidery on the neckpiece and trailing down to the bottom. Todd dropped into a chair shocked.

"Wow, ladies, you will blow their minds away." He stood up as he recovered from the shock and walked around them to inspect the dresses. The girls smiled as the clerk checked them over. They took the dresses off and packed them into the car.

Mid-June

The sunny afternoon greeted the girls as they walked out of the spa resort. "Oh, that felt good," Nicole said as she twirled in the sun. "I still can't believe Todd paid for all of us," she stated as she caught up to the girls on their way to the car.

"I think he's trying to make up for what he missed out on," Stacey replied as she got into the car and drove home. The ladies changed into dresses for the dress rehearsal. "It's nice to be back in La Crosse, it's a nice change of scenery." Nicole laughed as they did each other's hair.

"Everyone misses you around here, where are you guys settling down?"

"Derek is going to Stout and I will be working at the YMCA. During the summer, Derek will be a life guard at the public pool in Menomonie."

"So, when do you start?"

"In a week, so our honeymoon is shorter than we hoped but we need the jobs." They finished getting ready and went out to find the whole family ready to head to the church. Grandpa West started arranging them and started the run-through. Aunt Addison was singing and one of the church ladies was playing the piano for them. All the flowers and decorations were ready to be set up in the morning. The run-through went flawlessly and they all went out to eat. Derek held Stacey's hand as he drove to the restaurant.

"I can't believe it's finally happening," Stacey smiled.

"I was thinking the same thing." He parked the car and leaned over the armrest.

"I think you should kiss me," Stacey chuckled as she turned her head to meet his.

"I think you're trouble," she whispered as their lips became closer. Derek closed the distance as Stacey's hand went behind his neck. Her hand slowly went down to his chest then gently pushed him away. "We should join the family," he pulled her in for another kiss then let her get out of the car. The whole family was there, all three families and they talked until the restaurant kicked them out. Derek drove her home and parked in front of the house.

"This time tomorrow night, we will be together forever." Stacey set her hand up to his cheek and rested it there. Derek turned his head into her hand and kissed the inside of her wrist.

"I love you," she whispered as she reached her hand to open the door. Derek reached for her other hand and kissed the inside of her wrist then pulled her in for a kiss.

"I love you too, my darling," Derek let Stacey get out of the car and watched her walk into her parents' house.

———⁓———

The phone rang, bothering Stacey, and finally, the sound went away. A few minutes later, she heard someone open her door and walk in. "Stacey, the phone is for you." She reached her arm out of the blanket and pulled the phone under the blanket to talk.

"Hello,"

"Good morning sweetheart," she pushed the covers back and looked at the clock.

"I'm supposed to be on my way to the hair salon right now," she heard Derek chuckling over the phone. "You don't want a stinky bride do you?" His laughter became louder. "Derek, I'll see you at the altar, love you." She jumped out of bed and ran into the bathroom while tossing the phone to Adam. After the shower, Laura drove her to the hair salon to get her hair done up. When they arrived, Nicole, Opal, and Nicole's sister were getting finished up. "Why did no one wake me up?" She asked feeling a little rushed.

"You seemed so peaceful, we didn't want to disturb you besides we are right on track," Nicole said hoping Stacey would relax. Stacey dropped into the chair and took a deep breath. The hair artist started doing her hair.

"Thanks, the extra rest felt good." They were done in record time and on their way to the church to eat and then get dressed. Christian carried in a tray of sub sandwiches as they organized everything. They ate and then did their make-up before putting their dresses on. The photographer took pictures while they got ready. Christian and Nicole's father walked in and stood there speechless. Tears welled up in Christian's eyes, "Daddy, don't make me start." He walked up to her and hugged her, careful not to crush her dress.

"You seem calmer than the boys. They are like tigers in a cage pacing." Stacey laughed at his comment. "They want to be married to you. They are so excited." The girls went up, ready to go before the brides. The dads stayed for a few pictures then they headed up ready to walk down the aisle. Opal and Chase walked in front of Stacey and Christian and Nicole's party followed. The wedding ran beautifully. And in the end, after they were announced to the world, they skipped down the aisle out of the church and the crowd came to congratulate them. Stacey was giving hugs when she felt someone's arms around her waist.

"Hello wifey," Derek whispered into her ear before she was pulled away again for a hug. They greeted everyone and took pictures before heading to the reception hall. A limo drove each couple over to the hall with their party. Stacey turned to look Derek in the face.

"Hello hubby," they laughed then they talked to Opal and Chase. As the limo arrived at the hall, Derek kicked Opal and Chase out.

"Give us a minute," he asked while closing the door again. Stacey looked at him suspiciously, "I just want a kiss without people watching." Stacey laughed as she leaned into him. He closed the distance watching her eyes; Stacey closed hers as his lips touched hers. He put his hand on the side of her neck underneath her ear and pulled her in to deepen the kiss. They heard a tap on the window and separated before the door was opened.

"Come out and join the party," Adam yelled knowing he interrupted them. He held out his hand and she accepted it as she climbed out of the limo. They were bombarded with people and pictures as they walked into the reception hall. The main table was long as all the members of both parties sat up there. Stacey was sitting in between her two favorite guys, her husband, and her twin brother. After the dinner, half of the tables were cleared for a dance.

"Let's let the two newlyweds have the first dance of their lives together as husband and wife." Derek offered his hand to Stacey and spun her in for a slow dance.

"I am going to enjoy being married to you, Mrs. Derek Rysner." Stacey laid her head against his chest.

"I think I'm going to enjoy it too." The song ended and a new one started then Derek got tapped on the shoulder.

"May I dance with my sister?" Derek kissed Stacey before he handed her over to Adam and danced with his sister-in-law. "I can't believe the wedding finally came and that we got married to amazing people." Stacey smiled as she loosened Adam's tie.

"That looked a little tight," she commented, "It finally happened and now our families will grow up together and grow old." They watched as their guests joined them on the dance floor.

"Did you hear that Todd is moving to Wisconsin?"

"I think I heard something about that but I wasn't sure if it was a rumor or not," Adam confirmed it then the person they were talking about tapped on Adam's shoulder. Adam handed her off to Todd. "So, I have heard you are moving closer."

"I am, while I was here I decided I wanted to move here and be close to my family."

"What about the family that adopted you?"

"The couple that adopted me were older, they died five years ago due to a heart attack and cancer. That's when I found out that I was adopted and I wanted to find my biological parents." Stacey kept her mouth shut to not mention that her mother was raped and hoped her mother had told him. "Do you know who my father is?" Stacey shook her head, honestly not knowing the answer. Stacey and Derek danced the night away with their families and friends. At midnight the reception hall was empty and cleaned up.

"Stacey, let's go to the hotel," Derek said, she hugged her family before they left and got into the limo. "Drive around for a little bit," he told the driver before he got in. Stacey looked at him with a questioning look. Derek cuddled in with Stacey not giving her an answer. After she relaxed, Derek started talking. "I wanted you to relax a little before we arrived at the hotel. I can see it in your eyes; you have some anxiety because of Aaron. You're scared that it's going to come back, the memory of it will pop up." Stacey turned her head to look him in the eyes.

"When did you become so intuitive?" He shrugged his shoulders and kissed the top of his head.

"Dallas told me that Jayne had anxiety before their wedding night, so I watched for it and I saw it when I mentioned that we should go." The limo started to slow down and Stacey looked out the window to see their hotel. The hotel was all lit up to welcome them. Derek got out first as Stacey gathered up her dress and Derek helped her out. They signed in and walked up to their room. Derek opened the door and then picked Stacey up to carry her into their room. The room was huge. It had a king-size bed with a two-person Jacuzzi, couch, and balcony. Derek helped Stacey unbutton her dress then she went into the bathroom to change into a bikini. When she walked out of the bathroom, Derek was in the tub already with two glasses of sparkling grape juice. Stacey climbed in and sat next to him, relaxing her muscles in the heat. Derek handed her a glass, "Here's to our marriage and making a new family." They tapped the glasses together and took a drink. Stacey moved behind Derek and gave him a back massage. After a while, he moved behind her and massaged her back. He kissed the back of her neck as he massaged her lower back. When he was done, he carried her out of the Jacuzzi; they dried off and laid down in each other's arms.

"Derek, I love you," Stacey whispered.

"Stacey love, I love you too." They fell asleep in each other's arms. Stacey dreamt of their future of kids and growing old together. It was a wonderful dream and a wonderful night with the man she loved in his arms and God's.